RISE OF THE TEMPLE GODS

HEIR to the DEFENDANTS

Works by K.L. Bone

Rise of the Temple Gods Series
Rise of the Temple Gods: Heir to Kale
Rise of the Temple Gods: Heir to Koloso
Rise of the Temple Gods: Heir to the Defendants
Rise of the Temple Gods: Heir to the Prophecy (coming soon)

The Black Rose Series
Black Rose
Heart of the Rose
Blood Rose
Silver Rose (coming soon)

Tales of the Black Rose Guard Series
Shadow of the Rose (coming soon)
Daughters of the Rose (coming soon)

Other Novels
The Indoctrination

RISE OF THE TEMPLE GODS

HEIR to the DEFENDANTS

K.L. BONE

CHAPTER I

KYLE STOOD BEFORE THE TEMPLE of Ziazan, with no memory of how he had come to be there. Lined with forty steps on either side, the open-aired structure featured a high, domed ceiling supported by four enormous white pillars. Gazing in wonder, Kyle climbed the steps. The marble, long scorched by centuries of smoke and flame, now appeared pristine, absent all traces of the ceremonial fires lit for those heroes who had risen, and fallen, before him.

When he reached the top, Kyle realized he was not alone. Two men stood on opposite sides of the stone floor, garbed in robes of gold, which shimmered in the light of Kale's three suns. Holding a silver sword, the man standing closest to Kyle had pale skin and shoulder-length blond hair tied neatly back. The other man was equally pale, but his hair was black, and he clutched a gold sword.

"We don't have to do this," the blond called. "I don't want to fight you."

"Because you are weak," the dark-haired man taunted.

"We can find another way."

The dark-haired man approached his opponent, his expression unreadable.

In response, the blond took a step forward, balancing his stance and adjusting his hands on the hilt of his silver blade. "Please," he tried again, "we don't have to do this."

The man with dark hair thrust his sword toward the blond's left side. The two blades collided, and clashing metal rang through the silence. Kyle attempted to intervene, but found himself frozen in place.

The two adversaries circled in a swirl of golden robes. The gold blade again thrust forward. Violently, weapons met in the air, sliding against each other. Both men stepped back.

The dark-haired man approached the stairs, where Kyle watched in growing frustration. The blond followed, thrusting his silver blade toward his opponent's chest. In defense, the dark raised his weapon, deflecting the blond's blade harmlessly to the side. Swords clashed again as both men moved, shattering the air around them.

"What's going on?" Kyle's words fell on deaf ears.

The blond moved forward. He thrust his sword at his opponent's right side.

The dark-haired man jerked left and twisted, side-stepping the attack. In a continuous, smooth movement, he raised his blade high and swung the golden sword in a downward stroke. The blond raised his own weapon barely in time to stop the blow, struggling to maintain his footing. He pushed up, fighting to keep the blades safely above him. Abruptly, the dark-haired man pulled back, lifting his blade and throwing the blond off-balance.

As he stumbled, the dark-haired man turned in a full circle and thrust his golden sword into the blond's right side. The injured man cried out, falling to his left as his opponent rushed forward, kicking the blond's injured flank.

The blond screamed in pain, losing his grip on the silver blade's hilt. The two men locked eyes on each other for only a moment before the dark-haired man plunged his blade down, sinking it into the blond's chest.

Kyle could hear the sickening sounds of breaking bones which accompanied the plunging sword, followed by the painful wheeze of the man's final, gasping breaths.

From his position on the steps, Kyle remained trapped. He watched, unable to help as the impaled man grew still, blood staining the purity of the white floor on which he lay.

The victor reached down and, to Kyle's surprise, closed the fallen man's eyes. "I'm sorry," he said. "I wish there had been another way."

A deep, gruff voice arose from behind Kyle's immobile position. "You have done well."

"I didn't do it for you. I did not want this."

"And yet," *the voice countered,* "you made your choice."

"Damn you," came the man's reply. "There was no choice. Not after what he had done, and would have done still."

"Ah, my lord, but there is always a choice. Always."

A deep growl reverberated through Kyle's bones as the fallen man's body burst into flames. The fire rose upon the still form, blending with the man's golden robes before spreading across the marble. In reflex, Kyle attempted to rush back down the stairs, but remained unable to move.

"No!" Kyle exclaimed as the flames warmed his pale skin. "What do you want?" Genuine fear laced his plea at the fire's approach. He willed his body to move, to no avail. Flames reached him, tiny sparks jumping to his robes before bursting to new life, consuming the silver threads. Intense heat burned Kyle's eyes and blurred his vision. The world transformed into a sea of flame, which licked its way along his skin. He shrieked as his hand reddened and burned.

"Death, Lord of Koloso," the voice growled, overpowering Kyle's screams. "Death to those who love them."

"Kyle!" Brandan's voice pulled him from the nightmare to the safety of his palace chambers. Attired in pink satin, Brandan had been standing guard between the chambers of the crown princess and the young captain. "You called out in your sleep," Brandan explained as Kyle jerked from the silver blankets to stare down at the smooth skin of his unburnt hands.

Heart racing, it took several breaths before Kyle could manage to say, "A dream."

"Must have been a bad one."

"Yes," Kyle answered, his eyes traveling the familiar room, decorated entirely in silver, from the thick draperies to the cushions covering the chairs. After confirming they were alone, he turned back to Brandan. "What time is it?"

"Almost sunrise."

"Okay." He nodded as his pulse slowed. "I will go ahead and prepare for my shift."

"As you will," Brandan replied. He moved toward the door, but paused as he reached it. "Kyle, I know you're captain to the future queen, and that creates a new level of protocol, but if you ever want to talk. ."

"I will let you know," Kyle replied. "Thank you, Brandan."

"Glad to be of service," he said before leaving the chambers.

Once alone, Kyle raised his hands and gently rubbed his fingers against his temples. Another in a line of ceaseless dreams. Each featuring the same two men, killing each other over and over again. Always with the same warning.

Death to those who love them.

CHAPTER II

PRINCESS MARIANA STARED AT THE endless pile of papers covering the wooden desk. It seemed for every stack she managed to read, three more magically appeared. After reviewing an account regarding a water dispute between two mid-level lords, she'd had enough. "I'm supposed to fight my sister," she wondered in renewed disgust, "for the right to spend the rest of my life doing this?" She shook her head. "I don't understand why anyone would want to be queen."

Then why do you? a voice asked from the back of her mind. *If we had only attended the same temple...*

She once asked her father why they'd been sent to different temples. Less than satisfactorily, the late prince had merely stated it was her mother's wish that one of the twins be trained at the Temple of Koloso, where Annabelle had served as the golden student. Similarly, he'd desired Mariana be trained at the Temple of Kale.

"*Besides,*" he'd added, "*it would not have been fair to force one of you to wear silver, when you both had proven yourselves worthy of gold.*"

Mary understood the reasoning, but could not help harboring resentment against the decision made so long ago. Instead of being raised as partners and friends, the twins had been trained to be bitter rivals. In fact, Mary could not remember a time where their relationship as sisters— as twins—had measured equal to the importance of showing absolute loyalty to the temples in which they had been raised. These circumstances were not unique to royalty. Members of a temple were fiercely devoted, and often hostile toward each other, including within one's own family, blood relationships a far and distant second.

Even the title of princess had meant little to Mary, until it became apparent her aunt might not bear a child to her uncle, the king. Mary had been treated like any other temple student during her younger years. Any special consideration had been attributed to her success in the tournament matches, as opposed to royal birthright.

She wondered, not for the first time, if her sister's upbringing had been different. Had being the younger twin, trained in the lower-ranked of the two temples, forced Ameria to lean more heavily upon her royal title? Was Ameria's desire to claim the throne in the best interest of the kingdom, or merely a way to prove she no longer deserved to stand in her elder sister's shadow?

Mary sighed, adding these questions to the pile, which seemed as never-ending as the stack of papers on her desk. She walked to her chamber doors, calling to the men who stood on the opposite side.

Moments later, Brandan entered the room and knelt before her. "My princess."

"Rise," she instructed, taking several steps in his direction. "Send for Lord Chiro. Tell him to come to my study at once."

"Of course, Your Highness. Will there be anything else?"

"No. That will be all."

Dismissing Brandan, Mary returned to her desk. The requested chief advisor arrived quickly, dressed in full-length satin robes over matching clothes. An accomplished man and former Silver Defendant, the High Lord of Turbamentum once served as partner to Mary's mother at the Temple of Koloso, and was Kyle's father.

Entering the room, Lord Chiro gave a bow similar to the one previously offered by Brandan, causing Mary to shake her head. "I told you before, my lord, I do not require such a show of submission from the head of my Royal Council."

"And as I have also said, Your Highness, the gesture is a show of respect, not submission."

Mary motioned him to rise. "My lord," she began, "I want to know why I am being inundated with so many trivial matters? Is this not what the Royal Council is for? To attend the lesser matters so I may devote time to the more important challenges facing the kingdom?"

Chiro cleared his throat before answering. "I assure you, my princess, the council has sorted through the matters brought to your attention as carefully as—"

"Then tell them to do a better job," she said crossly. "I don't have time to decide where, exactly, the line between two provinces touch, or who should have rights to a particular side of a lake."

"Forgive me, Your Highness. The issues are not so much about boundaries or lakes as they are about keeping the higher-ranking lords happy."

"What does it matter if I'm too busy dealing with petty squabbles to train for the fight I must win to keep my throne?"

Chiro paused, stepping closer to Mary, his silver robes gliding behind him. "Would you prefer for me to handle more of the smaller disputes, my princess? Even those that may involve other lords of rank equal to myself?"

"Yes," Mary answered. After a pause she added, "Actually, I'd like to have Princess Annabelle assist you in doing so. The other lords will likely be more receptive with her involvement."

Chiro nodded. "Your mother's inclusion in matters of state is a good idea. Though, a suggestion, if I may?"

"Yes?"

"I would advise you continue to oversee the matters involving Serenitas yourself."

"Lord Riccard's province?"

"Yes." He nodded. "I believe Lord Riccard would find anything less than your personal attention an insult; he is not a man known to forgive a perceived slight."

Mary nodded. "Fine. Bring Lord Riccard's concerns to my personal attention. I want the rest directed to you, my mother, and the Royal Council."

"Yes, Your Highness." Chiro bowed at the waist, then asked, "Will there be anything else?"

"Yes," she answered. "My lesson with Master Jiro has been cancelled today. I would like you to ask Kyle if he would spar with me in the training room. In say, ten minutes from now?"

"Of course, my princess. I shall send him there at once."

"Thank you," she replied as he turned and vanished from the room.

Lord Riccard's name had not recently crossed her mind until Lord Chiro mentioned it. She had almost no memory of her maternal grandfather, save for a few vague images. A former Golden Defendant, Riccard's achievements were approached by few, and matched by even fewer. One of the most powerful men in the kingdom, his reputation as a high lord stood equal to Lord Chiro's; a reason that likely contributed to the two lords' reputed dislike of each other.

The story was common enough. Two powerful men, trained at rival temples, each vying for more control over lands that shared a common border. Both with an equal share of royal heritage. Mary wondered why no one had suggested Riccard's inclusion on the Royal Council. Perhaps because of the rivalry with Chiro?

Mary made a mental note to speak with her mother on the matter. She drew a deep breath and started the short walk to the palace training room.

CHAPTER III

PRINCESS AMERIA RODE TOWARD THE village of Helans. The Silver Defendant, Lord Stephen, rode on her left while the captain of the Serenitas Guard, Lord Yarin, rode on her right. The two men appeared remarkably similar; both had brown hair streaked with gray, hazel eyes, and expressions hardened by time. Lord Stephen was garbed in silver robes of his defendant status while Lord Yarin wore the deep blue of the high lord he served. A former Red Defendant, who had served under the late Master Leo, Yarin had been Lord Riccard's captain for nearly twenty years.

As the party drew near the village, the two rode ahead of the princess. "Open in the name of her Royal Highness Ameria! Heir to Serenitas, Golden Student of Koloso, and Princess of the Kalian bloodline!" As Lord Stephen finished calling out her titles, the wrought iron gates swung open, allowing the riders to gallop through. Lord Stephen and Lord Yarin paused to retake their positions on either side of the princess.

Ameria sat astride her horse, Argento, whose silver coat gleamed in the light of Kale's three suns, which burned brightly in the clear, violet sky. The party did not slow as they rode through the village, trampling the blue grass covering the valley at the edge of the Rainbow Mountains. The riders ignored dilapidated wooden houses, and barren rows of stands, which might have qualified as a market had there been more of them.

They rode to a series of elaborate tents raised on the village's south side. The pavilions, draped in Serenitas-blue banners, stood more luxurious than anything the local residents could hope to possess. The encampment belonged to Lord Karris, a chief advisor to Ameria's uncle, Lord Andrew. Without bothering to announce herself, Ameria dismounted in a sweep of golden robes, handing Argento's reins to one of the Serenitas guardsmen who rushed forward to greet her.

"Princess Ameria." He sounded out of breath. "We were not expecting you."

Instead of answering his implied query, Ameria nodded toward the largest of the five tents. "I'm assuming Lord Karris is in that one?"

"Yes, my princess," the guard replied. "I shall inform—"

Ameria ignored the man's nervous ramble, walking immediately toward the tent. She entered through a narrow drape of blue fabric into an expansive space within. A wooden table presided in the center, adorned with silk cloth under a vast assortment of fresh fruit and silver goblets. Along the back curtain, a seating arrangement including a sofa covered with plush, blue cushions and several equally elaborate chairs.

Lord Karris reclined on this couch, a goblet of wine in his left hand, which he promptly spilled as the princess entered with the Silver Defendant.

"Princess Ameria," he stammered, wiping at the liquid soaking his blue shirt. "What are you—"

"You missed your monthly report," Ameria said curtly. She took a step closer to the man struggling to rise to his feet from the lavish upholstery. "And I do believe, Lord Karris, we agreed things would go very badly for you if this village was not properly defended." Ameria paused, allowing the threat to settle over the lower lord, who never failed to displease her.

His eyes shifted nervously, left to right, avoiding the princess' direct gaze. "I assure you, my lady—"

Ameria's eyes narrowed as she interrupted him. "I seem to recall having already instructed you on which titles were, and were not, acceptable from a rank such as yours, Lord Karris." She took a step closer, anger blazing through her sapphire-blue eyes. "I believe in second chances, Lord Karris. But in thirds...never."

"Wait!" The lower lord realized his error, dropping to his knees before his princess. "Forgive me, Your Royal Highness." Fear laced his words. "I meant no disrespect."

"The next time you fail to address me by my proper title, Lord Karris, will be your last. Am I understood?"

Supplicant, he remained in a kneeling position, his eyes on the ground as he answered, "Yes, Princess Ameria."

Ameria gave a single nod, her eyes lingering upon the lower lord, but not granting him permission to stand. "Now, explain to me, *Lord* Karris, why did I not receive your monthly report?"

He searched for the correct answer. "I apologize, Your Highness. Events have been unfolding and I must have been remiss in my duties."

"Unacceptable," Ameria answered. "I gave you an order, my lord. And made it very clear I expected to be obeyed."

"I am sorry, my princess."

"Stand up," she ordered. "Give me a full report."

With a startling lack of grace, the untrained lord struggled from the clearly unfamiliar position. He lost his balance, and staggered forward a step, his cheeks reddening in embarrassment. Lord Karris, a lower-ranked lord of the Serenitas province, had been raised to the role of advisor through a chance friendship with Ameria's uncle, Lord Andrew. Normally, such a position would be held exclusively for those of higher-rank, individuals who had been trained in the famous Kalian Temples.

"Explain yourself, and the status of this village. I would advise you do so quickly."

"Your Highness," he began, "as you are aware, bandits have been stealing from the local villagers."

"Which is why you were sent."

"Yes, but you see, stopping them has proven more difficult than I originally thought."

"And why is that? It wouldn't be because you thought you could simply ride into the village, pitch your tent, and they would surrender while you gorged yourself on wine, would it?"

"Your Highness, the raids have slowed since our guardsmen arrived. However, those attacks that still occur have changed in nature. Where these bandits used to ride into the village and boldly take what they wished, they are now looting covertly, entering under the cover of darkness. They have also expanded their raids to two additional villages, forcing us to spread our men."

Ameria considered his words before responding. "So, in other words, Lord Karris, your efforts to stop these raids have proven unsuccessful and, instead of leading your men in the search, I find you seated on plush cushions drinking wine. Comforts those you have been charged to protect could never afford due to the theft you have failed to stop."

"My princess, I assure you, I have been out—"

"Choose your words carefully, Karris. Lying to a member of royalty, let alone one who is set to become the next Lady of Serenitas, if not your queen, is treason."

Karris' eyes went to the floor. Ameria watched him draw a nervous breath before speaking. "My princess, I have worked diligently, as have my men, in attempts to stop these attacks, as you ordered."

"Have you, at minimum, managed to catch any of these raiders?"

"Yes, Your Highness. Five have been taken into custody."

"Are they being held?"

"Yes, under the watch of my guards."

Ameria nodded. "I will speak with these men."

"Speak with them?"

"Yes. I will have the names and whereabouts of their companions. Should they refuse to provide the information, I am perfectly willing to make an example of them. These deeds will not go unpunished, Karris. Not under my rule." Karris raised his eyes from the ground to meet Ameria's, shifting nervously. "Take me to them," the princess commanded. "Now."

CHAPTER IV

PRINCESS MARIANA CLUTCHED THE GOLDEN hilt of her blade tightly in her left hand. Standing across from her was the silver student of Koloso and the acting captain of her guard, Kyle. He stood taller than her, and she was forced to tilt her head to meet his emerald eyes, accentuated by the angry welt that ran from eyebrow to cheek. Her heart ached at the sight of the scar, placed there by her own blade.

Saved by the gods in exchange for the life of Mary's own temple partner, the princess spent many nights struggling with the guilt of her choice. Unknowingly as it may have been, she was still the one responsible for sacrificing Marcus to ransom Kyle. The life of a Kolosian for a Kaian. An act unthinkable between the two temples whose rivalry typically superseded all. Yet somehow she had come to love Kyle in spite of this required hatred, allowing her best friend to die to save the life of the man she should despise.

Only when standing upon the training room's gold and silver mats, could Mary free herself of the constant burden. Here, in these spare hours, she allowed herself to concentrate fully on the heavy blade in her hand. The practiced motions coming as naturally to her as breathing, her heavy conscience was temporarily set aside.

She stood calmly as she awaited Kyle's next attack. It came in a blur of silver as he lunged forward, swinging the sharp blade toward her right side. Mary twisted her arm, colliding the side of her sword against Kyle's with a loud clash. Both stepped apart, separating their blades briefly before he again swung his sword, this time with enough force Mary was driven several steps back as her blade met his. Mary moved left, their swords sliding against each other. As if a well-rehearsed waltz, both took a step away, offering a brief respite before Mary lunged forward, thrusting the tip of her blade toward Kyle's chest.

He jerked to the right, causing Mary's sword to miss his body, while bringing his blade in an upward motion. It crashed against the bottom of

K.L. BONE

Mary's weapon, forcing her arms up as she fought to maintain her grip upon its golden hilt. Without pause, Kyle shifted into a downward stroke, thrusting his sword toward her now exposed torso.

Mary pulled back, but not before the tip of Kyle's blade cut into the golden cloth covering her body, her pale skin saved by the multiple layers she wore. She stumbled backward, clutching her blade tighter and softly cursing. Kyle stood patiently across from her, allowing both Mary and himself to catch their breaths.

Kyle wiped his brow on a shimmering silver sleeve. "Shall we call a pause?"

"Why?" Mary struggled to slow her heart rate enough to offer a steady smile. "Have I worn you out already?"

"Not even close," Kyle answered, returning the smile before he swept his sword toward Mary's right. She met his challenge and the two champions continued their dance across the gold and silver mats. Mary swung her blade toward Kyle's right, but he stepped away. She swung a second time, aiming high.

Kyle ducked under the blade, rolling across the mat until he reached the opposite side of the training floor. He stood, adjusted his grip on the hilt of his blade, his fingers partially covering the engraved horses, and prepared for her next onslaught.

Mary followed him across the floor, but paused before she attacked, searching for the angle that would provide the best advantage. She finally decided to step left, which had a slightly wider area provided than to the right. She swung her blade, but Kyle parried. As their swords collided, Mary pushed against Kyle with all her strength, forcing him to push back.

She stepped right, removing her blade so swiftly Kyle fell forward, his back foot rising from the ground. Mary used the loss of balance to her advantage, raising her sword and bringing it down hard on Kyle's, who stumbled, allowing Mary to turn her blade sideways and move the weapon against Kyle's throat.

Her heart pounded as she stared at him, her breath labored. Though believed by many to be the best hand-to-hand champion in the land, Mary's skill with a sword was considered sub-par to the Champion of Koloso. To have beaten Kyle was a rare feat, and a testament to how hard she had been working.

"I guess your lessons are paying off," Kyle observed from the golden mat.

"It would seem so." She moved her sword and realized the edge was tipped with blood. "Oh my gods!" she exclaimed. "Did I hurt you?"

"Just a scratch."

Mary moved down to where he knelt, laying her sword upon the mat. A thin trickle of blood ran from his collarbone where the blade had sliced his skin. He was right, the cut was not deep, but as she pulled back the silver material, a second, older injury was revealed. The raised red blemish ran across the side of his neck to the top of his chest, placed there by her sister, the proclaimed Princess of Koloso. Fresh blood so close to the scar caused something to hurt deep inside Mary's chest. She reached down and tore a strip of golden cloth from her sleeve, then pressed it against Kyle's wound.

"It's okay," he assured her. "You don't have to..."

"I'm sorry. You are always telling me to be more careful and I..."

"Mary, it's fine. It's only a scratch."

A splotch of red soaked the center of the thin material, drawing Mary's mind back to the night Kyle had stepped between the sisters' deadly blades, almost costing Kyle his life. Blood had poured from his body that night, gushing from the artery slashed with Ameria's practiced precision. Deep red liquid had cascaded over the silver marble floor of the throne room, leaving both sisters kneeling in a pool of his blood.

"Mary?" Kyle's voice was soft. He lifted his left hand toward her cheek, then paused, curling his fingers against his palm, fighting the urge to touch her pale skin.

In response, Mary closed her eyes, attempting in vain to clear the vision of his dying form.

"I'm okay, Mary."

Your choice, Princess of Kale. Princess of Koloso. Your choice. The sinister words entered the confines of her mind.

"Mary," Kyle said again. "It's all right."

"No," she answered, opening her eyes, unable to hide her fear.

He leaned forward. "What's wrong, my lady?"

"I don't want to hurt you."

At her words, he lost the fight for self-control and pressed the tips of his fingers against her cheek in a gentle caress.

"It's not safe."

"Mary, please," he pleaded, forgetting everything but the terror shining through her eyes. A fear he had seen far too often. "Tell me what frightens you."

A shudder ran through her, prompting Kyle to slide forward against his will, slipping his arm around her. She pressed her cheek against his shoulder, closing her eyes as she attempted to drown out the voice she could never escape.

Your choice. The words of the wraith whispered for her alone.

"No." Mary pulled away from Kyle's embrace.

"Mary, please."

"No," she repeated, grabbing her blade and struggling to her feet.

"Mary, what scared you?" Kyle asked, rising beside her. "Please, my lady. How can I protect you, if you refuse to tell me what I'm defending you from?"

She turned back toward him then, stepping so close they nearly touched. "Kyle—" she pleaded. The single word interrupted by unsteady breaths as her heart pounded in a flurry of panic.

The wraith stood behind them, its wolf-like form covered in shaggy black fur. Slanted cat-eyes reflected the light like a single, sinister flame. The menacing creature did not speak, but merely stared in silent warning.

"What do you want?" she asked in a voice barely above a whisper.

"Nothing, my lady," Kyle answered the question he thought intended for him. "I only want to help you. Please, my princess, my lady...Mary. Let me help you."

Death, Princess. The wraith spoke to her alone. *Death to those who love you.*

The wraith took a step forward and Mary rushed past Kyle in a desperate attempt to place herself between them. She found her voice, which came out as more of a scream. "What do you want from me?"

Kyle jerked around, but saw nothing, the wraith having vanished into thin air. "Mary, what's going on?"

"No," Mary called. "Don't go!"

"I'm not going anywhere, Mary." Desperate to reach her, Kyle grabbed her arms, turning her around to face him. "I promised I would not leave you. I meant it."

"You should," she answered. "You should go far away from me. As far away as you can. I..." Hot tears spilled from the corners of her emerald eyes. "You should go."

"Please, my lady, won't you let me help you? I am trying to understand."

"You can't," she answered. "You can't help me."

"I am here to protect you."

Mary drew a trembling breath, managing to stop the tears enough to turn her gaze fully upon his. "Not even you can protect me from what I am."

The words stung. Kyle moved his hand from Mary's arm to the side of her face, pressing his palm against her cheek. "My lady."

"Princess," she corrected.

They stared at each other, until Kyle dropped his hand, allowing her to turn and leave the room.

Once she moved out of sight, Kyle turned and looked at the wall across the room, searching for an explanation. Had she been yelling at him...or someone else?

CHAPTER V

PRINCESS AMERIA ENTERED THE WOODEN hut, which served as the local jail. The men were housed in two cells, three on the left, and two on the right. True to Lord Karris' word, members of his own guard stood watch. The prisoners, who had been lounging on dirty cots, stood, curious about the new visitors. Flanked by men dressed in the blue cloaks of the Serenitas Guard, Ameria approached. She stopped in front of the poorly lit cells, well clear of the rusting bars, attempting not to curl her nose from the stench of urine and decay.

With the exception of one notably younger, the men appeared to be middle-aged. Their clothes were caked with dirt, chins covered with weeks of beard growth. Ameria considered them, allowing her gaze to trail over each, making eye contact as she swept their fractured line. Finally, she settled upon the one who appeared to be the eldest.

"You've been accused of robbing the goods and valuables from the people of this village," she spoke to him. "Are you guilty of such a crime?"

The man stared back at her, offering naught but an impudent stare.

"Let me try again, with a different query. Do you know who I am?"

"A temple bitch," came the response, but from a different man.

Ameria tilted her head toward the speaker, noting the glint in his eyes and combative stance. While all the men were unkempt, this man's clothes had been well-made. "A somewhat crude, though partially accurate answer."

"Oh? Are you not from the temples then?"

Refusing to be jarred by his offensive tone, Ameria instead offered the slightest hint of a smile. "Might I request the knowledge of your name? Or should I simply call you the rotting thief?"

"Rotten maybe, but not rotting." He gave a crude chuckle. "Step closer and I'll prove it to ya."

"Well," Ameria said, "not yet." A smile curved her lips, causing the thief's arrogant swagger to falter. "Your name?" she asked again, her piercing blue eyes bearing into his.

"Giles," he replied gruffly.

"And are you the leader of this merry band?"

"You could say that." He gave a cough. "I'd ask the same of you, but then you're nothin' but a child, aren't ya?"

"I assure you, Mr. Giles, rank and position has little to do with age."

He chuckled. "Aye, 'tis the truth. All about the size of yer sword, ain't it?"

Suppressing a chuckle of her own, Ameria turned to Lord Yarin. "Have him brought from the cell. I wish to continue this conversation free of this building's stench." Yarin nodded as Ameria added, "Bring the youngest one as well."

Once outside, Ameria drew a deep breath, grateful for the fresh air. Lord Stephen, whom she had left at the top of the stairs, resumed his place beside her as she moved away from the decrepit building. Lord Yarin, and additional members of the guard, followed shortly thereafter. Between them, Giles and the younger man shuffled forward, their arms bound in front of them and held tightly between pairs of guardsmen. The prisoners were stopped in front of the princess and forced to their knees.

"I would advise not getting too close," Yarin cautioned.

"Noted," Ameria replied, stepping forward in spite of his warning. "Mr. Giles," she began, "I can be a reasonable woman. I am also one who believes in truth above all else. Integrity is highly valued as the golden student from the Temple of Koloso, and as a member of this land's ruling family."

Giles looked up and eyed her again. "Now yer the one speaking in riddles," he said. "There's no woman in the Serenitas family."

"Ah, perhaps you do know more than you implied."

"I live on these lands. Kinda hard not to know who rules 'em."

Ameria nodded. "Then you would also know you are mistaken in your statement. That there was, in fact, a female born to the Serenitas bloodline."

He scoffed. "We're a long way from the palace, girl. And you don't look old enough to know what ta'do with that sword strapped to your side, let alone be the prince's widow."

Ameria forced a smile that did not meet her eyes. "No, my mother would be the widow."

"You're..." He looked her up and down. "You're a princess?"

Ameria nodded. "Yes. Princess Ameria of Koloso, to be precise. Tell me, Mr. Giles, would you consent to take a walk with me?"

Bewildered, the man nodded.

"Assist Mr. Giles to his feet," Ameria ordered. The guards hauled him up and Ameria waved her arm, motioning him forward. "I must beg your forgiveness at not having your chains removed. My guards insist until we, at least, have been able to speak on more reasonable terms."

Propelled by men on either side, he moved beside the princess, who walked down a worn dirt path through the village. In silence, they passed a series of wood houses, headed to the center of town. Many were poor and ill-kept, with rough mud and straw patching the walls. Dust covered steps led to splintered porches, and doors stood in dire need of repair. Where once a market appeared to have thrived, there was but crumbling remains and broken dreams. Baskets of molding bread were being offered alongside strips of meat cut so thin they could barely feed a person, let alone a family. Children, sickly thin, ran half-clothed over dying grass fields.

Astounding poverty on all sides, the town a decaying relic of what it had once been. At a barren merchant stall, with a series of wooden bars upon which food had once been served, Ameria paused and turned to the leader of thieves. "Tell me something, Giles, what do you see?"

"See?"

"Yes. When you view your surroundings, what do you see?"

Giles considered the options briefly, before giving a rough laugh. "What d'ya expect me to say, Princess? That I see a bunch of poor folks down on their luck? People I wronged?" He laughed again, a harsh, unpleasant sound. "I don't. I see a bunch o' weak peasants, not strong enough to stand up and protect themselves, or their possessions."

Ameria tilted her head. "Tell me, Mr. Giles, do you not feel any remorse for the circumstances you, and your men, helped to create? For the women and children who starve because of your actions?"

"Why should I?" he answered. "These people could've fought back. Instead, they let me take their bread right out of their hands. Do ya have any idea how much we've taken from this town?"

The first wave of true anger reached the princess' sapphire eyes, but she fought to keep the flames from igniting her voice. "You were never worried about being caught? About paying the price for your crimes?"

Giles laughed in earnest, unable to stop for several minutes. "Price?" he managed to say through the laughter. "Ain't no 'price' I ever seen. You know how long it's been since defendants were in these parts? Without them, it was easy pickins."

Ameria's smile slowly widened. Giles was not intelligent enough to see the cruelty which lay behind it. Lord Karris, on the other hand, took three wide steps to the left, attempting to vacate Ameria's field of vision. "Tell me, Mr. Giles, when it was announced a lord had been dispatched, with his men, to protect this town, did you then begin to worry about being caught?"

"You speak as though they have done more than sit in those purdy tents. Stupid luck caught me. I got drunk, and when I woke up, found m'self in a cell. Aside from the stench, I ain't seen a 'price' for nothin'."

Ameria's cold eyes slid to Karris, who took another wary step back. "I believe you are correct, Mr. Giles." She turned her eyes back to the unapologetic thief. "There has been a distinct lack of consequences, for your actions, and the actions of others who have committed harm against the village." She took a step closer to the man, whose cheery expression faltered, his laughter chased back by her icy tone.

"However, Mr. Giles, starting today, I can promise you, this will no longer be the case." She stepped back, turning to the abandoned booth, and ran her hands along the splintered plank of wood behind her. "Unchain his hands," she instructed her men, "and place them here, upon the wood." She watched the men follow her instructions in silence, speaking only after both hands had been secured flat against the weathered wood.

"Lord Yarin," she turned to her grandfather's captain, "I have a question for you."

"Yes, my princess."

"What is the penalty in my grandfather's kingdom...for thievery?"

Yarin drew a sharp breath before answering. "It would depend on the number of offenses, Your Highness. For a first, the loss of two fingers."

Ameria nodded. "And for a second?"

"Loss of the entire hand," he replied.

"What? No!" The words came from Giles, who attempted to remove his hands from the plank, but found himself held immobile by the surrounding men. "You can't!"

"I assure, Mr. Giles, I can."

Without further warning, Ameria withdrew her heavy blade and brought its sharp, silver edge down upon the thief's left wrist, severing his hand with a single stroke. A spurt of blood splashed Ameria's hand, and the sleeves of her gown.

The thief gave a blood-curdling scream, which echoed in the ears of those surrounding him.

Ameria stood aloof, leaning down to wipe her sword on the blades of blue grass beneath her before returning the implement of justice to its sheath. "Bind his arm," she instructed. "If he lives, please have the courtesy to remind him of the punishment for stealing a third time. I understand it is far less lenient. Bring up the others and see that they receive the same punishment."

"Yes, Princess," Yarin replied. Then he paused. "What of the boy?" He motioned to the youngest of the thieves.

"He will be last," she answered.

Standing beside her men, Ameria watched as, one by one, each man was dragged from the make-shift prison and suffered the same fate as their leader. By the time the rest were finished, the young man standing beside her shook in fear.

Ameria motioned for him to be brought forward and bound to the plank, now stained with the blood of those before him. "Since you are the youngest, I have an offer. You can be spared your companions' fate, if you provide me with the names of your fellow bandits and their current locations. Otherwise, I am afraid, in spite of your youth, you shall be held to the same standard of law as those you have just witnessed."

Shaking, the boy nodded. "I'll tell ye," he said in a panic. "I'll tell ye. I'll tell."

"Good," Ameria answered, but did not permit him to remove his hand from the restraints. "Proceed."

The boy provided names of the men in question, and the locations of their favorite hideouts, in an eager rush.

When he finished, Ameria turned to Lord Karris. "Did you get all that, my lord?"

"Yes," he answered, unable to fully disguise the fear in his voice. "I did, Your Highness."

"Good. I trust you know what to do with the information?"

"Yes, Princess. They will be found and punished for their crimes."

"They will. I expect no excuses this time. Do your job, Lord Karris, or you will find yourself with a fate worse than these men. Do you understand?"

He fearfully sank into a low bow. "Yes, my princess. Perfectly."

Ameria nodded and turned back to the boy. "Thank you," she said. "You will be held until we learn if the information you provided is accurate. I, in return, shall remain true to my word and not impose the punishment given to your companions." She cleared her throat and turned to the men holding him. "He is young, so let us consider this a first offense, as opposed to a second, thus holding true to both my promise, and to the law as my grandfather deemed appropriate for his province." She motioned to the man standing on her left. "Choose two fingers and see them removed. Not the thumb though. We want to remind him of transgressions, not cause a debilitating handicap."

"What?" The boy's eyes widened and he fought vigorously to pull his hand from the board. More men moved in, holding him still. "You said I wouldn't be punished!"

"No. I said that you would not be punished as severely as the others," Ameria answered. "This is the lightest of the permitted penalties. Consider it a reminder to never again commit such a crime."

"No!" he cried as a man, bearing a sharp, silver blade, came closer. "Please, have mercy! Mercy, my lady. Please..."

She looked at him with an expression of pity. "Were it my soft-hearted sister to whom you were pleading, mercy is what you might have found. But this is my province of the kingdom now, and though I have been accused of many things, a soft heart has never been one of them."

"Please," he begged, tears falling from his eyes as he jerked in fear. "Don't do this!"

The men looked to Ameria in question.

"Well," she asked, "what are you waiting for?" Without another word, she turned and walked back to Karris' tent as the boy's pleas turned to deafening screams.

CHAPTER VI

KYLE SAT IN HIS PRIVATE study with a stack of papers before him. As captain of the guard to the crown princess, it was his job to review any reported, or perceived, threat to her safety. However, his mind was far from the task. The fear in Mary's eyes from the previous night haunted him. *I know she is having trouble adjusting to the role of queen, but the fear. The absolute fear.*

She called the gods. Ameria's words echoed through his mind. *And the gods answered.*

Kyle knew something dark had transpired that night, but the act that resulted in his life being traded for that of Marcus' was something Mary had never spoken of. Her suffering pulled at his heart, driving him to entertain notions that would result in destroying his father's highly held convictions of honor. Dreams continued to plague him, becoming more frequent—two young men engaged in eternal combat, always resulting in death. "What does it mean?"

He stood from the chair and walked closer to the fire. Autumn was approaching and the nights were cooler. He pushed his hands toward the rising flames, allowing their warmth to chase the chill from his cold skin. "Mary, what do I do?" he asked, although he already knew the answer. "Do I take you away? Sweep you into my arms and ensure your sister will inherit the throne? My father is right. It would be so easy." He drew a deep breath. "Do I leave, surrendering you to the fate the gods have seen fit to bestow?"

Yet he knew he could no more bring himself to leave her than he could take her away. *She is a princess,* his father had said. *The one fate from which she can never escape.*

He shook his head. "Mary," he whispered. "Mariana."

Flames danced across the crumbling wood, the tips occasionally transforming from yellow to red, orange, and white. "Gods of Kale, hear my prayer. Guide me upon this path. Guide me in protecting this woman who has embedded herself so deeply into my soul."

A deep, gruff voice answered through the shadows. "*Beware calling the gods, Lord of Koloso. Beware.*"

He jumped, sweeping his eyes across the room. "Who's there?" he asked.

No answer came.

CHAPTER VII

MARIANA HAD CALLED KYLE TO her chambers. Finding her seated before a warm fire on the opposite side of the room, he bowed before approaching. "You summoned, my princess?"

"Yes," she answered, motioning him closer. "Please, sit down."

He crossed the room and took a chair beside hers. Evening had cast its shadow over the land and the room was lit entirely by firelight. The chairs were lined with golden cushions, which matched the drapes covering the windows. Mary was a vision, in a gown with thin straps that clung to her shoulders as her hair cascaded loosely down her back.

"Thank you for coming."

"When the princess calls."

Mary nodded. "Kyle, I must make a request of you."

"Of course, Your Highness. I am at your service."

"I am not sure you are going to like this one."

Kyle straightened in his chair, centering his gaze on Mary. "What has happened, my lady?"

"I have heard a great number of things, Kyle. Specifically, rumors and whispers about the men who killed my father and Master—" She had to draw another breath before she could finish her sentence. "Master Leo."

"You have secrets to tell?"

"Yes. For starters, the killer's father was a defendant."

"What? A...defendant?"

Mary nodded. "His name was Nathan, and he was banished for the murder of a teammate. Only...it is possible he was innocent."

"He murdered a teammate? Wait...innocent?"

"Yes. The woman had been injured during a battle. Nathan claimed she died of her injuries. However, it is also conceivable Nathan killed her on the way to the temple healing chambers."

"Why would a defendant have done such a thing?"

"Because the woman was engaged to my father, the prince, but my grandfather wanted my mother on the throne enough to start a civil war among the provinces over an inflated slight. Potentially, in order to avoid further loss of life, Nathan took steps to ensure my father's love did not survive the journey. And, there's another reason..." She shook her head, casting her eyes down.

"Mary, what is it?"

She forced herself to draw another deep breath and meet his gaze. "Some versions of the events suggest Master Leo ordered her killed."

"Master Leo? Ordered the death of a defendant?" He shook his head. "You can't believe that."

"I don't," she answered. "Or at least..." Pain seeped back into her voice. "I don't want to."

Kyle slipped from the chair to his knees to take her hands into his own. "I'm sorry, my princess."

Mary's teeth dug lightly into her bottom lip. "I don't know what to believe, Kyle. Defendants led me into a trap meant to claim my life. A temple master attempted to kill my sister. Now Master Leo may have ordered a man to kill my father's fiancé, then banished the defendant who followed his orders, punishing not only that man, but his children as well. Children who have now come to claim their vengeance." She moved her hand, slipping it more securely into his grasp.

"What do you need, Princess?"

"My sister. I cannot envision going after my father's killers without her."

Kyle nodded. "Shall I send a message?"

"I tried that already. Lord Louis informed me she is at Sanguis Castle."

"In Serenitas? What is she doing there?"

"I'm uncertain, but I wonder if she is doing the same thing I am—searching for Father's killer."

"If it was your grandfather who threatened war, he might be the one to ask what actually happened."

"Yes," Mary agreed. "I imagine he would be, which is why I suspect Ameria is searching for the same answers."

"What would you have of me, Princess?"

"Speak with my sister as someone she trusts. Tell her this is an issue which transcends our anger and impending fight. The prince was her father as well, and I don't think it appropriate to..."

"Make these decisions without her?"

"Exactly. I don't know who I can trust, so I need the message delivered by..."

"Me?"

"I hope she will be more receptive to you. I could send Jiro, but he's helping your father govern the council."

Kyle stared, then nodded. "If you think it is best, Mariana, I shall accept this quest. Though I wish..."

"I know," Mary replied. "But I think this message will be best received coming from you. She may listen, where she would refuse to heed all others."

"I understand. I will go, if this is your desire."

"Not my desire," she answered. "But what is required."

"I will leave at once."

"Not so fast. I don't want you to go alone. Take Brandan."

"No, Mary. He's my acting second. I don't want to leave you without both of us."

"I have Master Jiro and the Golden Defendant at my side. I'll be fine. Please, Kyle, for my peace of mind, take Brandan with you."

He reached a hand up and cupped the side of her face. "Are you certain?"

"Yes. Take him, and at least three others you trust. Ride from here to the closest Kalian temple. From there, transfer to the Temple of Koloso, and ride to Lord Riccard's castle."

"The Temple of Dektra would be closer."

"Traveling to Koloso will raise fewer questions, and allow you to ride your own horse, which I know you would prefer."

"I shall leave at once, my princess." He pulled away.

"Wait."

Kyle froze as she raised her hand to touch his cheek, then surprised him further as she kissed him. Not a gentle expression, but a forceful, passionate gesture, which transformed to a lingering embrace as he slid his arms around her.

When she finally broke contact, unshed tears threatened to spill as she fought for breath. "I love you, Kyle. Right or wrong." She choked. "Please come back to me."

"I will, Mary," he answered, as she leaned forward and kissed him a second time. This caress was more controlled, more purposeful than passionate. He held her, a tremor betraying her resolve. Then, in a breath so soft it was barely audible he said, "Right or wrong, Mary. Right or wrong."

When she regained control, he pulled back and laid a kiss on the back of her hand.

"I will complete this task, and return to you swiftly." Kyle stood and bowed one last time. "I bid you *adieu*, Mariana."

He turned, leaving Mary alone in the room of dancing flame and flickering shadow.

CHAPTER VIII

HAVING SUFFICIENTLY MADE HER POINT on how the laws of the land were to be enforced, Princess Ameria returned to her grandfather's castle. Despite this province being foreign for the majority of her life, the land called to her, as though a piece of her soul had always dwelled within the ancient stone halls.

Dismounting from her silver stallion, she passed Argento's reins to a waiting guardsman and entered the stone fortress. The echo of her heels followed as she walked down a series of hallways. Entering her mother's old room, which had been assigned to her, she planned a bath to rid herself of her journey's stench and the sweat of the hard day's ride.

She paused at the sound of her uncle's voice, drawing her farther down the corridor.

"You cannot be serious!" Andrew's voice boomed. "I am your son!"

The unmistakable sound of her grandfather's words answered, "A position you were born to, but have never been worthy of holding."

"Honestly?" her uncle asked in disbelief. "Because I never wore your precious gold? Do you know how many lords would be overjoyed to have their son wear the silver of Kale? Even your arch rival, Lord Chiro, has a son and heir who wears silver!"

"Silver to a worthy opponent. To a princess of the realm and, thus far, an undefeated champion of the Kalian temples. Chiro's son was never born, nor meant, to wear the golden robes. You, on the other hand, lost to your own partner. You never earned a leadership position on the defendant team, and you lost all but one of your tournament rounds...including to your own sister."

"And was she, dear father, not a worthy enough opponent to lose to? My *sister*."

"Not when she faced you wearing silver robes."

"So what?" he answered, anger lacing his words. "I wasn't as perfect as my precious sister. I lost one fight to my partner and you have made me pay dearly for that defeat! I have been denied your pride and love all my life. But to disinherit me? For a girl barely more than a child?"

"That child is my granddaughter. A proven royal champion of golden rank. A princess, if not future queen, of this kingdom. An offspring worthy of bearing my name and title. She *will be* the next Lady of Serenitas and, should she become queen, the title will pass to her children."

"Father, you cannot be serious!"

"I find that I am rarely anything else," the high lord answered his son. "And the legalities are already done. From this moment, you remain in this castle only by my good graces, and those of Princess Ameria."

"Father, if you do this, I swear I will—"

"Will what?" Ameria interjected, stepping into the room.

"You!" Garbed in the deep blue robes of Serenitas, Andrew wheeled to face her.

"It is good to see you as well, Uncle." Ameria walked toward him, keeping her hand loosely on the golden hilt of her silver blade. "Though I find it distressing to return from my mission and find you issuing threats against a high lord of the realm." She turned to where both Yarin and Stephen stood in the doorway, drawn by the same angered tones which had prompted Ameria to investigate. "Tell me, Silver Defendant, do you find this exchange distressing as well?"

"Yes, my princess," Stephen replied. "Most distressing."

"Surely I must be mistaken." Ameria continued moving toward Andrew. "What I perceived to be a threat must have instead been naught but a misunderstanding between family. Is that not so, my dear uncle?"

He met her with an icy stare. "If you believe, for one moment, that I am going to sit by and allow you to take away my birthright—"

"Ah," she interrupted, "but I do." Ameria took a step closer, and lifted her sword fractionally from its scabbard. "I expect you to accept what your father, and sworn lord, has deemed best for both this province, and the people who reside within it. I also expect you to comply with this demotion as you have all the other ones in your life—without resistance."

"You know nothing of my life!"

"We are both children of this land, Andrew. And of the Serenitas bloodline, are we not? Both sworn to do what is right for its people. Are we not alike in this endeavor?"

"We are nothing—"

"Forgive me." She raised a hand, the gesture stilling her uncle's words. "Perhaps you are right. I, after all, know nothing of disappointing one's parent, lord, and sovereign. Nothing of losing fight after fight. Nor of the shame you must carry at being such a failure in the eyes of your family, both royal and not."

"How dare you!" He stepped toward Ameria.

"Come any closer," Stephen warned from a few paces behind the princess, "and you will forfeit more than your title."

Ameria kept her gaze steadily on her uncle, who stopped moving at the threat issued by the Silver Defendant. "I believe, Uncle, there is no call for violence. Wouldn't you agree?"

Andrew looked from Ameria to Stephen. He reluctantly took several steps back, distancing himself from his royal niece.

"I'll take that as a yes. Now, as the new heir apparent, I am charging you personally with oversight of Lord Karro's efforts to rid the border villages of local raiders. You may take your personal guard to assist you with this task."

Her uncle blanched. "You're...what?"

"Ordering you to the villages to assist your advisor in his thus far insufficient efforts to fend off the bandits."

"Ordering me...into the field?"

"Who better to trust, with this most important of tasks, than a member of my own family?"

Andrew turned back to face his father. "Disinherited and cast out on the same day?"

"No one has cast you out," Riccard reprimanded. "You have been given a command by your future high lady and princess. No more, no less."

He turned back to Ameria, but she spoke first. "I am a princess of Kale," she said. "And even I was not above going out into the field when needed. Why, Lord Andrew, be appalled at being asked to carry out an act which the Princess of Kale herself was not above doing?"

He met her sapphire eyes with searing heat. "Such calculated malice. You must be your mother's daughter."

"And Riccard's granddaughter," Ameria answered with a cold touch.

"Angelia was right! She always said you would never see me as worthy."

"Andrew!" Riccard's tone caused goosebumps to rise on Ameria's skin. "You are not now, nor are you ever, to speak that name. Your sister chose her fate. You are dangerously close to sealing your own."

In the subsequent silence, Riccard's words fully spread through the room.

Ameria cleared her throat. "I am sending you, Andrew, to protect our people on the outer edge of the province. Something you have continually failed to do. You view this order as a punishment, when in fact, it is an opportunity to return to your father's good graces. A chance to regain the honor you have lost before facing our ancestors in the rainbow halls. The hope that, when you die, you'll know you made a difference, for the better, in this realm." She drew a deep breath. "I will tell you, as I have previously informed your advisor, I believe in second chances. You will never be a high lord, it is true, but you could still become a good knight. The choice to do so, Uncle, is your own."

She took a step, closing the gap between them as the Silver Defendant moved beside her like a shadow. "I believe in second chances," she said again. "But in thirds—never. If you are to be my loyal lord and subject, then I suggest you learn this now. You will obey me, Uncle, if you ever again wish to stand in my, or your father's, presence."

Andrew bowed his head. "I shall leave at once, my lady. As you command."

She nodded, stepping aside, allowing him to walk past her. When Andrew's footsteps faded, she turned to her grandfather. "It would be insulting to ask if you are certain of this choice, so I shall spare us both and assume I know the answer."

"That would be wise, Princess," Riccard answered. "It is time my son earns his way in this world. I only regret that I did not force him to do so long ago. You shall inherit this province and, should you become queen, its title and wealth will pass to your second-born."

Ameria nodded, then bowed at the waist to the older lord. "I shall take my leave, Grandfather. Know that I will work every day to ensure I never give you cause to regret this decision, nor dishonor the faith you have placed upon me this day."

"Thank you, Princess. I am sure you will never give me cause to do so."

Ameria turned and left the room, gliding through the cold halls tainted with the dank smell of approaching winter. When she reached her chambers, Ameria called for her grandfather's captain, Lord Yarin, who entered the room at her bidding.

"Your Highness."

"I have a question for you, my lord, if you would allow me to ask."

"You are the princess, my lady. I shall answer any question to the best of my ability."

"Did you know my aunt?"

Caught off-guard, Yarin stumbled over his answer. "Your aunt, by which you mean..."

"My mother's sister, Riccard's youngest daughter."

"Briefly."

"The way my uncle spoke of my dishonored aunt today troubles me. I wish to know...were they close as children, or perhaps even as young defendants?"

"I believe so, my princess."

"Speak frankly, please. The answer is important."

Lord Yarin stared at Ameria, then admitted, "Lord Andrew was heartbroken when his sister was banished."

Ameria considered his words before taking a step closer, lowering her voice, though there was likely no need for her to do so in this far wing of the castle. "Thank you for your candor, Lord Yarin. Would you please ask the Silver Defendant to attend me?"

"Of course, my lady." He paused. "Forgive me, but is there anything *I* might help you with?"

"That depends on where your loyalties lie, Lord Yarin. Lord Stephen's are with me out of a mixture of fear, and the faint hope he will be able to maintain his position after I wear the golden robes. Fear and hope, my lord. A very powerful combination. And a trust I know he would not dare to betray."

"I assure you, my lady, you are my lord's granddaughter and chosen heir. I would never dream of—"

"Even if what I ordered could potentially bring harm to one, or more, of Lord Riccard's discarded children?" she challenged. "How deep does your loyalty go, Lord Yarin? To strictly your lord and his chosen? Or perhaps instead, do they reach the children you helped to protect and train?"

"Your Highness," Lord Yarin answered, "my loyalty will always be to the high lord and his *chosen* heir. I know my duty, to this land and you, as both his heir and a princess of the realm."

Ameria considered him, then made her decision. "Come closer, my lord. Tonight we speak in secrets."

He did as instructed, moving to take a knee in front of his princess. "How may I be of service, Your Highness?"

"This will be a mission requiring great secrecy."

"Of course."

Ameria nodded. "I want you to follow my uncle."

"Your uncle?" he asked, confused. "What do you mean?"

"If he goes to the village, as ordered, you may return with the private satisfaction my suspicions proved unfounded. However, if not..."

Lord Yarin shook his head, "I don't understand. Where else would he go?"

Ameria stared down at Lord Yarin. "He may go to the village.

However, he may, just may, go to see my father's killers. And if he does, you will lead me straight to them."

CHAPTER IX

LIKE THE ROOMS OF ALL temple students, the interior of Kyle's private quarters at the Temple of Koloso matched his rank, from the silver cushions covering the chairs to the coverlet across the expansive bed. The only contrasting item was a wooden desk, where Kyle now sat, and even that was draped with a shimmering satin that matched his robes.

Now the highest-ranking of the silver students, Kyle lamented on Marcus' death. Raised as competitors from birth, the two men had often found themselves at odds, both on and off the mats. The contention not only due to their competing temples, but it could be traced back to their warring families as well. A nephew of High Lord Riccard, Marcus could potentially have been named the heir of Serenitas, while Kyle would be the heir to Turbamentum.

An uneasy history lay between the provinces of Serenitas and Turbamentum. A rivalry that had existed even before the time of Kale, if the stories were to be believed. Both families had connections to the royal bloodline with multiple princes and kings born to each province. Though they rarely engaged each other in true battle, history whispered of behind-the-scenes intrigue with deaths allegedly caused by members of the other lineage.

Historically, the two families hailed from different temples; the likely cause of the ancient disdain. The heirs of Serenitas, including Lord Riccard, attended the Temple of Kale, while Turbamentum heirs attended the Temple of Koloso. Many of the supposed assassinations were in the name of advancing not only one province, but the temples each hailed from.

It had been an unprecedented act when Lord Riccard broke this tradition by sending his eldest daughter, Annabelle, to the Temple of Koloso instead of Kale. Having only met the high lord once in his youth, Kyle was uncertain why Riccard had chosen to send his daughter to the silver temple instead of the gold. His best guess was the siblings had likely been sent to separate temples in order to optimize their chances of both wearing golden robes; they were too similar in age to compete in separate classes. Kyle wondered if the Serenitas Lord would have made the same choice, had he known it would be Annabelle, and not Andrew, who would bring honor to his ancient name.

Perhaps I can ask him, Kyle thought, only to immediately dismiss the notion. All of this had taken place before he was born and mattered little now. It would take a united front, of both families, to face these new challenges. Not only delivering justice to Leo and Eadmund's killers, but to also keep the kingdom intact with the twin princesses' fight looming on the horizon. A task that Kyle wondered at the possibility of, with each temple plotting the demise of the other on a regular basis.

Kyle pressed his fingers against his temples, rubbing firmly. He was tired. Met with a storm, which continued even now, it had taken several days of hard riding to reach the Temple of Kevera. Additional hours were spent arranging passage through the enchanted portals, present only at the thirteen temples, land blessed by the gods. Now at the Temple of Koloso, the riding party had chosen to rest in hopes the inclement weather would pass before they continued their journey. Grateful for the respite, Kyle remained leery of the rest his body craved.

The dreams were growing worse, making prolonged, deep sleep nearly impossible. The same two men, dueling. Never at the same location, and always resulting in the death of one warrior. Lowering his hands from his face, Kyle wracked his brain for who the two men might be. As usual, he drew a blank.

Frustrated, he rose from the chair and reclined on the bed. It was only in the privacy of these familiar chambers, that he allowed his thoughts to drift to Mary.

I love you, she had confessed, before sending him on this quest. Yet, even then, an unknown fear had shone through her eyes. *You should stay away*, she had cautioned only days before sending him from both the palace and her.

"I don't know what to do, Mary," he spoke aloud to the silent room.

Even you cannot save me from what I am. Her words were an echo of his father's counsel. Mary was the future queen, and as such her fate lay beyond the control of even their own hearts.

I should have given in to her pleas. Ameria would be queen, and Mary would be in my arms. I could spend the rest of my life making her happy. He turned, tossing on the pillows. His princess and sworn queen had begged him to wash her pain away. A fervent plea that had threatened to overwhelm every caution he had ever put into place. He'd resisted. Was he a fool for refusing her?

Yet he knew, deep down, that was not the case. Mary had sworn before the gods to honor the vow of blood and arms. An oath he loathed more with each longing glance. He adjusted his head against the feather pillows, resolved at last to surrender to exhaustion.

But there was no comfort to be had, even in his dreams.

CHAPTER X

❖ ⋙✦⋘ ❖

KYLE STOOD IN THE KOLOSIAN *Temple's training room. Dual-colored mats lined either side of the expansive silver floor, each area draped with satin curtains matching the mats they thinly veiled. He walked down the center row, lightly touching each of the colored cloths. Above him hung a chandelier filled with candles giving off soft light, which combined with blue flames of a massive fire burning in the center of the isle.*

He paused when he reached the fire, staring at the blue flames licking their way across thick strips of crackling wood. The fire cast shadows on the satin and the dark stone walls, surrounding him. Helplessly mesmerized, he drew shallow breaths to avoid as much of the smoke as possible.

A sharp sound drew his eyes past the fire. Tall doors separated the standard training area from the space reserved only for the highest-ranked students and leaders. To Kyle's surprise, he found the stately doors not of their normal silver, but of gleaming gold.

Kyle stepped left, moving around the fire to approach the golden threshold. As he remembered, the same intricate spirals were embedded into the metal. However, as he reached the doors, he found something new. The mark of Kale. An outline of a blade, its hilt surrounded by a golden crown, symbolizing the celebrated lord as rightful king. Along the circlet of the crown was the outline of a dagger, with a miniature ruby for its tip, the only splash of color against the otherwise golden sheet.

"Gold?" Kyle said, turning the word into a question. "Why is the mark of Kale on the door of Koloso?"

"Beware." A gruff voice seeped into the room. "What is seen cannot be unseen."

The doors opened of their own accord, parting to reveal the room within. Featuring a mat draped in layers of gold and silver satin on one side, and rainbow on the other, the room seemed familiar enough. Except, on the back wall, hung a portrait Kyle had never seen. Portraits were traditionally frowned upon in the temples, the belief that such an accurate depiction held the power to prevent a soul from resting peacefully in the Golden Halls. Of the few that did exist, many were burnt by religiously devout temple members, many decades before he was born.

Entranced, Kyle stared at the framed image, and the frozen eyes of the two men who haunted his dreams. The tall blond was garbed in robes of gold, while his companion stood an exact height in shimmering silver. Kyle studied their somber faces, searching for a hint of recognition.

"Fear to the fearless," *the deep voice came again.* "Hope to the hopeless."

Kyle turned to his left, and discovered that wall had changed as well. In place of temple banners, there was a sheet of gold.

"Mercy to those who hate them," *the growling voice rose.*

He walked forward until he reached the wall, his eyes deciphering lines etched within the panel. Rough images, of each Kalian temple, were outlined within the gold, accented with splashes of corresponding color. The temple of Ziazan stood at the top, outlined in a mixture of jewels, representing each of the Kalian temple colors. Below Ziazan, the Temple of Koloso, barely visible, while the Temple of Kale stood outlined in silver.

"What?" *he asked in confusion, running his finger over the etching's outline.*

"Death to those who love them."

He traced his fingers lower, over the Temple of Dektra, down to the temples of Kevera and Proelium.

"Destiny."

He froze when he discovered what seemed to be an additional temple. Presuming a mistake on his part, he went back to the top and counted. When he reached fourteen, he shook his head and counted again. "Twelve, thirteen, fourteen."

"Fourteen? There should be thirteen."

Puzzled, he turned and found the portrait of the two men now appeared on the opposite wall, their sapphire and emerald gazes burning through him. Only now they were joined by another framed painting, this one of two women Kyle knew well.

He stepped forward, allowing his eyes to fall into the depths of Mary's, frozen in time beside her sister. Clasped in her hands was the hilt of a golden blade, while Ameria stood with a sword of silver. He compared the two portraits. The same hair, dark and blond, the same eyes. Only the color of their respective robes was different, with Mary's black hair standing out against golden cloth while the dark-haired man wore silver.

"I don't understand," *he spoke aloud, though to whom, he was uncertain.*

"Princess of Kale. Princess of Koloso. Heir to both," *the voice answered, only this time followed by a deep-throated growl that made his blood run cold.*

He turned toward the sound and saw something moving in the shadows against the far wall. "Who's there?" *he asked, his voice lacking its usual confidence.*

"Destiny."

"Destiny?"

"Heir to both."

Kyle turned back to the portraits, those depicted so similar in not only hair and eye color, but in height, bone structure...what did it mean?

"Beware the twins of Kale," *the deep voice boomed through the room.* "Beware."

CHAPTER XI

BLADES CLASHED, RINGING THROUGHOUT THE stone chamber. Ameria clutched the hilt tightly, maintaining her grip despite dripping sweat soaking her golden robes. Breathing hard, she stepped back, moving the sword close to her body as she awaited the next attack.

Across from her, in Lord Riccard's training rooms, Lord Stephen's silver robe and short brown hair clung to his equally damp skin. He eyed the princess, through labored breaths, on the same gold and silver mats that Ameria's mother, Princess Annabelle, had once held a sword for the first time.

Stephen lunged toward Ameria, his blade sailing to her left. Ameria moved right, sending Stephen off-balance as his sword met only air. Ameria turned, bringing her blade high for a downward stroke on Stephen's exposed arm, attempting to use his precarious balance to her advantage. He threw himself across the room, hitting the golden mat and rolling, holding his sword above him so not to cut himself. At the edge of the mat, he struggled back to his feet.

Ameria did not pursue him, instead pausing to wipe both of her hands on her clothes. After adjusting her grip on the hilt of her blade, she widened her stance as Stephen moved back across the mat. Her heart rate was elevated, but not excessively so for having been on the mats for the past hour. The attacks had become progressively slower, energy being conserved for more accurate strikes.

Stephen stepped closer. Ameria watched him with calm eyes. He took another step. Ameria moved without warning, swinging her blade toward his right. He moved to block her. The two swords met in mid-air with a loud clang. Ameria twisted, stepping away from Stephen before swinging her blade again. Stephen moved to block her, and she decided to take a chance, moving her sword down, throwing herself toward the ground as she did so. In a semi-controlled fall, she swung her blade, ducking under Stephen's as the tip of her sword bit into his leg.

Stephen jerked back with a sharp cry. "Gods!" he called, moving his free hand to the torn cloth quickly staining with blood. "We're not at the temples, you know."

"Oh come now, it's not deep," she scoffed.

"It could have been."

Ameria rose to her feet. "Trust me, Lord Stephen, should a day come when I intend to cause you serious harm, you'll know."

The air stilled at her words.

Breaking the silence, Ameria broke the building tension with a smile. "Here." She walked to where her grandfather kept a kit for injuries. Removing the required supplies, Ameria assisted the Silver Defendant to a chair and knelt to dress his injury.

"Please, Princess, there is no need for you to—"

"As though I've never seen blood," she dismissed his protest, tearing the material covering his lower leg. "This will sting," she warned, before splashing the wound with antiseptic. He inhaled sharply, but otherwise gave no indication of discomfort.

Ameria had been taught basic healing skills, as had all trainees, at the Temple of Ziazan. A temple devoted entirely to the worship of the gods that offered no combat training, Ziazan was located between the two highest-ranking of the Kalian Temples, on the border of the Turbamentum and Serenitas Provinces. Every student spent at least a year at the most sacred of the Kalian temples, learning everything from Kalian histories, identification of healing herbs, meditation, and ways to honor the temple gods. Skills Ameria was grateful to have.

She only vaguely remembered being taken to the temples. Barely five years of age, she struggled to understand why her parents would abandon her to the care of strangers, though she was told it was the Kalian way. Jiro had been kind to her, she could recall that much. Though, it was a distant level of kindness, more like her strict mother than the father who had read her stories and embraced her warmly. Her father told tales of heroic knights and valiant quests, always promising one day he would lead her, and her sister, on such adventures.

A broken promise. No sooner was Ameria named to the Temple of Koloso, than her Kalian father abandoned his youngest daughter, spending the few visits his position allowed with Mariana at the Temple of Kale. Her father was not unkind. He was simply never there. Never attending so much as a single tournament match, let alone a personal visit, if her sister was not in attendance.

Instead, Ameria developed a distant relationship with her mother, the former golden student of Koloso. Princess Annabelle kept her apprised on the comings and goings of the court, shifts in power between ruling families, and other details her mother believed she, as a princess, should familiarize herself with. It had never, precisely, been a warm relationship, but better than the utterly non-existent one with her father.

After his murder, Ameria did not particularly miss the man he had been. She'd never really known him. Any chance of that had been destroyed by the long-established rivalry between the Temples of Kale and Koloso, powerful enough to cause even her royal parents to declare an unspoken loyalty to the daughter who attended their chosen institution, and an aloofness toward the twin who did not.

Instead, Ameria mourned the relationship she had longed for, and the knowledge it would never be. Her determination to find his killer was one more of principle and honor, than anger or grief. Instead, Ameria's fury was directed at her sister's decision to watch their father die and allow his killer to live.

The thought made her blood boil anew. How could any true servant, let alone ruler of the realm, watch its prince and golden master be struck down, and not be willing to sacrifice whatever was necessary to ensure it would be the last life the killer would ever take. How could Mary have stood there and let him get away? Her inaction was infuriating. True, doing so may have cost Kyle's life, but that was a debt any Kolosian would have paid. The good of the realm must come before all else. Something her soft-hearted sister continually failed, or refused, to understand.

"My lady?" Stephen's words drew her from reflection. His leg was fully wrapped, a faint pink line coloring the white strip where blood collected on the opposite side. She had no memory of tightening the bandage, having been so lost in her thoughts.

She glanced up.

"Where were you, my lady?"

"Forgive me," she said, standing from her kneeling position beside the chair. "The cut was shallow, it shouldn't scar." She tried to resist, but was unable to keep her eyes from slipping down to her wrist, where hideous mutilations marred her once-perfect skin. She generally hid the unseemly welts, but during training, she bared her arms to ensure nothing would impede her ability to grip the hilt of her blade. Ameria walked across the room to collect a pair of golden gloves, which she slid over her hands.

"You should not view them as a mark of shame, my lady."

"What?" Ameria asked, turning back to the Silver Defendant.

"Scars should not be viewed as a mark of shame," he clarified. "I assure you, no one else sees them that way."

"Easy for you to say." Ameria fiddled with her covered fingertips. "I am a princess."

Stephen stood and approached the younger woman. "A warrior princess. One who, I have no doubt, whether queen or Golden Defendant, shall lead men into battle one day." He reached forward, his fingers stopping just shy of her arm. "With your permission, my lady?"

Ameria stared at him unsure, then nodded. Taking her hand, Stephen pulled off the gloves. Her fingers, even calloused from constant swordplay, were practically smooth in comparison to her wrists. Punctured and burned by flame, the splotchy skin was pink with ugly white lines crawling toward a circular, deep blotch, where the bones of her wrists had completely pierced through. For several horrific months, Ameria feared she would never again be able to use a blade.

Until one night, during a raging storm, the wraith had come, materializing before her for the first time. "*It will not do*," the wolf-like creature had said in a voice more growl than words. "*It will not do*." With a breath, he had healed the injuries to her arms. But the scars remained, bringing a fresh wave of disgust every time she looked at them.

Stephen lifted her hand, aligning the scars with her eyes. "These scars, My Princess, are a sign that you have faced great danger and survived. That you did not surrender. You have suffered, it is true, but you also fought through the challenges placed in your path. Don't you see, my lady? These scars are a sign of bravery, not weakness."

Ameria stared at the Silver Defendant. She had never before considered Stephen a man of particular wisdom. Nor of great bravery. In fact, this was the first time she could recall ever having considered Stephen with significant respect.

A deeper voice entered the conversation. "He is correct, Ameria." She dropped her hands to face her grandfather. Draped in golden robes, his right hand rested on the top of a matching cane, the face of a wolf with jeweled eyes carved into the shimmering metal. "You may as well show her."

Stephen took a step back, turning to face the High Lord of Serenitas. "I feared it would be..."

"Inappropriate?" Riccard suggested. "To show an unaccompanied princess of the realm, bound to wed a man of higher birth than you?"

Stephen nodded.

"Show her anyway."

The man in silver shifted uncomfortably.

"An order, not a request."

Stephen complied. Both Ameria and Riccard watched in silence as he removed his belt, placing his sheathed blade on the floor. Next he removed his outer robe, before pulling his long-sleeved shirt above his head. When he raised his left arm, he revealed a thick, faded scar, which ran from his shoulder down his side, before vanishing into the silver cloth of his trousers.

Ameria took a step forward, studying the old wound. "From a blade?"

"Yes," Stephen answered.

"Why..." Ameria took a breath to form the proper question. "Why was the injury not healed?"

Stephen stared at the ground.

Riccard answered, "The injury had healed before he returned to the temples. Therefore, the magic did not smooth the scars."

"Oh?" she asked, but did not remove her gaze from Stephen's side.

"He was held captive," her grandfather explained, "by an old nemesis of Master Leo's. He captured some members of the defendant team, oh...it must have been ten years ago now. They were tortured for months before Leo's team was able to track down the villains and slay them."

"How many defendants were taken?"

"Eight."

Ameria stepped to her left, circling the Silver Defendant, her eyes gliding across his chest as she noted additional scars, everything from shallow cuts to faded burns. She realized the marks ran along his left arm as well, sporadically dotting his arm down to the elbow. She tried to recall a time when she had seen the silver lord in short sleeves, but could not bring to mind any such occasion. Now, she knew why.

"This is not a story I know."

"Failures are not something the defendants prefer to remember. And this story would not have been appropriate for the seven-year-old you were." Riccard gave a wave of his hand. "You may replace your shirt, Lord Stephen."

The Silver Defendant obeyed, slipping the satiny material back over his head before reaching down to pick up his robe.

Ameria considered Stephen with a newfound sense of understanding, and regretted her harsh critique of his mettle at Lord Edward's funeral. He'd had good reason for not following the late Golden Defendant on his mission to find Nathan's children. The last time he had embarked on such a quest, he had paid dearly.

After drawing a deep breath, she walked toward the door, leaving her gloves discarded on the training room floor. But when she reached the doorway, Ameria turned back to the Silver Defendant. "A question, my lord?"

"Yes, Princess."

"Eight were taken prisoner. How many survived?"

Pain crossed Stephen's face and Ameria knew—the answer was one.

CHAPTER XII

KYLE AWOKE FROM THE DREAM in a cold sweat. Morning had come, light pouring through a far window, though not with the same radiance of both the royal palace and the Temple of Kale. Deep in a valley, the Temple of Koloso was forever shrouded in the shadows of the surrounding mountains. Legends claimed it had not always been so. That the mountains had actually risen around the once-prominent temple. Though, of course, there was no way to be certain if the stories were true.

Kyle rose to a seated position on the bed, swinging his legs over the side so his feet could touch the floor. He raised his hand, rubbing his temples as he closed his eyes.

Beware the twins of Kale.

He had little doubt now the voice spoke of Princess Mariana and Ameria. But why he should beware the woman he loved, and his temple partner, he could not fathom.

Well, on second thought...perhaps he should fear Ameria, at least to a certain degree. She won't be happy when she learns about my affection for her sister. But then again, neither was my father... Kyle sighed internally, thinking again of his tormented love. Even in his dreams, she'd seemed forlorn, the burden of a crown she did not desire weighing on her shoulders.

Her golden-haired sister had seemed less sad than unreadable, cold sapphire eyes revealing nothing of the soul within. Ameria had always been the hard one. A princess trained, as he had been, to be more ruler than person, with the responsibility and expectations unwavering, no matter the cost. Emotions, for a leader, must be abandoned to do what is right for the kingdom. Choices are to be made with a clear, level-headed thought process, never on a whim of the heart.

Kyle had assumed, from a young age, he would one day wed the youngest Princess of Kale. That his children would bear royal, though distant, titles until the day his eldest became the high lord in Kyle's place.

Expectation of the match was one of the reasons he, and not his older sister, had been named Lord Chiro's heir.

He had not seen his sister since the day she'd been initiated onto the defendant team, though he had heard she performed quite well, advancing through the ranks to hold the fifth-highest position on the team. Five years older than Kyle, Sasha had been the golden student of Koloso, winning ten of her twelve tournament rounds. She would be a contender in the thirteenth tournament as well, where Kyle was certain he would see her name high within the ranks of invited champions.

Pushing these thoughts aside, Kyle pulled out a set of fresh silver garments. He dressed, tying his robe into place with a matching ribbon, marking his Kolosian status. Reviewing the dream again in his mind, Kyle decided to walk the familiar stone corridors to the archive room, where he was greeted by the smells of aging ink and leather from the collection of bound books and ancient scrolls, each painstakingly transcribed by the temple scholars. Here lay the entire history of the Kalian temples, documenting their roots back thousands of years, with the histories of those families who served them. Following the catalog system he had been taught as a child, Kyle pulled several scrolls from the dusty shelves and spread them gingerly across a table on the left side of the room. He scanned the documents, searching for the meaning behind his dream. "Fourteen," he muttered. "But there are only thirteen temples."

When he found a temple list, he counted. Thirteen. He pushed that scroll to the side and selected an older one. Kyle counted again. "Eleven, twelve...thirteen." It made no sense. He flipped to the next. Placement changed on this version, Koloso in gold, Kale in silver. Kevera third instead of Desoto. But there were still only thirteen.

He reached for another. This one, dated over three hundred years ago, also had Koloso in the golden rank with Kale in silver. Three hundred twenty years—Kale gold, Desoto silver and Koloso red. Surprised, Kyle had never known either of the current top-ranking temples had been anything other than gold and silver.

He kept flipping. Three hundred fifty years. Four hundred. He paused. This was new. The temple of Desoto ranked gold. Temple of Eversus, silver. "Eversus?" Kyle spoke the temple name aloud. There is no such temple.

Yet here it was, written neatly in the ancient scroll. Returning to the shelf, he pulled additional parchments, opening the yellowing and brittle paper as gently as he could. Four hundred twenty years. Another temple he did not recognize, Aurum.

Aurum was ranked gold. Eversus silver. He searched further, scanning the document until he found the tournament records. *Championship Tournament, Championship round. Kale of the Temple of Eversus vs. Koloso of the Temple of Aurum.* He scanned lower. *Semi-championship rounds: Kale of the Temple of Eversus vs. Rachel of the Temple of Eversus and Koloso of the Temple of Aurum vs. Evelyn of the Temple of Aurum.* Kyle scanned lower. *Tristan of the Temple of Eversus vs. Jerald of the Temple of Aurum.*

He went back, thumbing through additional scrolls, searching for anything on these mysterious temples. A piece of folded paper fell out of one of the rolls. He picked up the carefully creased sheet and cleared additional space on the table. Opening it gently revealed a map so old he feared it would crumble at his touch. His emerald eyes scanned the document. A temple, which he knew to be Kale, presided over the northeastern corner of the map. Below it, the Temple of Ziazan. Then Koloso.

No—wait! Not the Temple of Koloso. The Temple of Eversus. "What?" The temples of Koloso and Kale were nowhere to be seen. In their place, the temples of Aurum and Eversus were listed as the highest in the land. He scanned further, going over names both familiar and unfamiliar. Fourteen names. No thirteen, but a familiar symbol, denoting a temple, where it should not have been—in the forest of the Periculum Mountains.

"What?"

A sharp pain burst through his fingers, causing him to drop the map. He pulled back, shaking his hand from the pain as the paper ignited and burned, the ink melting as the parchment rolled, paper blackening under the flame. "No!" he called, using his robe in an attempt to snuff out the fire.

His efforts proved futile against the spontaneous blaze. The tiny parchment now nothing but a pile of smoldering ashes lying atop the charred table. "By the gods," Kyle whispered. "What is happening?"

Then came the increasingly familiar warning. *"Beware the Twins of Kale."*

CHAPTER XIII

◆◆◆◆

PRINCESS MARIANA GALLOPED A HAPHAZARD route over the grassy fields surrounding the palace grounds. In an increasingly crowded court, these excursions had become more necessity than luxury. Stolen moments where she escaped the responsibility that otherwise never left her shoulders. Normally she'd have a royal escort. However, after promising herself she would remain within the palace gates, Mary ordered the stable boy to silence, while tossing him a golden coin to ensure he would remain so.

With both Kyle and Brandan gone, Mary struggled with isolation more than ever. The castle walls were strange and hollow; the rooms more vast than her presence would ever be able to fill. *It shouldn't be this way*, the bitter thought rolled through her mind.

Her father, the late Prince Eadmund, and Master Leo, had a presence, an aura surrounding them. The kind that drew men to them in times of need. The kind that others would follow blindly into battle. Their very being filled every corner of the enormous palace rooms, colossal in comparison to those she had called home in the Temple of Kale. Every time she thought of her father, and master, she realized how inadequately she was prepared for the tasks that fate and birthright now forced upon her.

Did Kale ever have such doubts? The revelation that Koloso and not Kale had been born to rule, contrary to the stories she had been told as a child, awoke conflicted feelings within her. The popular story was, of course, that King Kale and his younger brother, Prince Koloso, had fought a great evil where the younger of the brothers had been killed. The realization that Kale had been the younger made her feel strangely closer to him. Had Kale, being forced to take the throne at the unexpected loss of his brother, felt as Mary did now? The thought that Kale might have also felt as lost comforted her. Kale had managed to sit upon the very throne she now found herself thrust upon and still remain a hero. *If Kale could do so, could she not as well?*

At a tall stone wall surrounding the palace grounds, she paused, allowing her golden horse, Sherwyn, respite. She dismounted, pulling a thick blanket from the bag tied to Sherwyn's saddle and, with a sharp snap, spread it on the ground. Two of Kale's three suns were still high in the sky, providing late afternoon heat, while the third had just touched the horizon on its descent. Grateful for the momentary stillness surrounding her, Mary lay down on the blanket, closing her eyes against the brilliant sunlight.

She had received a report, delivered by a messenger from the Temple of Kevera, that Kyle and Brandan had safely reached the Temple of Koloso. They were preparing to continue on their journey towards Serenitas, where Mariana's maternal grandfather, Riccard, reigned as high lord. Mary could only recall having met him once, as a young child, and it was a vague memory at best. To her knowledge, Ameria had never ventured to his lands either. Learning her sister had taken up residence there was surprising. Mary wondered what secrets her grandfather might have divulged to her estranged twin.

More than this, Mary worried for Kyle. Had she done the right thing by sending him away? Was she protecting him from the wraiths, or had she put him in even more danger? Trusting no one, how she longed to speak to Master Leo one last time. To beg his guidance, and ask him for the truth of the terrible accusations lodged against the man she had thought capable of no wrong.

What a Golden Defendant you would make. His final words were a haunting taunt she could not escape.

"What did you mean?" she asked aloud, knowing there would be no answer. "Did you mean I should give up the throne? That I should take your spot as the Golden Defendant and temple master? Give my sister the throne she covets?" Anger infused her words as she spoke to the figment in her mind. "You told me I had to be queen. You said there was no choice! A Kalian must sit upon the throne! Why would you say that? Why would you make me doubt everything? Why, Leo!" Tears filled her eyes and she was grateful to be alone with her fears.

But she was not alone.

A deep growl answered her. "*You cannot escape,*" the wraith hissed, "*your destiny, Princess of Kale. Princess of Koloso. Heir to both.*"

Mariana's weeping ceased instantly at the increasingly familiar sound of the wraith's gruff tone. Her breath trembled as she opened her emerald eyes and rose from the blanket. Near the top of the hill above her, he stood: the black wolf-like creature, who was no wolf at all, but something far more dangerous. Its eyes glistened like jewels. "*Hail Princess.*" The words formal, yet menacing. "*Hail.*"

"What do you want?" Her voice was barely a whisper, but she knew her words would carry to the pointed ears of this menacing creature. "Tell me."

"*So young. Always young. But never so beautiful. Always a prince. Never a princess.*"

"What?"

"*Different from those who came before. Yet, the same.*"

"I don't understand." Her voice remained a fearful breath.

"*The ones who came before. Always a prince. Never a princess.*"

"Before? You mean...my father?"

The wraith gave a gruff laugh. "*Not worthy. Not chosen.*"

"Chosen for what?" she demanded. "Stop talking in riddles."

"*Heir of the ancient bloodline. Heir of prophecy. Heir to royalty. Heir of...*" His words trailed. He stilled—waiting.

"Kale," Mary finished for him. "Heir to Kale."

"*Yes,*" the wraith hissed.

"Heir to Koloso."

"*Both. Heir to both.*"

"Princes. They were princes?"

"*Mercy to those who hate you. Death to those you love.*"

"I don't understand!" Heat rose in her voice. "Why? Why must I lose those I love? Is it because I am on the throne? Tell me what I must do."

"*Twins of the ancient bloodline. Fear to the fearless. Hope to the hopeless. Mercy to those who hate you. Death to those who love you. That is your destiny, Princess of Kale, Princess of Koloso, heir to both.*"

"Please," Mariana pleaded, "just tell me. I don't want anyone else to die."

The reflected light in the wraith's eyes dimmed, and something akin to pity filled the creature's gaze. Yet his words offered no answers. Only a warning before he vanished, as though evaporating.

"*The hour draws near. Beware, Princess. Beware.*"

CHAPTER XIV

PRINCESS AMERIA STOOD IN AN expansive stone chamber supported by wide pillars, at the heart of her grandfather's ancient keep, Sanguis Castle. Once, this fortress, and not the glass palace where her sister now resided, had been the center of power in the Kalian kingdoms. A stone structure that had stood over a thousand years, it would remain standing after her time in this world was done. Everything about this land spoke of ancient power. From that strength, Ameria's confidence grew under the tutelage of her grandfather, Lord Riccard.

Ameria had difficulty understanding why her mother had kept her from this wise man. A teacher worthy of advising the queen she hoped to one day become. One who had consulted royalty for decades, and would continue to do so until his last breath. A believer in the ancient traditions Ameria had been taught to value in her childhood, and clung to as she became a young woman. The father figure she'd never had, her own father abandoning her due to the ancient temple rivalry.

"Many rulers," her grandfather elucidated, "when faced with making a choice in a dispute between two lords, will side with the one of higher rank."

"But not you," Ameria replied, having observed his decisions during numerous court audiences.

"Nor should you," he advised. "If you always side with the lord of highest rank, then your people will mistrust you. They will find other means of resolving their disputes instead of bringing the issue before you. While I cannot say rank should be utterly disregarded..."

"Decisions should be made based on the merits of the case."

"Yes, exactly. I tell you this, not because I do not believe you already know it to be true, but as a simple reminder that, when you one day rule this land, you must remember all concerns are worthy of a fair hearing. If you do this, you will gain the trust and respect of those who live on these lands. A trust you will need, if you expect them to follow you through darker days."

"Do you expect trouble, Grandfather?"

He eyed her directly. "If the wraiths have awakened, then I have no doubt of it, Ameria. The time draws near, and you must be ready for what fate has in store for you."

"What is this fate?" Ameria pressed. "I don't understand. This story, this prophecy? What does it all mean?"

"Not here," Riccard cautioned, walking forward while motioning for her to follow. He led her through a series of stone hallways, her steps echoing along the dimly lit corridors until they emerged to a balcony. A light wind greeted them, blowing stray strands of Ameria's golden hair behind her. An orange glow cascaded over the previously purple sky, with a few streaks of pink tinting the edges of scattered clouds, creating a prism of colors.

Her grandfather did not stop until he reached the far balcony, placing his arms on the stone ledge. Ameria stepped beside him, but refrained from speaking, allowing the high lord to continue in his own time.

"What has the wraith said to you, Ameria?"

"'Fear to the fearless. Hope to the hopeless...' The list goes on. He always ends it with calling me the heir to—"

"Both bloodlines."

"Yes."

"What do you make of it?"

"It has something to do with Kale and Koloso, but for the life of me, I don't know what."

Her grandfather nodded, without turning her way. "What do you know of them, Ameria? Of Kale and Koloso?"

"Enough to know something isn't right," Ameria answered. She touched the hilt of the blade tucked into the sheath at her side. "This bears the mark of Kale. But it's silver. My sister's, the mark of Koloso, but it's gold. They should be the other way around. High Priest Louis told us the stories were wrong." She shook her head. "Legends say Kale was the eldest and Koloso the youngest. That Kale was gold, and Koloso silver. Priest Louis claims the opposite. But..."

"Yes?" Riccard prompted, finally turning his green eyes to Ameria's blue.

"Louis maintained it did not matter. The prophecy. The swords. The wraith. But I know it's all connected. It must be. I just...I can't put the puzzle together."

"It's true," Riccard said, drawing a deep breath of the cool air tinged with the scent of fresh grass. "Kale was the younger brother of Koloso. Koloso, heir to the throne, and the golden-ranked champion of the land. Kale, the younger, was silver."

Ameria nodded. "I figured as much. But...what does this have to do with me?"

"Your birth was foretold, Ameria. Fated the moment your uncle, King Derik IV, refused to marry my daughter, your mother."

"Because of the war?"

Riccard shook his head. "No. Not because he refused your mother, specifically. There were dozens of brides he could have chosen from. But rather, in his refusal to select a bride trained in the temples, he broke thousands of years of tradition.

"Your uncle refused to heed the warnings of those who had come and fallen before. He refused to heed anyone, his lust for his queen, and her family's wealth, overrode all of his common sense. Your aunt was beautiful, of course, but combined with her wealth, and the idea she was not pre-determined, made her very appealing to your uncle. More so than any bride the high priest would have approved."

"You said you had warned them, that the wraiths would come."

"I thought it would be a slaughter," Riccard confirmed. "That the wraiths would come down, as they had centuries before, to kill your uncle and any who dared to support such a grave transgression. That your father would become king. But when you and your sister were born, I realized, as did many others, the fate your uncle had brought upon this kingdom was far worse than the mere slaying of a king."

"I don't understand."

"There is a prophecy about twins of the ancient bloodline, Ameria. An oracle written in blood."

"Yes, the wraiths keep repeating it. 'Death to those who love you.' But I don't understand. How do I stop such a thing from happening? How do I—"

"That, Princess, is something you must discover on your own. I can no more help you to escape your destiny than I could avoid mine. The path you have chosen is one of danger and great trials, but as to how you survive it, only you can decide."

"Why won't you help me? Why lecture me if not to offer guidance?"

"I would if I could, my lady. But there are rules that even I, a high lord, Golden Defendant, and your grandfather, cannot break."

CHAPTER XV

◄•►◄•※•►◄•►

KYLE SAT ASTRIDE STERLING. THE silver stallion had been given to him by Master Jiro on his fourteenth birthday. It would take two days to ride from the Temple of Koloso to Sanguis Castle, where defendants had confirmed Princess Ameria had been residing. In the twelve-year partnership he had maintained with Ameria, Kyle had never once heard the golden-haired princess speak of her grandfather. And to the best of his recollection, Kyle had never seen his partner with the high lord either.

Has he ever attended our tournaments? Kyle thought about it, but could not recall having seen Riccard at any of their competitions.

Kyle was sure he would learn more about Ameria's decision to join her grandfather when he arrived. They had decided to divide the journey, pausing at the Temple of Dektra, the fourth-highest-ranked of the thirteen Kalian Temples. *Or was it fourteen?*

They rode all day, Brandan never leaving his side. The party remained mostly silent as they glided through the ever-present mist of the Rainbow Mountains. Light sparkled around them, a prism that colored the air reflecting in jewel tones. The fog blanketed these mountains, thought by many to be blessed by the gods, as the mountains of Periculum were supposedly cursed.

He pushed these mental wanderings from his mind as the party approached the Temple of Dektra. As tired as he was, the rest of the men must've been exhausted.

Kyle turned to address his party. "Good day's journey, everyone. Get some rest. We will ride out again at the second sun's rise."

After affirming nods, the men handed their reins off to a group of young students who'd run from the front of the temple to assist the knights. As Kyle dismounted, he handed Sterling's lead to a boy, perhaps twelve years of age, who wore golden robes, signaling he was of the highest-ranked younger pupils.

Generally there were thirty students at any given temple, divided into three classes. The youngest were those recently selected for the temples. The second group was in training to be admitted to the third, advanced team. Only advanced students competed in the coveted Kalian tournaments, reserved for the best contenders from each temple.

"Thank you," Kyle told the boy.

"At your service, my lord," he replied with a respectful bow, but his brown eyes did not follow his downward movement.

Kyle considered ignoring the curious gaze, but found himself asking in spite of his better judgment, "Do you have a question?"

"I..." The boy hesitated. "Well..."

"Go ahead."

"My lord, you're the silver of Koloso. I watched you fight last year. You're on a mission, and probably very tired but..."

"If you would like a sword demonstration," he guessed the boy's request, "then you are correct, I am exhausted. However, were I to get something to eat, and a full night's rest, you might find me in your training room at the first sun's rise."

The boy's face lit up, unable to fully suppress a smile, failing in his attempts to maintain a respectful manner. Kyle offered a quick grin of his own, watching the boy relax at his action. "What's your name?"

"Mathew," he answered, "but they call me Matty."

"Matty," Kyle repeated, turning to his silver horse whose reins the boy still held. "This is Sterling. Do you think you can get him bedded down for the night, and find him something good to eat? He's more exhausted than I am."

"Yes, of course, my lord."

Kyle maintained his smile. "You take good care of him, and I will see you in the morning."

"Thank you!" Matty answered excitedly, reaching up to take the harness firmly in his hand. Kyle watched as the horses were led towards the stables, then turned to the temple entrance.

The Temple of Dektra was the lowest-ranked of the Kalian Temples within the Rainbow Mountains. Sparkling lights surrounded the area, giving off a luminous glow in the evening light. White marble steps were embedded with quartz crystals, offering a pink twinkle, which complimented the rainbow mist. High columns supported the building, across which were draped sheets of pink satin, a deep color reminiscent of the sky's flush as the third, final sun dropped below the horizon.

Despite the appearance of the white marble and pink crystal, no one should be fooled into believing this temple was softer than others. Within dwelled some of the most ferocious warriors in the land. The temple master, Eric, had once served as the highest-ranking Red Defendant, under the late Master Edward. Garbed in robes of the same sunset-pink, Master Eric awaited him at the temple entrance.

"Lord Kyle," the temple master addressed him, running his fingers through his short blond hair before reaching out a pale hand in greeting.

"Master Eric," he answered. "You did not need to greet me personally."

"I wanted to. It brings the Temple of Dektra great honor to house the champion of Koloso."

"We thank you, and your temple, for the hospitality."

"It is our pleasure."

"My men are exhausted. We would be grateful for food and rest."

"Of course, my lord. Food is coming off the stoves as we speak, and rooms are prepared."

Kyle nodded and entered the white door set against marble stones, ducking slightly to not disturb the pink cloth which draped the entrance. Eric followed a few paces behind, remaining silent as they walked into the kitchens. Deciding on simple soup and bread, Kyle sat down at a rectangular wooden table. Brandan took a seat beside him, while Eric sat across.

"My lords," Eric began, after allowing both men time to eat, "I'm aware you are on a mission for the crown princess. While I would never seek to intrude, I would be remiss if I did not ask if there is anything I, or any other member of this temple, could do to assist you on your quest."

Kyle glanced at the temple master's brown eyes and, after consideration, understood what he was asking. "Are you afraid, after what happened with the late temple master, that the queen seeks vengeance, or has mistrust for your temple?"

Heat crept to Eric's cheeks, and he cast his eyes down in shame.

"Believe me, Master Eric, if the queen sought to punish this temple for the attempt on her sister's life, she would never allow me to sleep under your roof. You have nothing to fear, my lord. At least, not from me, nor any of the men riding with me."

"I don't understand what possessed Phillip." Eric's words were laced with a deep-seated pain. "How could he, a master of this temple, and a former defendant, have tried to kill a princess of the realm? And only moments after her own father had been killed?" He forced himself to return his eyes to Kyle's. "I am ashamed, my lord, to have had such treachery in our temple and to not have known."

"Do you have any idea why he attacked Princess Ameria?" Kyle inquired. "Were there signs of strange behavior, or..."

"He spent a great deal of time in the archives over the months leading up to...well..."

"The assassination attempt," Kyle finished for him.

Eric nodded.

"Would you show me to those rooms? I doubt I will find anything, but it's worth a look."

"Of course, my lord."

"Shall I go with you?" Brandan asked from beside him.

"No," Kyle answered his second-in-command. "Get some rest. You were up even earlier than I this morning."

"Thank you," Brandan answered, "but should you need anything..."

"I will send for you at once," Kyle assured him.

Brandan offered a weary smile.

Kyle rose and followed the temple master down a series of hallways. The temple's interior was composed of the same crystal-encrusted marble as the exterior. Arriving in the archive room, it appeared to be nearly identical to the one at the Temple of Koloso. Eric led him to a wall where a series of scrolls lay upon a narrow desk.

"These are the last documents Phillip read through, before he was summoned to the palace. News of the king's illness was unexpected, and he left before he had time to put everything away. I've pored over these pages, and can't find anything out of the ordinary." Eric lit several half-burnt candles as Kyle stepped closer to the desk.

"Thank you. I shouldn't be in here for very long."

"Take as much time as you wish, my lord. Please be sure to extinguish the tapers when you leave."

"I will." Kyle moved to take a seat in the desk's wooden chair. After Eric left, he smoothed the curled scrolls, his eyes scouring the ancient transcriptions. For the most part, there was nothing out of the ordinary. Downright boring actually. Pages describing various tournaments that had been fought over the centuries. More discussing the history of the Temple of Dektra.

Finding nothing of particular interest amid those parchments, he stood, grabbing one of the candles to light his way, and moved toward the archive shelves. More temple history. More reviews of tournaments, from the very old to the very recent. Browsing aimlessly, he reached a section that seemed lacking, even of the dust layer that clung to other surfaces. Whereas other cubes were stuffed near-to-bursting, only a few rolls remained in this cabinet.

This must be where Phillip pulled the scrolls from. He reached over his head, into the mostly empty cabinet, and pulled out the remaining spools. More temple history. About to give up, he noticed the persistent dust had been swept away from the back boards. Curious, he pressed against the paneling and one gave way, revealing a secret compartment. Holding his breath, Kyle reached inside to find a stack of yellowed parchment. Carefully, he removed the documents and returned to the desk. After clearing enough space to flatten the yellowed pages and bringing the candles closer, he studied the faded script.

If you are reading this, you have been entrusted with secrets remembered by few. It is imperative, for the good of the kingdom, these secrets remain shadowed in nature; it is equally important they never be forgotten.

I write this against my heart, which has known nothing but friendship from my lord and king, the most noble and just ruler this land has ever known. Yet I recognize, deep in the confines of my heart and conscience, this is a truth which must be told, for the safety of this kingdom, and those to come. For this reason alone I now break my silence, which I once swore on bended knee to maintain unto death. I beg of the gods, and my fallen lord, to forgive the transgression of this traitor's hand.

The story we told is a lie, and if the kingdom knew, we would horrify the very people such lies were meant to protect. For the love of our people, we made a hero of a villain, and have honored, time and again, the memory of a man whose name should have been stricken from history. In this action, we ourselves have become the villains. The grief our late ruler suffered transformed him from the heroic man we once praised to the tragic shell seen only by those of us who knew the truth.

I leave this as a lesson, a story of caution. There existed a man who betrayed us all, but also one who protected us fiercely—and paid a terrible price. In upholding the falsehood, he became a broken man. The propaganda would ultimately break all of us, in ways we will never fully understand. Yet there are times when such a deception is necessary in order to mask a far more terrifying truth.

A truth which begins, as most do, with a myth none wanted to believe. A story. A prophecy. A horror even our lord and king, the great Kale himself, and his beloved brother, were unable to escape.

"Fear to the fearless. Hope to the hopeless. Mercy to those who hate you. Death to those who love you...and beware the twins of the royal bloodline."

Kyle's breath caught as he read the lines that echoed through this dreams. He turned the page.

CHAPTER XVI

In the Time of Kale & Koloso

PRINCE KALE SWEPT A HAND through the short strands of his dark hair, his green eyes considering those assembled in Sanguis Castle's vaulted stone chamber. "This threat must be answered," he urged. "Too many lives have been lost already." He searched the faces of those around him, most of the royal court nodding their agreement, but a few with blank, schooled expressions. Kale's gaze finally settled upon the golden-haired man seated immediately to his right. "Please, Brother, allow me to ride out. I will take our best men and join our army gathered in Turbamentum. Hopefully, Tristan will lead with me, and I'm sure other men will volunteer."

"Aye," a blond-haired man spoke from his left.

Kale turned to the speaker. Tristan had trained with him at the Temple of Eversus. Together, they had led many victories as friends and teammates.

"I guessed as much," Kale said with a brief smile, "but didn't want to speak for you."

"Like I'd allow you to take all the glory for yourself," Tristan answered with a soft chuckle.

Kale turned back to his brother.

The king paused in consideration, scanning the faces of those around him. "I have heard your concerns," the king addressed those gathered. "I would speak with my brother alone on this matter, and we will reconvene shortly."

"Yes, Your Majesty," a chorus of voices answered as those gathered rose and shuffled from the room.

When all had cleared, the king moved to take the seat across from his brother's, leveling his deep blue eyes with Kale's. "It's too dangerous," Koloso said. "You're the crown prince. I can't have you risking your life."

"Protecting the kingdom is my job," Kale countered. "Even more so as the crown prince."

"I need you here, by my side, Kale. Not off on some distant battlefield. I cannot run this kingdom by myself."

"Running the kingdom is your job, Brother. Yours and those advisors you appointed."

Koloso sighed. "Kale, please, I detest giving you orders."

"Then don't. These are not random attacks. This is an army under the direction of a powerful enemy. They have already taken over the mountains of Periculum, carved a path through Usqub, and are now threatening the Turbamentum province. How long before they reach the temples or Serenitas? How long before they reach our very gates?"

"Kale, I do not doubt the validity of the threat being presented. But I also have faith the Lord of Turbamentum can handle this."

"I don't doubt his capabilities either. This is the greatest threat we have seen in our lifetimes. We have treated them casually, because they are limited in number, but the army has defeated everyone they have fought. More alarming, they are paving a path as opposed to conquering lands."

"What do you mean?" Koloso asked.

"Don't you see, Brother? They are not trying to take control of Usqub or even Turbamentum. They are headed somewhere. To here, or to one of the temples, I know not. Though if I had to guess..."

Koloso raised his gaze to more squarely meet his brother's.

"I believe they are targeting the temples, defeating our warriors one by one."

Koloso shook his head. "Their pattern has been chaotic, and they have by no means moved toward a specific temple. In fact, they've gone around them. Seems like a stretch."

"True, but that works to their advantage. As temple champions come to face them, due to the chaotic pattern, they rarely do so together, in an organized manner. I have no idea who is leading this force, but I believe—truly believe—the only way to stop these attackers is to meet them with a united front. Otherwise, I fear when this force reaches us, we will be outnumbered and outmatched."

"I agree the situation is dangerous, which is all the more reason why I want you to stay here, in the castle. In recognition of the threat, I will agree to send Tristan to assist the High Lord of Turbamentum."

"Come on, Koloso," Kale said in an exasperated tone. "Tristan and I have fought every battle we've ever faced, together. You cannot forbid me to go with him. If anything happened to him, I would never forgive myself."

"By the same token, if anything happened to you, when I could have kept you—"

"What?" Anger seeped into Kale's voice. "Kept me safe with the children?"

"Kale, please."

"I am a knight of this realm, and it is my duty—nay, my responsibility—to protect this kingdom from all threats! Do *not* forbid me to do my job, Brother."

"Do not *force* me to forbid it. I don't want to, but I will."

"Please, Koloso, I..." Kale paused, searching his brother's blue eyes. "I would be ashamed to ask the men to fight without me."

Kale stared at his brother, and briefly thought his golden-haired twin might relent. At least, until his sapphire eyes darkened and he anticipated what his brother would say before the words fell upon the air.

"I'm sorry, Kale. I really am, but I need you here, in the castle and by my side. We must show a united front. Trust the men to do their job and handle these bandits."

"Warriors," Kale corrected. "They are far too dangerous to be simple bandits."

"Bandits or warriors," his brother conceded, frustration seeping into his words, "I will not permit you to engage these men yourself. You will remain here, your rightful place as crown prince. I will send the men you requested, and Tristan in your stead, to represent the crown."

"Please..."

"I will hear no more on the matter. My decision is final."

Kale parted his lips to speak, only to close them. He cast his gaze down to hide the anger flaring in his emerald eyes.

"Say you understand," Koloso demanded.

Kale drew a deep breath and forced himself to answer, "I understand, my *king*."

"You may go. Have Tristan return for his orders."

Kale gave no further acknowledgement before removing himself from the council chambers. He spoke briefly to those standing outside, struggling to keep the anger from his words. As those gathered shuffled back into the room behind him, Kale walked down the gray stone halls until he reached his own quarters. He managed to enter his room without incident, but once within, was unable to contain his frustration. He reached into the closet for anything he could find, in this case a silver goblet. Without bothering to check its contents, Kale tossed the chalice across the room. It hit the stone wall with a sharp clang before clattering to the ground

Kale was not normally one for outbursts, yet he'd been frequently disturbed since his brother's ascension to the throne. Though trained at different temples, both had once held a similar vision for the kingdom's future. However, with each passing day, Kale found himself more and more in opposition to his brother's commands.

He's becoming just like father, the thought filtered through Kale's mind.

Neither had been particularly close to their late father. As a second born son, their father, Derik I, had never expected to become king, let alone give birth to the future one. Derik had never thrived in the temples. When he was sixteen, and his twenty-two-year-old brother had become king, Derik begged for permission to leave the temples. His brother had granted the request, allowing Derik to return to the palace instead of completing his training.

Derik had believed that the temples were unnecessary. Their legends and teachings, little more than frightening fairytales to keep the undereducated in line. From stories Kale was told later in life, Derik had been reluctant to surrender his own children over to the temples. However, when his older brother died in an accident while hunting wolves in the Periculum Mountains, their father assumed the throne and was required by the high priest to do so, lest risking an open rebellion from the very knights he counted upon to protect both himself and the kingdom.

Derik I's reign was not considered a great success, his rule saturated with unusually harsh choices, and frequent occurrences of taking punishments too far. A trend that Kale was surprised to see his brother now continuing.

At their respective temples, the brothers had been treated as equals to the other highly-ranked students, enough so that Kale spent the majority of his youth without realizing he was different than those around him. In fact, he had been seventeen before his first "royal" function—a dinner held in his brother's honor so their father could introduce Koloso as the kingdom's next ruler.

Even then, Kale had thought little of the title. He would never rule. His destiny was to protect the kingdom, riding with the elite knights, before eventually becoming a temple master and training the next generation. He had always known this would be his destiny; had never dreamed of another.

Well, except once, when he had fallen for the beautiful brunette, Rachel. A woman whose deep green eyes, the most common color of the Kalian bloodline, called to him with a power he found difficult to explain. She'd been named a knight of the realm two years before Kale's own tournament rounds, where, as predicted, he had taken silver to his brother's gold. Rachel's success in the temples solidified her place as the future queen, turning her eyes and heart solidly towards his brother.

Kale found solace in the fact he no longer had the potential to be with Rachel, making it easier to come to terms with the idea of a celibate temple master life. His deepest relationship would be with the gods, to whom he planned to devote his life. He had thrown himself fully into the development of his faith, and in leading the knights of the kingdom, defending his people from all threats, from the highest to the lowest in rank.

"Every life is precious," the high priest had told him. "And every soul worthy of protection."

Once, Koloso had believed this to be true as well. Yet, since becoming king, Koloso seemed to be forgetting this most important of lessons with increasing abandon. Only yesterday, he had put a young man to death. The crime? Stealing a horse, which was later found unharmed. Certainly the man deserved to be punished. Locked in the tower for a time. But death? That was beyond extreme. Others had been severely beaten, sometimes with Koloso himself witnessing such events. Distasteful. Speaking out for milder punishments put Kale at odds with his brother in increasing frequency. He was confused by it. He had never known his brother to be cruel prior to taking the throne.

Kale had never imagined the day his brother would fail to recognize a legitimate risk to the kingdom, nor prevent him from fighting to protect it. This troubled him even more than the boy's death. At twenty-four, his brother was considered a young king. "It will take some time for him to learn the role," Temple Master Jonathan had reminded the younger twin.

Yet the longer Kale stood by his brother's side, the worse, and not better, his temper became. To be honest, Kale would have welcomed a chance to escape the palace, even without the looming threat.

The incursion had begun with a few seemingly random incidents in the northwest corner of the kingdom. The Temple Master of Bellum, Galen, was killed while out for his morning ride. When his golden student, Caden, went to investigate why his master had not returned, he also lost his life to the same mysterious villain. Kale had been saddened to learn of Caden's death, a good man and an even better friend. His body had been transferred to the Temple of Ziazan, where proper funeral rites had been provided, including Kale's personal presence to mourn the loss of his friend. Bellum was the third-highest-ranking of the temples.

In spite of great efforts, led by both the temple students and many knights, the killers were not found. Everything seemed quiet for some time. Months later, news reached them from the province of Usqub that villages were being raided by a group of warriors, though the number of men seemed to increase with every report.

More knights were sent in an effort to stop the raids. To everyone's surprise, the villains evaded capture, while the number of funerals for Kale's friends increased. What was at first subtle, became glaring to everyone, it seemed, except the king. Even when Eleanor, the daughter of the High Lord of Flos, was killed, his brother did little more than sign a letter of condolence. Kale, on the other hand, consoled the grieving mother and paid respects to the fallen warrior.

"What the hell is wrong with him?" Kale asked no one. While he had respect for the Lord of Turbamentum, and trusted the two warriors being sent, he could not shake the feeling something was amiss. Something he could not see that should have, by all rights, been right in front of him.

Drawing a deep breath, Kale left his chambers, and headed toward the temple training quarters. Gliding down the steps, he walked past the areas reserved for those of lower rank. Beyond them, the gold and silver mats showed signs of wear.

He stepped onto the pad, determined to lose himself in a few hours of physical training. It helped relax him, returning him to what he knew— a temporary escape from this foreign world of diplomatic scheming and backdoor politics.

"Need a sparring partner?" a voice called as Kale withdrew the blade from his side.

He turned and found himself facing Tristan. His oldest friend, Tristan had been brought to the Temple of Eversus at the age of three. They had bonded instantly, and maintained a devoted friendship. The son of a powerful high lord, Tristan was destined to one day govern the province of Serenitas. He had never been daunted by Kale's princely status, a fact for which Kale was eternally grateful. "Sure," Kale answered with a smile. "Come on over."

Stepping onto the mat, Tristan drew his own sword, freeing the silver blade from the black scabbard on his left. He untied the belt from his waist, laying the sword's sheath aside. Kale did the same, allowing more controlled movement without worrying about the extra weight. He then moved toward the center of the mat and adjusted his grip on the hilt.

"So," Tristan said, standing a few paces from him, "I understand you will not be joining us."

A fresh wave of anger rose through Kale, which he was unable to mask from his expression or words. "Not by choice."

Tristan offered a quick bow before moving a second hand to his blade, tightening his grip. "Never occurred to me it was."

Instead of answering, Kale stepped forward, bringing his blade down to Tristan's left side. Tristan met the motion and the two swords clashed, the sound of colliding metal ringing through the dank air. It echoed off the stone walls as both men stepped back, adjusting their grip, before Kale again lunged to Tristan's side. Tristan jumped back, stepping beyond the range of Kale's sword.

"The likelihood of this threat being something I cannot deal with—" Tristan twisted right to block another swipe of Kale's silver sword, the clash forcing a pause to his words. "The odds are highly unlikely."

"I don't doubt that," Kale said, anger collecting in his voice. "However, that does not change the fact that you, along with others I care about—" Their swords clashed again. "Are riding into danger and my *king*..." the word sounded foul, "is refusing to allow me, a protector of this land, to do my job!"

Kale swung his blade. Both men fell to silence, forcing themselves to focus on the movement of the other. Tristan leaned low to thrust his weapon in an upward angle toward Kale's midsection. Kale parried, moving his blade sideways, knocking Tristan's sword harmlessly to the left. Tristan used the momentum from Kale's blade to step behind the prince, twisting to bring the blade to Kale's side. Kale turned barely in time to stop him, the two swords colliding with great force, sending both men several steps from each other. Kale's hand touched the mat, an unsteady grip on the sword, but he kept from completely falling. Tristan did the same, drawing a deep breath before standing and moving his second hand back to the hilt.

The two men paused, each waiting for the other to move. This time, Tristan attacked first. He jumped toward the prince, sliding to his knees to strike up. Kale jerked back, but it wasn't fast enough, and the tip of Tristan's sword sliced through the outer layer of Kale's silver robes.

Tristan assessed the cut. "Perhaps this isn't the best idea, using blades outside of the temples."

Kale stared at him, his breath labored from the repetitive swinging of the heavy sword. "Perhaps you are right." He lowered his blade to his side before offering his hand.

Tristan took it, allowing the prince to assist him from his kneeling position. Once standing, he placed his hand lightly on Kale's upper arm and gave a gentle squeeze. "Feel better?"

"Not really."

"I can take care of this one."

"I know," Kale replied, resignation replacing his previous anger. "I can't even explain it really. I just have a bad feeling about this one."

"I understand."

"You do?"

"Of course. If it were you who had been ordered to face some nameless villain, and I were ordered to stay, I would feel the same. However—please don't hate me for this—I can also see your brother's point of view. He has not wed, which means until he has and Rachel is with child, the throne is vulnerable. Like it or not, you are his heir."

Kale gave a half-hearted chuckle. "Me as king, could you imagine? God I would hate it. Do you see how my brother spends his days? Meetings and disputes, appeasing two lords who are fighting over which side of a fence a tree can be planted."

Tristan stared before breaking into a teasing smile. "That may be true, but on the other hand, he will get to leave those meetings and go to the private chambers of a certain brunette."

Kale swiped lightly at Tristan's shoulder, who moved away from the intended slap. "That's my brother's fiancé and your future queen."

"And none of this changes the color of her hair."

Kale laughed.

"If you had been king, she would have been *your* intended bride."

"True," Kale said. "But for reasons beyond my understanding, she has always seemed to like Koloso better."

"You don't think the fact that marrying him will make her queen has anything to do with that extra layer of attractiveness?"

"That's enough," Kale scolded, unable to keep the laughter from his voice. "I think she loves him."

"You're probably right."

Kale stepped to the edge of the mat, and placed his sword back into its silver sheath, before securing it again around his waist. Across from him, Tristan did the same with his leather one. "Thank you for sparring with me," Kale said. "I needed to just..."

"No problem," Tristan replied. "Anytime."

"When do you leave?"

"At first light."

"In other words, around noon when you finally decide to force yourself from your bed?"

"Hey, would you get up early knowing you are trading in satin sheets for the battlefront? Especially now with the frost rolling in every morning."

Kale laughed. "Yes, I suppose that is one perk of being forced to stay."

The two walked the stone path, but mutually paused when they reached the doors.

"Hey," Kale began, "I know I don't need to say this, but...be careful out there."

Tristan turned to his friend and nodded. "I will."

"I mean it. Something about what's going on, just...isn't right."

"I have learned, over the years, that your instincts are annoyingly right. If you think something is wrong, I will proceed with the utmost caution."

Kale held his friend's gaze. "I hate to sound parental, but..."

"I will send regular reports. Every few days, if you wish."

"Thank you." Relief slid through him, releasing some of the tension from Kale's shoulders.

"If it were the other way around, I would hope you would agree to do the same. Will be strange, going into a fight without you."

"I would do so, gladly," Kale replied. He briefly embraced the man beside him before returning back to his chambers.

CHAPTER XVII

3 Months Later - In the Time of Kale & Koloso

KALE SAT IN THE DAILY council meeting over which his brother had appointed him to preside. Two minor lords stood before him, arguing over their proclaimed rights to the same pond, which their horses often enjoyed lounging by. For years, the body of water had been shared amicably. When one of the lord's fathers died the previous spring, the inheritor built a fence around his property, including the pond. Now the two men presented their dispute, each buoyed with a list of additional petty grievances.

How these arguments merited royal attention, Kale would never understand. Nor why he, the crown prince, was expected to resolve such ridiculous disputes. After pretending to listen closely to the lower lord's rambles, Kale reached the end of his patience. "Enough!" he said. "I've heard more than enough."

"But, my lord, I am not even halfway through my list," the younger of the two protested.

"Yes, you are. In fact, you are well over the limit of grievances I am willing to entertain." Kale cleared his throat. "Your families have shared this water source for generations. I see no reason not to continue to do so. The fence is to come down immediately, and the two of you will learn to share from this point forward."

"But, my lord!" the younger exclaimed. "It is on *my* property!"

"It is the crown's property," Kale countered. "All land is. And I am ordering you to share, otherwise I will find in favor of the other lord right here and now."

"This is highly outrageous."

"No," Kale answered in a frustrated tone. "What is ridiculous is that I am sitting here listening to this petty squabble to begin with. Now resolve this, and stop wasting the crown's time. You will share, or you shall lose all rights to the location in question. Is that understood?"

The younger man looked as though he wanted to argue, but Kale's glare made him think better of it. He remained silent, allowing the elder man to speak in his stead. "I am sure he understands, Your Highness. We shall resolve this matter peacefully, per your instructions."

Kale nodded and stood from his chair, causing both men to enter into a low bow. "Please don't let me see either of you here again on such insignificant matters."

"Yes, my prince," both men mumbled.

Leaving the room, Kale turned left in the stone corridor, his mind already far from the dispute. Instead, his thoughts remained singularly on the fact that Tristan's reports, which had arrived like clockwork every three days, had ceased. His best friend had been silent for nearly a month, and Kale's sense of foreboding increased with each passing day.

He stepped briskly through the gray chambers of Sanguis Castle. When he reached the exterior doors, he recognized one of the men standing guard. "Michael," he greeted.

"Your Highness."

"Have there been any dispatches for me today?"

"No, my lord, I am afraid not."

"Are you sure? Nothing from Tristan?"

"No, Your Highness."

Kale gave a sigh of frustration, shaking his head. "I should've heard from him by now."

He turned from the guard and walked back into the corridors, recalling the words of Tristan's last letter. He had reviewed it so many times over the past few weeks, he'd memorized the contents.

My lord and Prince Kale,

Things took a tragic turn this week as the eldest son of the High Lord of Turbamentum, Lord Lancel, lost his life during watch. Devastated by the untimely death of such a knight and friend, I'm plagued by the guilt that I should have done more to ensure the safety of those around us.

It did not occur to anyone he could be attacked only steps from his father's encampment, and in broad daylight no less! Strange as well that no one heard the fight, as Lancel was within easy audible range. This, more than anything, concerns me. If he had yelled, someone should have heard him. Which leads me to a far more disturbing notion...he did not scream.

Why would he not have shouted? Not have called out for other knights who stood so near to where he fell? I have determined, from my own examination, that he was killed at close range. I fear what you suspected, my prince, may be true. There is more to these attacks than is easily seen.

I will continue to proceed with caution and remain, as always, your devoted friend and protector of the realm.

Tristan Desoto

A message such as that, and then no news for weeks, left Kale overcome with the feeling that something was terribly wrong. Lancel had trained alongside Tristan and him at the Temple of Eversus. A valiant knight and loyal friend, this loss affected Kale more than any of those who had passed before. It would have taken a skilled knight indeed to have killed their friend. Kale wondered if he had been set upon by multiple assailants instead of one.

Why did he not yell for help?

Frustrated, Kale walked down the halls until he reached the doors to his brother's chambers, and waited while one of the guards announced his presence. Acknowledging he required permission to see his own twin brother agitated him further. He waited impatiently for his brother's consent, entering the chamber without bothering to thank the guard who opened the door before him.

In golden robes, Koloso sat on the sofa, blending with the satiny cushions. At Kale's approach, he stood. "Hello, Brother."

"Brother." Kale also chose the familial title.

"Do you need something?" Koloso asked, retaking his seat as he motioned for Kale to do the same.

"Yes," Kale answered, as he sat across from his brother on an identical sofa, a rectangular table occupying the space between them. "I still have not heard from Tristan. In order to find out why, I request your permission to travel to Turbamentum."

Koloso sighed. "Are we back to this again?" he asked. "I thought I had made myself clear."

"That discussion was months ago, when you believed the Turbamentum lord could resolve the threat on his own. Now his son and heir is dead, and Tristan, who has written me faithfully, has not been heard from in weeks. I must oversee this situation, if for no other reason than to ensure there is some semblance of order to whatever is going on."

Koloso shook his head. "I need you here, to help me—"

"Help you what?" Kale interrupted. "Oversee water disputes from some idiotic kid who was never taught to share? Really? How is that possibly more important than making sure our kingdom, and those who are sworn to serve it, are kept safe?"

"Kale, please listen."

"I am done listening! Are you reading these reports, Brother? Lancel is dead!"

"Kale, I'm sorry for the loss of your friend, but—"

"People are dying! Our people. Friends who stood by our side. The children of our high lords, temple masters, and those sworn to defend the realm. They are dying, and you hold me here, for...for what? I don't understand. I was not trained to be a royal, I was trained to be a knight. Let me serve you the way I was trained to do."

Koloso waited for his brother's words to fade. "Tell me, Kale, do you trust Tristan?"

"What?"

"Do you trust him? He's fought by your side for nearly two decades. So, do you trust him?"

"Of course. What kind of a question is that?"

"Then trust him to do his job. I'm sure his updates have merely been delayed due to the pursuit. According to my dispatches, they are not even in Turbamentum anymore, but are instead approaching the Periculum Mountains."

"Periculum?"

Koloso nodded. "My last report stated they were pursuing the bandits back into the mountains. That is likely why you have not heard anything from Tristan. He's traveling and doesn't have time."

Kale considered his brother's words. It could be possible this was the case. Yet... "No," Kale said aloud. "Tristan knows how important his reports are to me. He promised to send them regularly. Traveling or not, he would have sent something to me by now."

Koloso sighed. "You are being paranoid."

"Then let me prove you right," he replied. "Allow me to go to the front and verify everything is fine. I promise to return immediately after speaking to Tristan, if that is your wish. But please, Brother, let me go."

"I'm sorry, Kale. Things are not as they once were. As king, it is my duty to make choices for the safety of this realm, including protecting you, until another heir has been conceived. Like it or not, the fact remains you are the crown prince."

"I don't care. You are forcing me to take the actions of a coward."

"I've heard enough. You are not permitted to leave the palace grounds, and that's final."

"What if Tristan dies?" Kale challenged. "If he is hurt? If something is wrong and we're sitting here, completely dismissing his plight?"

"Then his death would be a tragedy. I would mourn the loss of such a man. But at least I will not be mourning the loss of a brother as well."

The words reached Kale, but not enough to subdue his anger. He stood and pronounced, "If Tristan dies, and I could have saved him, you *will* be mourning the loss of a brother, because I will never forgive you."

Without another word, Kale turned and left the room.

He threw himself into a full workout, hoping the exercise would lessen the tension that stiffened his frame, but even the physical exertion did little to quell his anger. He still seethed as he lay awake later that night, sleep finding him only after hours of endless staring at the ceiling.

CHAPTER XVIII

In the Time of Kale & Koloso

TRISTAN LAY ON A THIN *mat, his riding party camped at the edge of the Periculum Mountains. During the pursuit across Usqub, their faceless enemies had grown more bold, killing the son of a high lord only steps from the tight cluster of tents.*

No one who survived the raids could seem to provide a name, face, or even a specific description of the men they sought. Every report was different, making it appear as though no village was ever attacked by the same man. Perhaps those who did attack repeatedly only left dead behind.

The men took shifts and, after a hard day's ride followed by hours of guard duty, Tristan was relieved to finally fall into the sweet oblivion of sleep. Deep in slumber, he lay blissfully unaware of the dark-robed man who stood only a few paces away.

Creeping forward, the man had slipped into camp, slitting the throat of the two guardsmen who had stood on the northern side. He had ignored the majority of those sleeping, seeking instead the red robes of Kale's highest-ranking friend.

The hooded man moved silently, his long, silver blade naked in his gloved hand, splashed with blood from the two guards already killed. He moved to his knees beside Tristan, whose defendant rank garments were revealed by the blankets he'd twisted during restless sleep. Placing his sword on the ground, the assassin pulled a short knife from his side. He aligned the sharp edge with Tristan's throat and pressed it firmly through the skin, cutting the vocal cords before digging deeply into the airway beneath. As Tristan's eyes opened, he tried to scream...but it was too late. A soft, gurgling sound would be the last he'd ever make, his green Kalian eyes staring into matching ones as sight faded.

The hooded man twisted the blade, ensuring his work was done, before slipping from the camp as he'd appeared, unnoticed and unheard.

"Tristan!" Kale awoke from the dream, calling his friend's name. He sat up, breaths coming in harsh gasps that failed to drown out the quickened pace of his heart.

"*Yes.*"

He turned, his eyes searching the darkness, but there was no one to be seen.

The voice came again, "*Yes.*"

"Yes?" Kale repeated the word, fearing the meaning. "You mean, Tristan is...He's..."

"*Soon,*" the whisper was deep, more of a growl than a voice. "*Soon.*"

"No!" Kale fought to restrict his breathing. "Please, he can't. He's my friend, a hero in this realm."

"*Then why do you send him...to die?*"

"I didn't. I wouldn't."

"*You are the better warrior. Yet you hide here, safe while your friend nears his last breath.*"

"My brother ordered me to stay. He won't listen."

"*Then yes, Kale, prince of the ancient bloodline, your realm's hero will die.*"

"Please, no."

"*Save him, twin of the ancient bloodline. Save your friend, if you can.*"

"Who are you?" Kale demanded.

"*A messenger.*"

Kale searched the room, but saw no one in the darkness. "Show yourself!"

"*All in good time, Prince Kale. All in good time.*"

"A messenger for whom? What, by the gods, is going on?"

"*Death,*" the voice came softer than before, more distant. "*Death to those who love you.*"

"No!" Kale rose from the bed, grabbing his sword. "I won't let him die."

A gruff laugh echoed through the room, fading as though the speaker moved farther away, before quieting altogether.

"Show yourself!" Kale called again. "Tell me who you are!"

No answer came. A chill spread. There was a truth to the stranger's words that could not be denied.

Dressing, Kale wrapped a thick, leather belt around his silver robes, securing his jewel-encrusted scabbard against his hip before sliding his sword securely inside the worn material. Moving to the desk, he composed a brief note. Absconding from the palace, under the cover of darkness, he mounted Sterling before the first of the three suns touched the sky.

A few hours later, as light from the second sun filtered through the square window of Kale's chamber, the note was found. With Koloso's name transcribed on the sealed scroll, it was hastily carried to the king's chambers. He accepted the missive without comment, waiting until he was alone to break the fresh wax.

Brother,

I find I must disobey your explicit command. Tristan's life is in imminent danger. A voice came to me, bearing what I fear to be a message from the gods themselves. These are no ordinary bandits, Brother, and knowing this now with certainty, I beg you to prepare the kingdom for this threat, should I fail in my endeavor to stop them. The gods speak through dreams and whispers. Beware, my king, this force that comes from the Periculum Mountains.

This transgression is unforgivable, to disobey a king in such a blatant and direct way. Instead, I plead with you as my friend, my brother, my twin: Beware the gods, Koloso. They have awakened, and I fear with them comes a force born of a darkness that will spread across this land.

I ride to fulfill my duty as a knight of this realm. To defend the kingdom, its people, and my king from this unknown force. I pray I see you again.

Your Devoted Brother,
Prince Kale

Koloso finished reading the letter, turning toward his desk and laying the curled paper onto the wooden surface. "So," he spoke aloud to the seemingly empty room, "it would seem he has done as you predicted and disobeyed my orders."

"*Yes,*" came the deep-throated reply.

The king turned from the desk to face the creature a few paces behind him. Standing nearly six feet tall on all fours, the wraith's mangy black fur covered his agile form. Perfectly motionless, he appeared to be made of stone, yet to glance into his reflective, cat-like eyes, was to know it as instead the stillness of a predator watching his prey.

King Koloso was not afraid as he turned to face the wraith. "Kale has gone to the mountains of Periculum."

"*As you knew he would. Your brother defies you at every turn.*"

"It would seem so."

"*As we predicted.*"

Koloso nodded. "It's strange. Shouldn't my brother's desire for my throne make him want to stay in the palace, where it's safe?"

"*Instead of becoming the hero of this land? Leading the men who will loyally follow him, in spite of your orders to do otherwise?*" The wraith gave a rough laugh. "*Returning not only as a savior, but with an army loyal to him alone?*"

"I see. You're right, as usual. My brother's refusal to heed my commands, and the loyalty of the men to him over me..."

"*Must not be allowed to stand.*"

The king stared at the god's messenger, falling deeper into his haunting eyes. "No. It cannot."

Koloso stepped across the thick rug covering the stone floor, calling for his guard.

Within seconds, his captain appeared, garbed in deep red robes. "My king." The guard dropped to one knee.

"My brother has left, in defiance of my express orders and is, even now, racing toward the Periculum Mountains. Gather the highest-ranked of the royal guard."

"Yes, my king. Would you like me to follow or detain him?"

"Neither. He is riding to his death, which I, as a brother, cannot permit. Your charge is to accompany me, while I intercept him, and finally put an end to this threat, which has caused Kale such concern. I will not see my brother die."

The captain nodded, moving cautiously so not to turn his back to his sovereign until he reached the door.

Once the captain had departed, the wraith gave a deep, low growl before vanishing, leaving Koloso alone in his chambers. The king walked back to the desk and opened a drawer. Inside was a stack of handwritten letters, delivered over the recent weeks. Letters meant for his brother, Prince Kale.

CHAPTER XIX

In the Time of Kale & Koloso

KALE RODE DIRECTLY TO THE Temple of Dektra, where he was greeted by the temple master, who was thankfully unaware of his defiance of the king's orders. Unwilling to waste time on pleasantries, he exchanged only a brief word with the master before moving into the temple's training center, where the magic of the Kalian gods had always been strongest. There, he called upon the powers that had been conferred to him the day he had become a knight of the realm. "Critous," he spoke the name aloud.

The power of transportation could only be used to travel from one Kalian temple to another. Stories claimed the gods had blessed the land at these sites, declaring the locations to be where their temples would rise. Some questioned the myths, of course, but for Kale, the more he lived in these trying times, the more he believed the legends, which had been conferred to him as a child.

He focused on the Temple of Critous, specifically a room almost an identical match to the one where he now stood. As he concentrated, specks of light gathered around him, like flashes of sun glinting off a glass panel. "Critous," he said again. More lights appeared, becoming brighter, causing the entire room to sparkle. They grew so bright he was forced to close his eyes, and even then, the brilliance invaded his vision. A slight tingle began in his fingertips, then moved to crawl across his skin. The lights blended to a single flash and then vanished, leaving Kale blinking, spots blurring his vision. He wiped at his eyes, rubbing the corners.

"Prince Kale?" he heard the voice behind him, and turned to see a boy who looked perhaps thirteen. Garbed in silver robes, his breast pocket had a purple sword, the Temple of Critous' symbol.

"Yes," the prince replied, "I am Kale."

The boy dropped to one knee and placed both arms straight on either side of him in a traditional Kalian bow. "I did not know you would be here, my prince."

"I did not have time to properly announce my arrival. Please, stand."

The boy did as the prince instructed, a curious glint in his intelligent eyes.

"Would you please send for Master Carolyn? I must speak with her at once."

"Of course, my prince. I shall fetch her immediately."

The boy ran from the room, leaving Kale alone in the chamber. The Temple of Critous had been constructed of gray stone, the walls embedded with amethysts, creating a purple gleam against the blue fires that burned along the far walls. He stood in the violet glow, silent until he heard approaching footsteps.

Draped in purple robes, Master Carolyn was a tall woman with brunette hair and deep green eyes. "Prince Kale," she welcomed, sounding out of breath. "Forgive me. We were not expecting you."

"Nor should you have been," Kale replied. "I came in much haste and am afraid there was no time to send news of my pending arrival."

"Of course." Carolyn offered a brief bow. "How may I be of service?"

"I have come to join the Lord of Turbamentum's party. They have journeyed this way in pursuit of bandits. I recently learned the high lord's son was killed in this endeavor, and have come to ensure his life will be the last they take."

"Ah, yes, I was very saddened to hear of the high lord's loss."

Kale nodded. "I was wondering if you had any information regarding their specific whereabouts?"

"Yes, my lord. They rode from here not two days ago, heading toward the Temple of Aurum."

"Best I leave at once then. May I respectfully request the use of one of your temple's stallions?"

"Of course, my prince. You honor our temple by doing so."

"It is I who am honored by your generous assistance. I shall promise to do my utmost in protecting whichever steed you allow me to ride on this quest."

Master Carolyn offered a second bow. "Allow me, Prince Kale, to also replenish your provisions."

"That would be much appreciated."

She turned, and Kale followed her down a series of stone hallways, each splattered with the same amethysts that had been in the training rooms. Pausing by the kitchens, Carolyn procured two flasks of water, along with a generous provision of bread and dried meat, sealing them into a leather satchel before handing the bag to the prince. "These should help and the meat, at least, will last for some time."

"I thank you," Kale said, grateful for the supplies he'd been unable to gather in his flight from the palace.

"Of course, Your Highness."

She led him through more hallways, before emerging out of a pair of towering stone doors. They walked down a series of steps and paused by the fountain at their base. Nearly ten feet high, its inner layers were lined with amethyst, which caused the pouring water to appear violet as it splashed in frothy layers along the edge. A strong, icy gale blew across this western side of the kingdom.

"This chilly wind will fade when the third sun rises," she said. "Have you brought an extra cloak?"

"I have."

"Very good." She motioned him forward. "Shall we go to the stables?"

The wooden barn was also painted in faded plum and the horses inside had thick purple coats. These beasts of burden, Kalian legends maintained, were blessed by the gods. When a new foal was born, they would be transferred to the temple that matched the coat color. In the temple he had been raised, for example, all the horses were silver, like Sterling. However, unlike the gold and silver stables where there was a single, uniform color, Critous horses came in varying shades, from lilac to dried grapes.

Carolyn walked past a number of steeds until she reached a horse with a shiny amaranthine coat, the shade a deep blend of purple and red. "This is Porphyrius. He's the fastest in our stables."

Kale stepped forward and stroked the horse's sleek neck.

In response, Porphyrius gave a soft snort as though aware of the journey to come.

"I'm Kale," he introduced himself to the horse. "I require your help."

"He will serve you well," Carolyn assured, opening the stall door and leading the horse towards the tack room. Once there, the horse was outfitted with a blanket and a leather saddle. Kale secured his sword and bag of provisions, then mounted while Carolyn held the reins. He patted Porphyrius' neck, accustoming the horse to his weight and touch before reaching for the reins.

Thus acquainted, he guided Porphyrius from the stables, pausing by the violet fountain to turn back to where Master Carolyn trailed behind him. "Thank you."

Carolyn nodded. "You are welcome, my prince. Though, may I suggest you leave as soon as possible, if you wish to avoid your brother knowing your location and ordering you back to the palace."

Kale's heart skipped.

Recognizing his shock, Carolyn rushed ahead. "Tristan spoke of your desire to join their journey, when I mentioned I had never seen him on a quest without you. I assumed, since you are here alone, and unannounced, you've traveled without your brother's permission. Ride quickly, my prince. I believe this threat is as you fear, and it will take our very best to secure the safety of this kingdom."

Kale stared, his mind reeling. Carolyn knew he was disobeying the king, and had assisted him anyway. "It could be viewed as treason, to aid me in violating the king's orders."

"A crime I gladly commit, for the safety of the temples, and the kingdom."

"Thank you."

"Go."

At the commanding tone, Kale turned and urged Porphyrius towards the temple gates. He lessened his grip on the reins, allowing the horse to dictate their pace as he became more comfortable with the unfamiliar gait. Heading north, they soon rode under a clear, violet sky. True to Carolyn's prediction, the breeze lessened and warmed, heated by the power of the three suns above.

CHAPTER XX

In the Time of Kale & Koloso

KALE RODE WEST TOWARD THE Periculum Mountains. He hoped he could catch the others before they reached the Temple of Aurum. He did not particularly desire to enter another temple, as Master Carolyn was correct, it would be much easier to force him to return to the castle.

The Temple of Aurum, the most western of all the temples, was a place he visited frequently. Koloso's status as heir to the throne granted him admittance to this highest-ranked temple, where Kale had instead trained on the opposite side of the kingdom, at Eversus, where his mother had served.

Because of this, he had always been closer to his mother than his father. She had named him, after some negotiation with her husband, after an ancient hero whose stories she adored. A prince who had led many battles against the darkness before succumbing to a hero's death.

Koloso had been named after their father's older brother, who had died before the twins were born. The death had deeply affected their father in more ways than simply making him king, or so Kale had been told. King Derik I wanted the memory of his lost sibling to live on in the legacy of his son and heir. In this way, both parents were satisfied with the naming of their twin sons.

Their parents had also trained at opposing temples, though their father left before completing the curriculum, and had never served as a knight of the realm. Their mother, Queen Claudia, was a daughter of the High Lord of Serenitas. She'd been a strong, loving woman, and a knight in her own right before becoming queen. A tall woman with blonde hair that smelled of lavender, she always seemed an unstoppable force in his eyes.

Yet, his mother had been unable to prevent the illness, which first stole her strength, then claimed her life. Kale had raged for days as her death approached, all the powers of the Kalian kingdom being unable to diagnose the pestilence that ravaged her body, transforming her in a matter of months from the towering vision he had always admired to a frail creature. He had cursed the gods, watching the life leave her.

Toward the end, Kale's mother took his hands in her own. "This anger, my child, it will not do. The gods have been good to me. They gave me a position where I was able to spend my life helping both those I held dear, and those in need of my protection. It has been my honor to defend this realm, both as a student, a knight, and a queen. They blessed me further, by allowing me two children I am proud to call my sons, who will continue my legacy. Defend the realm, Kale, and never forget those who need protection most are often of the lowest ranks."

"But, Mother, I don't want you to leave me."

"Kale." She had slipped her hand from his and reached up to brush a lock of dark hair from the side of his warm cheek, causing him to shiver at the touch of her icy fingers. "I will never leave you, my son and prince. I will watch over you, from the Halls of Heroes, as my own parents have long watched over me. No matter what your father may, or may not, believe, I promise you the realm beyond is real, and one day I shall see you again."

"Mother, please," he had pleaded. "Stay."

She had not. The life vanished from her eyes hours later as he clutched her cold hands.

Kale had been fifteen when his mother passed to the gods. His father, who gave no credence to the realm beyond, had attempted to have her body burned at the palace. The combined will of both brothers, along with several temple masters, convinced him to allow the twins to move their mother's body to the Temple of Ziazan. Claudia joined other deceased knights of the realm, greeting the flames, her ashes carried on the wind across the Rainbow Mountains.

A few years later, their father would follow her in death when overseeing a battle. In the camp where he should have been far from the fight, a surprise force had managed to infiltrate from behind. A stray arrow claimed the king's life. Koloso assumed the throne only months after his twentieth birthday, a role which Kale had never envied. The weight of the crown sat heavily upon Koloso's brow, putting the brothers at odds at almost every turn, finally resulting in this—Kale being forced to openly defy the king in order to do what was best for the kingdom.

These thoughts and memories ran in a steady stream through Kale's mind as he rode. A sigh of relief washed over him when he reached the top of the hill and found the High Lord of Turbamentum's green tents.

With a tug on the reins, he guided Porphyrius along the rocky path in a quick-paced trot, soon reaching the guards standing on the northeastern side of the camp.

"I am Prince Kale," he called to the men, slowing his approach, "here to see Lord Tristan."

The men stared, hesitating. Finally, one of them, garbed in red robes, spoke, "Please remain where you are. I shall summon Lord Tristan."

"Of course," Kale acknowledged, coaxing Porphyrius to a stop. "Do as you must."

"Forgive us, Prince Kale," the second man explained, shifting uncomfortably in his blue robes. "Security has been difficult, and we've never met before."

"I understand, and appreciate, your caution."

The man in red nodded before vanishing into the sea of tents. He returned minutes later, Tristan trailing behind him in bright red robes.

"Kale!" Tristan called.

"Tristan," he acknowledged, respectfully holding his position as instructed by the guards.

"This is the prince?" the blue-robed knight confirmed.

"The only one I know," Tristan answered.

Both men dropped down to one knee, touching the tips of their fingers to the ground. "Forgive us, Your Highness."

"Never apologize for doing your job." He dismounted, swinging his leg over the saddle to slip to the ground, commanding the kneeling men to rise as he did so. They obeyed and one stepped forward, offering to take Porphyrius' reins. He passed the horse to the man. "This stallion belongs to the Temple of Critous and has served me well," he told the knight. "Be sure to take good care of him."

"Of course, Your Highness." He walked Porphyrius toward the camp, leaving his partner to remain on guard.

Tristan stepped forward and offered his friend a greeting, touching Kale's shoulder. "It is good to see you, my friend. Though I must say I am surprised. Your brother seemed adamant you were not to come."

Kale gave a half-smile, but failed to hide the truth from his best friend.

"Oh? I see." He motioned his arm toward the camp. "Come, we shall speak in my tent and see about getting some refreshments."

"That would be appreciated," Kale replied, following his friend until they reached a tent near the center of camp.

Opening a flap, Tristan motioned Kale inside, then closed the cloth cover, tying it behind him. "Helps keep the bugs, and other unwanted things, out."

Kale chuckled, knowing his friend's distaste for the outdoors. "I imagine you've seen a few *critters* on this trip."

"A spider—as big as my hand!" Tristan huffed.

"I'm sure," he replied with a smirk.

"I'm not kidding! Woke up and found it crawling on my blanket."

"And, let me guess, it crawled into your jars of ink so you could no longer write me?"

A confused expression shaded Tristan's face.

"I haven't received a letter in nearly a month."

"I've written every three days. Are none of our dispatches getting through?"

"Koloso has been getting regular reports, I'm told, but I've not received your letters."

"I have been writing you with the same regularity this entire trip, every three or four days. And I almost always send the letters with the same batch as those going from the other commanders."

"That's strange," Kale replied. "Why would only your letters not make it to the castle?"

"I don't know." Tristan's eyes narrowed. "Unless..."

"Unless what?" As soon as Kale voiced the question, the answer became clear. "Unless someone wanted me here, and knew without your reports, I would come."

Tristan gave a single nod. "Troubling news."

Kale nodded. "Who would do that? And why?"

"Hard to say, other than we should proceed with even more caution now that you're here. Or perhaps have you escorted to the nearest temple."

"And do what? Hide as my brother would have me do?"

"If you are the target of these raids, then yes."

"I am *not* leaving." His words became heated. "I'm not a coward. I am a knight of this realm and I deserve to be here as much as you."

"It's not a question of *deserve*. You're the heir to the throne—"

"I don't care. I have no desire to be king. I never have. No one knows this better than you."

"Kale, please."

"You sound just like Koloso."

"Well, perhaps he is right."

"Don't!"

Tristan held up his hand, resigned. "Okay, Kale. You are, after all, the prince. You don't need my permission to be here."

"I did not come to fight with you."

"And I don't want to fight either. Let's go back to the beginning, okay?" When Kale didn't respond, Tristan added, "Please."

"Fine," Kale relented. "What is the situation?"

"We've chased the bandits into the mountains, but can never seem to catch up with them. Still clueless as to whom it is we are actually pursuing, or what they want."

"You still don't know?"

"Stories here and there, all of them conflicting. Some say they are blond. Some dark-haired. Some say as pale as any Kalian, others say..." He shook his head. "There is no consistency."

"Have you tried to get ahead of them?"

"We've tried, yes. But they always seem to be just over the horizon."

Kale paused, processing this information as Tristan moved to the back of the tent. Shuffling through a pile of cloth, Tristan withdrew a silver flask. "Water?"

"Thanks." Kale accepted graciously, flicking open the lid with a soft click.

"There's wine as well, but it's in the high lord's tent."

"Water's fine," he replied, grateful for the refreshing liquid after the day's ride. He took a drink. "I noticed there were only two men guarding the side of the camp."

Tristan nodded. "We add a few more at night."

"Wasn't the high lord's son killed in daylight?"

"Yes."

"Then don't you think there should be more guardsmen during the day as well?"

"I recommended as much."

"And the high lord refused?"

"One of his good-for-nothing advisors. Understandably, the lord has been a mess since his son's death."

Renewed sorrow touched Kale. "I was saddened to hear about Lancel. He was one of the best men I've ever known."

Tristan nodded. "I am so sorry, Kale, it happened on my watch."

"There was nothing you could have done. I read the reports. The attack happened fast, and silently."

"True, but I still feel..."

"We will catch these killers, Tristan. I promise."

Tristan drew a deep breath and nodded. "As I said, the lord is inconsolable and his advisors have proceeded to make one ill-advised decision after another. Probably the reason we have not caught the men we seek."

"I'm surprised he did not appoint you his advisor on this mission, since it is what you were sent to be."

"Oh, they ask my advice on occasion. They just never seem to take it."

Kale nodded, acknowledging the frustration in his friend's voice. "What do you say we pay the high lord a visit?"

"Do you have a plan?"

"Perhaps. First, we need to increase the number of men surrounding this camp at any given time."

Kale stepped toward the make-shift door and unzipped the flap. He stepped out, waiting for Tristan to do the same. Tristan leading, they walked to the high lord's tent. Easily recognizable by its silver exterior in a sea of green, Kale was unable to hide his surprise at the elaborate structure.

As though reading his mind, Tristan raised a hand. "I would assume this was his advisor's choice. I myself, would want—"

"It shouldn't be so easy for our enemies to identify which tent belongs to the high lord," Kale's words interrupted his friend's.

"Again, not my decision."

"I have known High Lord Charles for many years. He's more intelligent than this."

Tristan gave a quick nod, then moved toward the tent where a guardsman opened the silver flap. "He's with me," Tristan said, motioning to the prince. The guard nodded, allowing both men access to the spacious area. As Kale ducked to enter, he spied a rectangular wooden table in the center of the tent. Scattered across were silver goblets and flasks of what Kale assumed to be the wine Tristan had spoken of previously. Several men sat around the table laughing, each in the deep green robes of Turbamentum. Their speech was slurred, and even from feet away, alcohol perfumed the air from where great quantities had been spilled over the silver tablecloth.

"What is the meaning of this?" Kale demanded as he searched the room for the high lord. He was nowhere to be seen.

A gentleman with short, tawny hair turned from the table. "The meaning of what?" His voice was sharp. "Tristan! How dare you let someone in here without permission."

"My lord, if I may—"

"You know the rules."

"He has come to speak with the high lord," Tristan replied, moving to stand beside Kale.

"The high lord is indisposed. All matters of concern should be brought before me."

Realizing this incompetent man did not recognize him, Kale broached the issue, curious to see for himself how this man responded to the request for tighter security. "The high lord's son was killed during daylight hours. Based on this known risk, I am having difficulty understanding how it is that there are only two men guarding the camp's north side."

"Two is sufficient," the man replied, his speech slurred.

"Not sufficient to save the life of Lord Charles' son," Kale countered.

"How dare you speak in such disrespectful tones. Do you know who I am?"

"A drunken fool," Kale guessed, "whose incompetence is placing everyone in this camp at risk. One who is drinking when he should be chasing those whose death, or apprehension, was personally ordered by the king."

"Guards!" the advisor called, "remove this man from my sight."

"I wouldn't do that," Tristan spoke from Kale's side. "It is a crime to touch a prince against his wishes."

"A..." The man turned, fully looking at Kale for the first time. "What?"

"As I attempted to inform you, Lord Richard, before you interrupted, his Royal Highness Prince Kale has arrived."

"Prince?"

"Yes," Kale answered.

"The king's..."

"Brother would be the word you are searching for. I believe, my lord, you are inadequately defending this camp in the daylight hours. I insist on having the number of guardsmen around the camp tripled, and to speak with the high lord immediately."

"I will get him right way, my prince. Right away."

CHAPTER XXI

———◆◆◆◆◆———

ONCE THE PRINCE ARRIVED, THINGS *changed for the better. The camp became more secure, and we made progress through the mountain passes. Men were deployed to strategic towns along the trail, always in groups, inquiring into sightings of the men we sought. Soon, it became all too clear the path our enemies embarked led to none other than the Temple of Aurum. More than half-way along the trail, and unable to safely send scouts ahead, we had no way to warn the men and students of the impending threat. We could only pray and hope we would arrive in time.*

If only we had known the truth of those we sought. What we were about to face was far more harrowing than any of us could have ever imagined.

Kyle put down the letter, realizing with a start he had read through the entire night, in spite of his exhaustion. He blew out the much shorter candle as sunlight filled the room with a golden glow.

Kale traveled to the front alone, and against his brother's wishes? The story he had been told as a child was that Kale and Koloso had ridden together, as a unified team, to face a rising threat. And what of this Temple of Aurum? The second time he had seen the name in a matter of days, yet there was no record of it in the official history books. In fact, there were no temples in the Periculum Mountains and, to the best of his knowledge, never had been.

Then, of course, there was perhaps the most shocking revelation. *Koloso was the elder brother...and king!* Kyle had always been led to believe Kale had been the elder, and that his younger brother, Koloso, had died young. As a student of the temple that had been considered second-best for as long as he knew, the thought that Koloso, and not Kale, had been the elder and higher-ranked twin disturbed him. Why had he, along with the majority of those now living, been told a lie? Did the high priest know? And if so, what was the reason for keeping this secret?

Uncertain of whom to trust with this information, Kyle removed the scrolls carefully from the desk and walked down the halls to where chambers had been prepared for his men. He found Brandan seated on a sofa of red cushions.

"Up already?" Brandan inquired with a yawn. "Not that I'm surprised."

"Actually, I didn't get any sleep."

"Oh? More dreams?"

"Something like that," he answered. "Look, we ought to hurry, as Queen Mariana is anxious for the information we're to collect, but if I don't get sleep I'm likely to fall off my horse. I'd like to stay one more day."

"Another full day?" Brandan tilted his head. "Is everything all right?"

"I'm just...exhausted."

"I'm sure, after riding through that storm, followed by the pace we have been on since we left the palace, everyone would appreciate a day's rest."

Kyle nodded. "Would you inform the men?"

"Sure thing," he answered. "Wouldn't mind some more sleep myself."

"Actually, I have another assignment for you."

"Oh?"

"When we arrived, some kids asked for coaching. I said they might find us in the temple training room this morning. Since I couldn't sleep, I'll leave that demonstration to you."

He groaned. "Training? But I haven't had breakfast."

"Then I suggest you be quick about it. Their day started half an hour ago."

"You so owe me." Brandan let out a sigh, exaggerated enough Kyle knew he didn't actually mind.

"Consider it a *perk* of being second-in-command." Kyle smiled.

"I doubt they will find me a great substitute. They are, after all, expecting the *undefeated* Champion of Koloso."

Kyle sighed, fighting to keep his eyes open. "You're probably right. Tell them I'll be there tomorrow morning. Promise."

Brandan nodded. "Good enough."

"Don't forget to tell the men—"

"I will. Lie down. Even to me, you look exhausted."

"Thanks," Kyle said entering the room. He fell upon the still-made bed and was asleep before he found the strength to disturb the tucked in blankets.

By the time he awoke, the third sun was already high in the sky. Stretching, he rose groggily and made his way to the kitchen. He asked for a simple sandwich of cold meat and cheese before returning to his chambers where he reopened the delicate scrolls in the privacy of his borrowed chambers.

His mind reeled from the differences of this tale compared to the one he had been told as a child. With every page, he became more certain that within this ancient parchment hid a truth the temples could not, or more likely did not, want to believe.

CHAPTER XXII

In the Time of Kale & Koloso

KALE'S HEART HAMMERED AS THE riding party approached the Temple of Aurum. They stopped out of sight, not wanting to alert anyone to their presence. He feared what they would find upon their arrival.

"Don't worry," Tristan said. "We're not talking about a helpless group. It's the Temple of Aurum—the most prolific fighters in the land."

Kale forced a smile that fooled no one, least of all his childhood friend.

"Relax. I know you're having dreams, but..."

The prince moved Porphyrius as close to Tristan's mount as he dared, leaning in so he'd not be overheard. "More than a dream," he whispered. "The one I had...the bad one."

"About the camp being attacked?"

"Not the camp..." Kale drew a deep breath and confessed, "You were attacked, Tristan. Killed in your sleep."

Tristan's eyes widened as he stared at Kale. "But I'm not dead," he said, concern lacing his voice. "It must have just been a dream."

"A dream, yes, but... also more."

"What do you mean?"

"At the end," Kale searched for the words, "I heard a voice, Tristan. And when I heard it, I wasn't dreaming any longer."

"A voice?"

Kale nodded. "It basically said I needed to find you, and that if I didn't, you would die."

"So..." Tristan said, understanding dawning, "the insistence one of us always be awake. The extra security—"

"Tristan, I..." Kale shifted in his saddle. "You'll think I'm crazy."

"Try me."

"I think...I'm fairly certain, I mean—"

"Out with it."

"The voice came from a wraith."

Tristan leaned back in surprise, and his horse reared with him. "Whoa." He eased his grip on the reins that he had not realized he'd pulled. "A wraith? You mean, a messenger of the gods?"

"There was something about what he said, his voice, the certainty of the future and a..." He searched for the word. "A power. I didn't just hear the warning. I felt it, a living truth that could not be denied."

"Kale."

"I told you it would sound crazy."

Tristan digested this information and then said, "No, Kale. What is far more concerning is that it does *not* sound crazy. Not in the least. You are a prince and knight of this kingdom. If you say a wraith visited you, and that the gods themselves have taken notice, then I believe you. But what worries me most is why the gods have come to you." He turned his head across the field leading to the Temple of Aurum. "I now wonder, are we chasing these men? Or blindly following them into a trap?"

"I had been wondering the same thing myself."

"We must proceed with all caution."

"Hey!" a voice interrupted their conversation, pulling both men's attention to the fact they'd fallen steadily behind the rest of the riding party. "You two coming?"

"We are!" Kale called. "Got lost in conversation." Both men directed their horses back toward the center of the group.

When they reached the outer temple grounds, Kale raised his hand, signaling the party to stop. "We don't want to lead the men into a possible trap."

"I agree," Tristan said behind him. "How should we proceed?"

"Send a riding party to the temple, ask to speak with the master?"

"We don't want to let them know we have an army at their gates."

"True. And we don't want to approach hostilely if I am wrong and nothing is amiss."

"So we send a small party, say it's urgent we speak with the temple master. If something is wrong, they likely won't allow us to speak with him. If everything is fine, then we should be able to inform him of the situation."

"I'll—"

"You'll do no such thing!" Tristan cut him off. "If you want someone in charge to go, I'll do it. But there is no way I am allowing you to ride in there."

"Well, I'm not about to let you go without me."

"Fine. We'll send someone else."

Both men paused, and then, as though reading each other's mind, they turned to where Richard sat atop his horse, behind them.

"What?" he asked.

Neither answered, but simply stared in his direction.

"No," Richard said, realization dawning.

"No?" Kale asked.

"I mean...my lords, my prince, surely there is someone more qualified."

"More qualified?" Tristan flashed a smile Kale recognized held no sense of humor. "More qualified than you, chief advisor to the second-most powerful high lord in the land? Certainly not."

"More, my lord, I don't..."

"I agree," Kale added. "You are most qualified for this mission. And don't worry, I'll send a couple of knights with you." *For what little good it would do if the men we seek lie in wait*, Kale thought. "I'm sure you'll be perfectly safe."

Richard shifted on his mount, preparing for further argument, when a sharp look from Tristan made him think better of it. He bowed his head, casting his eyes downward to avoid looking directly at either knight, resigned to a reluctant acceptance.

"You are to go to the temple. You are to tell no one of your mission, or of this army's approach. Ask to speak with Master Fallon. Tell him it's a matter of the utmost important. Tell no one of the threat except the temple master. I will send with you knights who'll be able to confirm his identity. If you are not back in one hour, we will assume the worst, and prepare to attack the temple with full force."

Ten minutes later, the appropriate knights had been selected to accompany the lower lord. Kale watched Richard, flanked on either side, ride down the path toward the Temple of Aurum.

CHAPTER XXIII

In the Time of Kale & Koloso

THE SUBSEQUENT HOUR WAS AMONG the slowest Kale had ever experienced. Tension held the group enthralled. Was this a trap? Had they sent those men into danger? Were they hostages or worse, already dead?

Kale forced himself to push these thoughts from his mind. Worry would not help, and fear had no place. He instead sat in silence, awaiting news until, as the end of the hour drew near, High Lord Charles approached.

"It will do no good, to worry."

"I know," Kale replied, shifting to meet the gaze of the gray-haired lord.

"There comes a time when you realize all the caution and preparation in the kingdom cannot determine the outcome of a mission such as this. Sometimes, all that's required is faith and the belief that whatever happens here today is the will of the gods."

That's what worries me. Aloud Kale said, "I regret, my lord, in the haste of this quest, I have not properly offered condolences on the loss of your son."

Lord Charles bowed his head. "I thank you, my prince." He sounded tired. "My son was proud to serve the realm."

"I am certain he waits in the Halls of Heroes, beside the gods themselves."

Charles gave a bittersweet smile. "It is a comfort to know he died in service, and was granted the honors accorded to a knight of the realm."

"Lancel was a great friend. A man I was proud to train beside. Everything a knight should be."

"It honors his memory, and eases this father's heart, to hear such praise from one of princely rank."

The two men fell silent, waiting becoming more agonized with each passing moment. Kale finally raised his hand, motioning Tristan over to where he stood with the high lord.

Tristan approached, cautioning, "We ought to give them a few more minutes. We don't want to do any..."

"Any what?" Kale asked.

Tristan pointed toward the open field, drawing the attention of both Kale and the high lord to where he'd indicated. Heading in their direction was a riding party, which included Lord Richard and the two knights. However, it was the person riding behind them that made Kale's heart skip. Garbed in golden robes upon a matching steed, sat the unmistakable form of Koloso.

Chapter XXIV

In the Time of Kale & Koloso

KALE SAT STILL, ALLOWING THE party to reach them. At a loss, he bowed his head from where he sat in the saddle as others moved to the side, creating a clear path for the king to reach his brother.

When the hoofbeats ceased, the king was the first to speak. "Lord Charles. Brother. Lord Tristan."

"Your Majesty," they acknowledged in unpracticed unison.

Kale looked up, wondering if his brother would yell at him publicly, or wait until they were alone.

"The temple is secure," Koloso said. "I suggest you move your party there for the night. Rooms are being prepared."

"Thank you, Your Majesty," High Lord Charles replied.

Koloso leveled his gaze at his brother. "You and I will speak in private." He glanced toward Tristan. "The three of us."

Neither man spoke, but instead followed the king, each taking a position slightly to Koloso's side so as not to be covered with the dirt stirred by his horse as they rode toward the Temple of Aurum.

When they arrived, they passed off their reins to stable hands before entering the temple at the command of their king. They climbed up marble steps, and two guards opened the towering golden doors. Gold surrounded them: the hallway walls, pristine marble floor with dyed rugs, and curtains lined the windows, pulled back with sashes of matching satin, offering a shimmering touch to the material. As they passed the elaborate doors leading to personal chambers, they saw carved handles lined with priceless jewels, each matching the rank of the student or master who lived within. The wealth of this temple was immeasurable; the grandest of all, where future kings had trained for thousands of years.

Koloso walked down the corridor until he took a sharp left and opened one of the doors. Once the king's own room, he had borrowed the chambers of the golden student of Aurum for the duration of his stay. He took a seat in a chair, which as with everything else in the room, was draped with golden cushions, and motioned for the two other men to take seats beside him before turning to address his brother.

"What, in the name of the gods, are you doing here Kale?"

Surprised by the question, Kale replied, "Exactly what I wrote in the letter. Helping the men to destroy these villainous knights, once and for all."

"Villainous knights? Such a fancy title to give some low-level bandits."

"Those low-level bandits," anger filtered through Kale's voice, "killed the son of a high lord. Killed a temple master. Killed multiple knights of the realm *and* have managed to evade capture for months, despite sending some of our very best out to apprehend them. You can call them what you like, Brother, but their threat merits above some low-level bandit."

"You are giving them too much credit."

"And you are not giving them nearly enough! A temple master, Koloso. If nothing else, they are murderers. Not bandits."

Koloso held up his hands. "Okay, fine. They are killers. But this does not change the fact you deliberately disobeyed me. I ordered you not to come here. Told you, specifically, I required your presence in the castle." He turned his gaze to Tristan. "And as for you..."

"Hey, now wait a minute. I had no idea he was coming to join us. And for the record, I never stopped sending letters. I have no idea why they didn't arrive at the palace, since I sent them with the same dispatchers who carried all the other reports."

"The other ones made it, didn't they, Koloso? That's how, I assume, you knew to come here."

"Yes, the other reports were delivered, but none from Tristan."

"I swear, upon my honor, I faithfully sent letters. As to your brother, if you can't control him, how should I be expected to?"

Koloso sighed. "I suppose that's true. However, you should have sent him back to the palace immediately."

"I advised him to return."

Koloso scoffed in disbelief. "Unlikely."

"He did," Kale interjected, turning his brother's attention back to him.

"You should not have come."

"Well, it's a good thing I did or this group would still be lost in the woods, and nowhere near the villains you commanded be apprehended."

"What do you mean?"

"Lord Charles is bereft with grief. He aged a decade in the past few weeks, and let some fool of an advisor run the camp. I found the leadership drunk and ignoring Tristan's recommendations. The camp was only loosely defended." Kale shook his head. "It's little wonder someone was able to kill the high lord's son so close to camp, with that idiot in charge."

Surprise crossed Koloso's features. "You put this advisor in his place?"

Kale nodded. "Lord Richard was the advisor, whom we sent to speak with the temple master."

"Ah," Koloso said, "he seemed unusually nervous when he spoke to me. If he was already reprimanded by the prince, I would assume he would not want a similar lecture from his king."

"I would assume not."

"Very well then. As long as the oversight was addressed."

"It was," Kale assured him. "Now, Brother, what are *you* doing here?"

"Chasing you, of course. My reports indicated you were approaching the temple."

"If you think you are going to order me back to the castle, before these murderers are found, you can think again."

Koloso studied his brother before answering. "As much as I would love to remind you who is king here, Kale, I see now it would be pointless at this juncture. So instead, my knights and I will assist you in ridding the kingdom of this nuisance. You are right, bandits or not, they are killing the people we have been charged to protect. It will not do."

"Thank you, Brother."

"Tell me what you know."

"Not much, unfortunately," Kale replied. "They have ransacked multiple villages on the path through the mountains, the last one only yesterday. We feared they might have attempted to infiltrate this temple, which is why we sent only a few riders first. I did not want to risk leading the men into a trap."

"Good thinking," Koloso answered. "Have you discovered the identity of these men?"

"That's the frustrating part," Tristan said from beside Kale. "None of the stories are consistent. It is as though these attackers send in different men every time, and never the same combination. All the descriptions are varied. We can't seem to figure it out."

"Hmm," Koloso hummed. "Troubling indeed. Allow me to think upon this information. We'll meet tomorrow morning and attempt to devise a plan to flush these men out, once and for all."

"Thank you, Your Majesty." Tristan bowed at the waist.

"Yes, thank you," Kale said.

Thus dismissed, both men turned and walked from the room.

CHAPTER XXV

In the Time of Kale & Koloso

BEWARE, THE DEEP, GRUFF VOICE called through his dreams. *Beware.*

Kale awoke from a deep slumber, by a voice calling his name. The summons came from Lord Jerald, second son of Lord Charles, and after the death of Lancel, now his father's heir. He had served two ranks below Koloso at the Temple of Aurum, and was now second-in-command of the king's guard, a trusted advisor.

"What is it?" Kale asked groggily, wiping at his eyes. "What's wrong?"

"There was some unusual activity. We sent two of our knights, Seth and Warren, to investigate. They have not returned. The king asked me to make you aware of the situation."

"Let me grab my outer robes."

"Really, my lord, there is no need for you to go yourself."

"I am going," he said insistently. "That is not up for discussion."

"We could be walking into a trap."

"All the more reason to gather our best swords."

"But—"

"No buts. I am the prince, am I not?"

Jerald paused, then cast his eyes down in defeat. "As you say, Prince Kale." He stepped outside the chambers, allowing Kale to dress in privacy.

Kale gathered his outer robes, adding an extra layer to combat the night's chill. Lastly, he secured his silver scabbard, which encased a matching blade within, around his waist. Suppressing a yawn, he shook himself, hoping to stave off the exhaustion for a few more hours.

He left the room to find Jerald standing outside his door. "Really, my prince, you don't have to go."

This time, Kale did not bother to verbally acknowledge his statement, instead heading directly down the hall to the front of the temple. When he emerged, he found Porphyrius and another horse already saddled at the bottom of the stairs, and four additional knights whom Kale recognized as former teammates of his brother, all trained at the Temple of Aurum. After descending, he took his reins from a waiting knight, Lord Brent, and mounted.

Only after Jerald had settled into his own saddle, did Kale speak. "Okay, tell me again what is going on."

"We had someone, a young boy, come in from the nearest village. He reported some men had come into town, well-armed. All the villages have been asked to report such sightings, in case they are the men we seek. We sent a couple of knights, told them to observe only and report back. They haven't returned. It could be nothing."

"Or," Kale countered, "it could be exactly those we have been seeking."

Jerald nodded.

Kale searched the faces around him as Brent and others mounted their own collection of colorful stallions. A mostly-full moon provided plenty of light. "There are six of us?"

"Should there be more?"

Kale shifted uneasily and ultimately pushed his caution aside. "Six, plus the two men you have already sent, should be sufficient."

"As you wish," Jerald said. There was something in his voice Kale could not quite place.

"Do you feel we need more men?"

"No," he answered. "We are enough. Though I have had the king informed of the situation, so he may send additional men."

Kale nodded. "Let's ride."

Jerald led those gathered down the dirt trail through the mountains.

As the cold wind blew, Kale heard the wraith's deep voice. *"Beware."*

Beware of what? Kale asked silently. *Of whom?*

No answer came. Glancing around again, he saw only knights of the realm, men he had known since childhood. He kept searching, even as he rode along the dirt path. The cold wind grew warm. At first, Kale thought he imagined the temperature change. Yet as he rode, it grew hotter. *There is no sun out, the air should not be balmy. What in the name of the gods...*

Something caught his eye. He leaned left and was startled to see a wolf on the side of the path, hidden behind the trees. Its jeweled eyes gleamed in the light, so brightly. Kale thought it couldn't be real. The gods' wraith could not be here, standing in the shadows of the trees, yet somehow close enough his breath heated the back of Kale's neck.

Porphyrius gave a shrill shriek, rising on his back legs. Unprepared for the sudden movement, Kale fell, colliding with the ground. His horse shrieked again, pawing the air before landing in violent stomp of hooves, forcing Kale to roll to his side to avoid being trampled.

"What in the world?" Jerald said, pulling his own horse to a stop as Porphyrius turned and raced back toward the temple.

"Kale, what happened?"

"What is going on?" a second voice asked.

Kale couldn't answer, his eyes transfixed on the wraith's menacing form. Six feet tall on all fours, shaggy fur, a silhouette in moonlight, with sharp-fanged teeth protruding from his mouth. Faced with such a beast, Kale realized he had never understood fear before now. The wraith was here and terrifying to behold.

Questions surrounded him, but the voices were distant, unable to pierce the trance of the wraith's jeweled eyes. Others looked in the direction he stared, but could not see the danger that loomed before them.

Dazed, Kale pushed himself up to one knee, lowering his arms to his side in a show of respect to the gods' messenger. *My lord,* he spoke silently.

"*Listen,*" the wraith commanded. "*Listen, prince of the ancient bloodline.*"

As soon as the wraith's words were spoken, voices punctured the veil surrounding him.

"What is he doing?" an indistinguishable man asked aloud.

"Does it matter?" a second answered. "The five of us are here."

"This was not the plan."

The plan? Kale wondered. *What are they talking about?*

"He wanted to be present when we—"

"Let's get it over with."

"I suppose you're right," the other voice answered. "Let us be done with this foul task."

Unable to remove his eyes from the wraith, Kale's mind grappled to understand. Until the undeniable sound of swords being drawn from their sheaths cleared the fog of his confusion.

Jerald's voice rang through the air, "Forgive me, my prince."

"*Now!*" the wraith growled.

The spell broken, Kale's hand rushed to his side, withdrawing his own blade. Yet he knew it would be too late. The unseen sword sailed down. But to Kale's surprise, the attack was met by the sound of clanging metal.

Kale jerked his head, clearing his sword from its scabbard even as Tristan called, "Kale, get up!"

Kale twisted away, struggling from his knees, raising his weapon barely in time to stop the swing of a second blade. Outnumbered, five to two, Kale's eyes swept the area, searching for Lord Jerald, whom he found, much to his shock, standing beside Lord Brent, sword drawn.

110

Tristan pushed back his own attacker and stepped to Kale's side, guarding his right as the two champions stared at the other knights.

"What is the meaning of this?" Kale yelled.

The gathered men, whom Kale had trusted with his life, did not answer. Instead two of the men lunged at the prince, while another moved toward Tristan.

Keeping both hands on the heavy blade, Kale turned his sword sideways, managing to block both men at once, his knees bending under the weight of the attack. He twisted right, forcing both men to take a step back to maintain their balance as the blade they had been bearing down upon vanished, tipping them forward. Kale stepped behind Tristan, so they could fight back-to-back and better protect each other.

One of the men lunged to Kale's right side. Kale turned and met the man's blade with his own. The sound of clashing metal rang in the night air, carried on the wind.

The second man swept his blade to Kale's left, causing him to twist to stop the sharp edge from slicing through his skin. Kale slid his blade along the side of his opponent's. He pushed hard, throwing his weight into the movement. The man stumbled, allowing Kale an opportunity to step forward. He brought his blade to the man's side, then changed to a downward trajectory mid-motion. The prince's silver blade sliced deep into the would-be assassins stomach. The man screamed, his intestines spilling from his body.

Kale did not have time to observe this, as no sooner had he landed the strike, he had to stop another from slicing Tristan's back. The swords clashed again. Kale managed to maneuver his way back, between his friend and the man trying to kill them. A sword swiped to Kale's left. He jerked his own, sparks flying as the blades met.

Behind Kale, Tristan gained the upper hand on his opponent. A scream filled the air as the man he had been fighting fell, leaving the field three-to-two. Better odds. Brent took the place of his dead comrade, but Kale could only focus on the man in front of him.

A blade swiped to Kale's right side. Kale met the sword with his own, afraid to step away from Tristan. Kale thrust his blade forward, forcing the other man to take a step closer to the tree line. The man swung low, aiming for Kale's stomach. Kale took a risk, stepping back to avoid the strike, while raising his own blade, bringing the sharp metal down, aiming for the man's arm. His blade proved true, piercing the skin. Blood spewed as the man roared in pain.

The cut was not enough to stop the knight-turned-assassin, who adjusted his grip on the blade, now slick from his own blood. Kale caught movement from the corner of his eye and realized Lord Jerald moved in his direction. Desperate, and knowing he could not defend both himself and Tristan from their double onslaught, Kale gambled.

With a roar, he thrust his blade forward toward his attacker's chest, driving the man farther toward the trees. He swiped his blade again, then repeated the movement, progressing steadily closer to the forest's edge. When they reached the tree line, heated breath touched the back of Kale's neck. Only this time, his opponent detected the warmth as well. Both men froze, the other belatedly realizing what Kale had known since the first dream—something was terribly wrong. The knight whipped around, sword clutched tightly as he beheld the wolf-like form of the wraith.

Behind him, Kale stared at the creature again, a sense of reverence and terror overwhelming as the wraith met his eyes. Without ever breaking eye-contact, the wraith moved faster than Kale could follow and bit into the side of the man's neck with six-inch razor-sharp teeth. The knight did not even have time to complete a scream before the wraith pulled the man's writhing body deeper into the forest, vanishing from sight.

Without pause, Kale turned to see Tristan had his own fight, with Brent, well in hand. Trusting Tristan's skill, Kale turned his attention to Jerald.

"What is the meaning of this?" Kale demanded, still unable to comprehend why one of his brother's former teammates, and closest advisor, would be attempting to kill him. Jerald did not speak. "You call this honor?" Kale tried again to goad Jerald into a response. "Attacking me five-to-one?"

"Clearly, it was not enough."

"Why would you do this?" A realization came to Kale. "Your brother! Did you kill your own brother?"

"Not personally," Jerald admitted, his voice holding a trace of regret. "Yet it had to be done. He was far too loyal to you."

"How could you say such a thing?" Kale asked in disbelief. "He was your brother!"

Jerald raised his blade. "He was, and now, I will send you to join him in the Halls of Heroes."

"Why?" Kale demanded again. "You owe me that much."

"No," Jerald said, "I really don't."

Kale moved into a defensive position, widening his stance for balance, and adjusting the two-handed grip on his blade. The sound of clashing metal rang behind him in a steady rhythm as Tristan fought for his life. "I don't want to kill you."

Jerald's blade rose high before crashing down, a stroke of pure force that had Kale struggling to maintain his grip as the two swords met. The intensity of the fight was overwhelming.

Jerald followed him across the dirt path until Kale stopped, holding his ground. He drew a deep breath, the scent of fresh grass clearing his head before assuming a defensive stance. Jerald also paused, widening his hands on the black hilt of his blade. Both men stared at each other waiting to see who was going to move first.

Jerald rushed forward, swinging his heavy blade to Kale's right. Kale turned, blocking the intended blow with another clang of metal. Jerald turned, twisting tightly to bring his blade to Kale's opposite side. Kale jumped back, with Jerald in mid-turn, causing Jerald's blade to slide harmlessly through the air. As the blade swept by, Kale lunged, bringing his sword to Jerald's arm, and slicing into his shoulder.

With a roar, Jerald jerked back, injured but still lethal. Perhaps more so in his rage. Kale advanced, swiping high, forcing Jerald to bring up his blade to stop the blow. As their swords touched above their heads, Kale brought his knee up into Jerald's stomach, his sword crashing down.

Jerald slipped to his knees, having to hold his sword above his head in order to stop Kale's blade from striking him. Blades crossed, Kale pushed down, while Jerald struggled to keep the sharp edge at bay. Jerald gave a gruff groan from the strain, then threw his body across the ground, separating himself from Kale's sword. Thrown off-balance, Kale tipped forward and nearly fell. He fought to maintain his stance. Sweat pouring from his brow, Kale wiped his face with his sleeve, lest it blur his vision. The time he took to do this was all Jerald required to regain his footing.

Swinging his blade right, Jerald rushed toward Kale. This time, Kale stepped back, timing the swing. Kale twisted around Jerald, turning fully to his exposed back. The tip of Kale's silver blade entered Jerald's spine before emerging through his chest.

Jerald screamed, his own blade falling to the ground as his body crashed into the dirt. Kale shot a quick glance over to Tristan, whose opponent also lay dead at his feet. Turning to Jerald's dying form, Kale kicked away his blade and turned him on his back. Jerald screamed again at the jarring motion.

Knowing he had only seconds to live, Kale knelt down beside the knight. "Why? Jerald, why?"

"Must die," Jerald spoke through shallow breaths. "Kale. Koloso. Must..."

"Koloso?" Fear increased at the mention of his brother's name. "What about Koloso?" He leaned closer. "Jerald, what about my brother?"

"Die. Death. Ko...lo..."

With that last utterance, a final breath escaped Jerald's lips. His body went still.

"What about my brother? Is he in danger?" But Kale spoke to the dead.

He turned to the trees, seeking the wraith who, only moments before, had terrified him. "Are they trying to kill my brother?" He searched the trees, but the wraith was nowhere to be seen. "Speak to me!" he shouted.

"Kale, he's dead," Tristan said, assuming he was speaking to the lifeless form.

"Not him."

"What?"

"The wraith. I saw the wraith."

"The wraith?"

"He was here. He killed one of the attackers."

"Here? Why are the wraiths..."

Both men exchanged a glance. "My brother!" Kale said. "They must be trying to kill my brother."

"At least, someone is." Tristan whistled. Two golden horses came to his call. "I saw you riding out and worried something might be amiss."

"Thank the gods you did," Kale said, mounting.

"Yes. Thank the gods."

"We have to get back to the temple. The king's in danger."

Both men turned as one.

CHAPTER XXVI

In the Time of Kale & Koloso

KALE AND TRISTAN RODE SIDE by side, flying past the forest as they raced toward the Temple of Aurum. They were surprised to find another party riding their way. Also traveling quickly, so sudden did the others appear, Kale and Tristan were forced to pull their horses onto the side of the path to avoid colliding with the other riders. "Whoa!" the men called to their golden mounts, pulling on the reins to guide their horses to a gradual stop. They turned to face the oncoming group.

"Wait!" Kale called. "Don't go that way." His words trailed as he recognized his elder brother. "Koloso?" Kale shook his head. "What are you doing out here," he glanced at the two men riding with his brother, "and with so few guards?"

"I could ask you the same question," Koloso replied.

"We were led into a trap."

"A trap?"

Kale nodded, but with only moonlight, was uncertain if Koloso could see the movement, so he voiced his answer aloud, "Yes."

Koloso dismounted and stared up at his brother.

"We should get back to the temple," Kale advised.

"Not until you tell me what is going on," Koloso said. "I was told Jerald accompanied you. Where is he?"

Kale looked at Tristan. Both men dismounted to join their king on the ground. "We encountered a trap."

"What do you mean?"

"I mean, Brother, exactly that."

"Jerald is?"

"Jerald was the trap." Pain laced Kale's words, giving them a ring of sorrowful truth. "He..." Kale drew a sharp breath. "He tried to kill me, Brother. And if Tristan had not arrived in time, he would have succeeded."

Behind them, the two additional guardsmen dismounted their horses as well, moving closer to the group. Koloso took a step away from his brother. "He was my friend, my captain. Jerald trained at the temple with me."

"Koloso," he met his brother's gaze more directly, "tonight he, and four other men, tried to kill us."

"Jerald is dead?"

"I am so sorry, Brother. In self-defense, I had no choice." The words hurt.

Grief seeped into Koloso's eyes.

"I suspect he planned to kill you as well. Your name was on his last breath, and he spoke of death."

"Did he?"

"Yes."

Koloso closed his eyes, absorbing the news further.

"Brother," Kale spoke gently, "we should return to the temple. It will be safer there."

Koloso nodded, seemingly dazed. He turned to where Tristan stood a few feet away from Kale. "You saved him?"

"Yes, Your Majesty."

"Come here." He motioned Tristan closer, and the knight did as he bade. The king grasped Tristan's hand and lowered his head. "I am sorry, Tristan, that you were attacked tonight."

"I am happy I arrived in time," Tristan answered.

Koloso leaned forward, placing a hand on Tristan's right arm. He held him in a one-armed embrace, which Tristan returned. "I am so sorry."

Tristan gave a sharp gasp as the king pulled back and thrust a knife into his lower stomach.

CHAPTER XXVII

In the Time of Kale & Koloso

"Tristan!" Kale screamed his friend's name. He raced forward, catching him as he fell to the ground. "Tristan!"

Tristan moaned in agony, the sound pulling at Kale's soul. He looked up at his brother as sickening nausea overcame him. "What?" he spoke in uncomprehending disbelief. "Why? Why would you?"

"You took my right hand, I shall force you to watch yours die as well." Koloso's voice was sharp, cruel, a tone Kale had never known his brother to direct at him.

"I don't under..." Tristan's hand gripped his, drawing Kale's gaze. His friend's eyes were wide with pain and fear.

"Though," Koloso continued, "perhaps I should thank you for taking care of Jerald. After all, not only did he fail to kill you, it would seem he attempted to warn you with his dying breath. What do you think, Kale? Will his final words be sufficient to gain his admittance to the Halls of Heroes?"

"What is this?" Kale asked. Going into shock, Tristan's hand trembled under his. "You're my brother."

"Yes, a brother whose throne you covet, and whose men answer to you before me, their king."

"What are you talking about?"

"I know of your machinations, Prince Kale. That you desire my throne above all else. You undermine me at every turn. Question my authority in front of other lords and knights. Turn the men's loyalty from the crown to yourself. Openly refuse my express orders."

"You're insane!" Anger overrode Kale's fear. Anger laced with the agonizing twist of betrayal. "I don't want the throne. I have *never* wanted *anything* to do with it!"

"Then why do the men always defer to you? I am king! Ruler of this land. The eldest twin. Yet time and time again, the knights who should guard my right to this throne turn to you. Only you!"

"If I have done something to offend you...but this...this..." He looked up into his brother's sapphire-blue eyes. "Please, Brother, Koloso...Tristan has nothing to do with this. Please, just...I'll do anything. Please."

"Stop pretending!" Koloso's voice dripped with venom. "I know of your scheming. How you plot to take what is rightfully mine. You shall not have it!"

Kale stared into his brother's eyes, but saw a man he had never met glaring back. "This...these *bandits*." A fresh wave of nausea washed over him. "This was your plan. Your men. Your orders."

"Yes."

"A temple master. The son of a high lord. Countless villagers. Knights, loyal knights! All dead! On your orders!"

"All loyal men—to you, Brother. Only to you."

"No!" Kale screamed. His sword appeared in his hand. He did not remember drawing it.

"Ah," Koloso taunted, "there he is. The great Kale."

Kale's words were low, deep. "Tell me it's not true. Tell me you did not do this."

Koloso smiled. A sinister expression.

"Why?" Kale demanded. "Why Koloso? You're the king! You're supposed to protect the people!"

"Because this was the only way I could see you dead without risking rebellion. Here, away from prying eyes. Away from the castle, the temples, and the men who are loyal to you."

"I don't understand."

"Ah, but you do." He paused, allowing his words to carry their power over the cold breeze. "You are beloved, Kale. By the people, the knights, the temples. I, on the other hand, am not. It would not do to kill you in front of the kingdom. No, they would never allow it to stand. But..."

All fear had faded from Kale's voice, leaving only a dangerous anger. "But what?"

"You chased a villain into the Periculum Mountains, defying my express, public orders. You went yourself, with limited guards, to find said villains in a nearby village, but met them on the road instead. Outnumbered, you tragically die, leaving your bereft brother to avenge your death. You a fallen hero and I—"

"A murderer," Kale supplied.

Koloso smiled. "An unchallenged king, whose harsh rule will be justified for decades on the death of my dear, *beloved* brother."

A moan turned Kale's attention back to his best friend. "Tristan has nothing to do with this." Kale's voice softened. "Please, don't let him die."

"You, Kale, are responsible for Tristan's death. Had he remained behind, he would have been safe."

"Please, let him be taken to the temple. Show mercy, Brother, please."

"Mercy," the king drew out the word. "Mercy."

"Please."

"Hmmm," the king mused. He leaned closer to his brother.

Beware! The soulless voice of the wraith cut between the twins.

Kale reacted, lowering his blade, moving it over Tristan's sprawled form moments before Koloso's thrust down. The clash of their swords filled the air, followed by the screech of a nearby bird disturbed at the sharp sound. The two stilled, blades crossed above Tristan's shaking form.

Kale spoke to the two men standing beside the king. "If either of you so much as moves toward Tristan, I will kill you, your family, and anyone you have ever called friend."

Koloso stepped back and waited. Balancing his sword in one hand, Kale shrugged out of his robe, keeping his eyes on his brother. He cut the heavy garment into several jagged pieces. Tristan cried out as Kale maneuvered him to tie the cloth around the abdomen wound. Kale took a second strip and pressed down, attempting to slow the bleeding. He moved Tristan's hand on top of the poor excuse for a bandage. "I know it hurts," he told his friend. "Hold it as tight as you can."

"Kale," Tristan stuttered, "Kale, please...run."

He looked down into his friend's green eyes. "No. I can't."

"Don't die for me." His panted words were unsteady. "Run."

"No," Kale said, his voice resigned. "There will be no running, will there, Brother?"

"I am afraid not."

Kale nodded. He touched his friend's hand. "Serving with you has been my honor."

Tristan stared at him with only partially open eyes. "Live...live to serve..."

"Die for honor," Kale finished the Kalian prayer, "and glory to those who live and die in service to the temple gods."

Kale stood, his silver clothes blending with the moonlight while his brother's golden robes shimmered.

"Are you ready, little brother?"

"No one touches him while I still breathe."

Koloso nodded. "It is not *him* I want."

"Then yes, Brother, let us end this, once and for all."

Behind them, the gruff voice whispered, "*The choice is made.*"

CHAPTER XXVIII

—◆•※◆※◆•◆—

"WHAT?" KYLE ASKED ALOUD. HE re-read the line. Then read it again. And again. *Koloso and Kale?* His mind reeled. *It can't be true. This is some sick joke. This is...*

Yet the description. A blond in golden robes. A dark-haired man in silver. A fight to the death. A prophecy about the twins of Kale. How did it go again?

"*Fear to the fearless,*" a gruff voice slipped into the room. "*Hope to the hopeless. Mercy to those who hate you. Death to those who love you.*" Shadows gathered in the room that had nothing to do with the setting suns. "*That is your destiny. Heir to Kale. Heir to Koloso.*"

"Heir..." Kyle spoke the final line. "To both."

"*Yes,*" the shadows answered as they took form. "*Yes, Lord of Koloso, and you too have a part to play.*"

Kyle fought the urge to back away as the creature materialized. Thus he found himself staring into the slanted, cat-like eyes of a sinister black wolf. His breath caught at the sight. It towered over Kyle, sharp teeth protruding from the sides of its open mouth. With a low growl, its eyes narrowed until they were thin slits, holding no actual color but instead reflecting the evening light like glistening jewels.

The creature leaned closer, so close Kyle's neck was warmed by its hot, foul breath. "*Lord of Koloso. Heir to Turbamentum. Heir to Serenitas. Heir to both.*"

Under the weight of those deadly eyes, Kyle found it hard to draw breath. The wraith waited, allowing the young man to grapple with the riddle of his words. "I am not the heir to Serenitas."

The wraith stared at him.

Then, to Kyle's horror, it dawned. "Marcus was."

"*Yes,*" the wraith said condescendingly.

"But I..."

"Watch, Lord of Koloso, and know."

Kyle blinked. When his eyes parted, he stood in an ancient forest, old even in the time of the lords before whom he now stood—Kale and Koloso.

CHAPTER XXIX

In the Time of Kale & Koloso

KALE STEPPED AWAY FROM TRISTAN, walking across the dirt path to where his brother stood. The ground was relatively free of rocks and branches, the path having been used by riders of the Temple of Aurum for decades. Dry, there would be no puddle or mud to slip in while holding the heavy blades. Kale wiped his right hand on his silver shirt, ridding his skin of Tristan's blood so his fingers would neither slip off, nor stick to, the silver, jewel-encrusted hilt.

"Just us," Kale said.

"Yes," his brother replied. "At last."

Kale shook his head. "Do you honestly believe I want your throne, Brother? And even if I did, do you believe I would want it enough to harm you?"

Koloso stared across into his younger brother's eyes and hesitated. The voice of the wraith whispered in his mind, *"Are you going to fall for this act? So innocent, they speak of your brother. So loving and honorable. They flock to his call. That of a prince, not their king. He wants your throne, and he has the means to take it."*

Yes, Koloso answered without speaking, *but he is still my...*

"Your what?" the wraith spat. *"Your future king? Your future murderer? He wants your throne, Koloso. Are you going to let him take it?"*

No. Koloso tightened his grip and widened his stance. "You, Kale," his voice was low, "will never be king."

"I don't want your crown!"

"Denials and talk, while Tristan's life slips away." He gave a crude laugh. "Tell me, Brother, if it was you who lay dying on the forest floor, would Tristan be wasting time with chatter? Or would he do anything to save your pathetic life." He glanced to Tristan, who trembled in a fetal position. "You really should let me put him out of his misery. Perhaps I should do so now?"

He took a step toward the fallen knight when Kale screamed. "No!" A glint of silver reflected in the moonlight. Kale brought up his sword to clash with his brother's. Koloso stepped back, his eyes studying Kale's silvery form in the moonlight. Approach decided, Koloso stepped forward and thrust his blade toward his brother's chest. Kale arced his blade, deflecting the tip of the sword to the left, knocking it away from him, forcing Koloso to follow his sword to maintain his grip.

Kale swung his blade to his elder brother's left side. Koloso jerked back, causing the attack to miss. Kale drew his blade back toward his chest. The world around them faded, until each saw only the tall form of the other royal warrior. Koloso gazed into his brother's eyes. All hints of fear and suffering had vanished. Kale's features slackened as he slid into a world where only the sword existed. This, at last, was the brother Koloso had desired. This deadly warrior who knew only blood. This, at last, was the fight he sought.

Koloso drew a deep breath, allowing himself to slip into the same realm as his brother. He lunged forward, sweeping his blade to Kale's left side. Kale jumped, avoiding the sharp edge. Koloso took another step, this time thrusting toward Kale's right side. Kale twisted away.

Kale drove his own blade toward Koloso's chest. Koloso moved his sword low and then up. Mid-motion, Koloso jerked his weapon down and forward, the tip moving toward Kale's stomach. Kale jumped back, barely escaping the intended injury.

Koloso attempted to press his advantage, when Kale twisted around him, moving to his left side and swinging his blade. Koloso did not have time to turn, so instead brought his left arm down and attempted to throw his body in the opposite direction. He managed to keep the sword from entering his side, but was not fast enough to prevent the tip from slicing across his left arm.

Hissing in pain, but the cut was not deep enough to be disabling. Adjusting his grip on the golden hilt of his sword, Koloso defiantly stood his ground. Kale moved forward, swinging his sword to Koloso's left with all his strength. The blades collided, sparks igniting in the cold air between them. The metal sang as they pushed back and forth in a dance. The brothers separated, and Koloso immediately swung his blade toward Kale's right. Kale met the challenge again, their blades clashing in the air.

The swords of gold and silver moved up and down, each collision more ferocious than the one before. Kale swung high, his blade sailing toward Koloso's throat. He managed to duck, causing Kale's blade to fly harmlessly above him. Koloso raised his blade from the crouching position, aiming at Kale's exposed side. Kale jerked back, but not before his brother's sword pierced the silver cloth, grazing the skin beneath, though as with Kale's previous strike, not deep enough to cause serious injury.

Through labored breaths, Kale held his blade close and moved his left hand to wipe his sweat-covered brow with the back of his silver sleeve. Koloso stepped forward, lunging again, moving his weapon to Kale's left. Again, Kale blocked.

Koloso taunted, "Tristan's life is slipping away, Kale. Can you hear it, the sound of death pulling him into her tight embrace? Much longer and it won't matter who wins."

"Don't!" Kale shouted, moving forward in a flurry of anger. Kale's blade sailed to Koloso's left. Koloso parried, but the blades had barely parted before Kale swung again. Koloso blocked the second swing with his golden sword. The edges screeched as they slid against each other, before separating.

Kale took half a step back. He swung his blade again toward his brother's side, this time forcing more speed into the movement. The silver blade connected with gold. Kale twisted, using the force of the clashing blades to increase the speed of his turn. Momentum carried him completely around to Koloso's opposite side.

Koloso realized too late what his brother intended. Kale aimed the sword's edge low, slipping under his brother's partially raised arm and into his right side.

The king bellowed as the blade sank into his ribcage. He stumbled left. Silver tore through muscle to hit bone. The pain was agonizing. Koloso took additional steps to the left, desperate to breathe. Kale offered no respite.

Following his wounded brother, Kale swung his blade toward Koloso's injured side. In a burst of sheer determination, Koloso stopped the strike.

Kale raised his sword high and brought it down again. Seizing the opportunity, Koloso thrust his own sword up, stopping Kale's mid-motion. Koloso pushed hard, knocking his brother back a step and, as he did, used Kale's unbalance to jerk his sword down, slicing into Kale's left arm. Kale cried out, cursing in pain.

Both men paused to draw the breath necessary to continue. Pain wracked their bodies, which now ran on adrenaline alone. Koloso leaned awkwardly, pressing on his injured side, his breathing labored and painful.

Kale lunged, swinging toward his brother's right side, to be stopped by Koloso's weapon of gold.

In desperation, knowing he could not endure much longer before collapse, and that Tristan's life slipped away with each passing moment, Kale thrust his weapon to his brother's left. Koloso blocked.

Kale spun, twisting in a tight spiral. Koloso followed the movement, blocking Kale's sword with his own.

Between them, the voice of the wraith rose. *"Fear to the fearless."*

Kale turned. Koloso followed.

"Hope to the hopeless."

Kale faked a third twist, but actually brought his sword low and thrust straight. Unprepared, Koloso had already begun to turn in anticipation of a side-stroke. Kale's blade slid directly into his brother's stomach.

Koloso screamed and fell to the ground.

"Mercy to those who hate you."

Beyond all rational thought, Kale swung his sword, bringing it down on his brother's arm, slicing through skin and muscle, causing Koloso to scream again. Still caught up in a blood rage, Kale aimed and brought the sword down a second time, onto Koloso's wrist. The blade sank through flesh and bone to sever his sword hand from his arm.

"Death to those who love you."

"I don't believe you!" Kale shouted, then ignored the wraith. Ignored the other men surrounding him. His entire world narrowed to this man, this traitor, this murderer of innocents, of men he had fought beside, of friends he had loved.

A wheezing, pained cry broke through his dimmed world. "Kale," Tristan called, "he's your...brother."

Kale looked at Tristan, and then back to the writhing, screaming thing on the ground. "No," Kale said in a cold, dead voice, "he is not."

The necessity clear, Kale, prince and hero of the realm, thrust his blade down with all his strength, squarely into his twin brother's chest.

CHAPTER XXX

―――◆ ⊱❖⊰ ◆―――

KYLE AWOKE, HIS HEAD ON the wooden desk. He guessed it to be some time in the wee hours of morning. The last he could recall, the suns had been setting. Now, the room was pitch-black. He stood, shuffling to the fire in the corner, which had dimmed to glowing embers. Pulling a few pieces of wood from a neatly stacked pile beside the fireplace, he tossed them onto the embers. Fumbling to grasp a metal poker, he stirred the fire until flames emerged to burn along the wood, bursting to life and casting a blue light around the room.

He made his way back to the desk and proceeded to light a collection of candles.

Had he been dreaming? If so, that was the most real dream he had ever experienced.

Did I actually see Koloso and Kale fight...to the death?

Pushing the candles closer to the letter, Kyle continued to read where he'd left off. His heart quickened as he realized the contents were an exact account of his dream.

"By the gods," he whispered. "It's true. It's all true."

He flipped through the scrolls, scanning until he came to where the dream had ended.

Chapter XXXI

In the Time of Kale & Koloso

KALE RACED TO TRISTAN'S SIDE. His hands were cold to the touch. The silver cloth he had been holding against his stomach was now scarlet. As Kale leaned over him, he was assaulted by the coppery scent of his friend's blood. "Tristan, stay with me!"

Fighting back a wave of painful emotions, Kale shouted to the wraith, "Is this what you wanted?"

"*Yes.*"

"Tristan had nothing to do with it!"

"*He had a role to play.*"

"But dying isn't part of it."

The wraith stepped out of the shadows, his black fur outlined in moonlight. Reflective, slanted eyes, with no color of their own peered at him. A low growl emanated from the back of its throat.

"I fulfilled your prophecy," Kale said, his voice tight, controlled. "Save him."

"*Giving orders to the messenger of the gods, brave prince?*"

"I did what you wanted. Now save him."

The wraith leaned down. His hot breath warmed the dying man's clammy skin. Scorching heat washed over Kale. The wraith growled, and the sound carried on the wind, filling the forest. Kale stared into his eyes, refusing to move as the heat increased.

The wraith breathed again and flames burst to life, gliding across Tristan's red robes. Kale wanted to throw himself on top of his friend, but was unable to move, held captive by the wraith's malevolent eyes. He tried to scream his friend's name, but the word came instead a strangled whisper, "Tristan."

"*Ask me, twin and sole heir to the ancient bloodline.*"

"Save him."

The flames rose. Tristan gave a curdling scream. Then, the conflagration vanished.

Kale jerked his hands down, pulling the blood-soaked cloth from Tristan's body, peeling back layers of sticky material. A scar ran across his friend's stomach and side. An ugly pink, the injury looked months old.

"Tristan," Kale said, fear lacing his words.

Tristan drew a breath. "It..." He swallowed hard and tried again. "It doesn't hurt." He began to rise to a seated position.

"Don't."

"It's okay." Tristan sat up. "It doesn't hurt at all."

Kale raised his head and looked up. The wraith stood by the forest's edge.

"*Prince Kale, sole heir of the ancient bloodline. You have served the gods well.*" The wraith bowed his head in Kale's direction. "*Your Majesty, I bid thee farewell.*"

"Wait!" Kale called. But the wraith vanished.

Kale turned back to where his brother's lifeless form now lay. He walked to his body, and fell to his knees. The adrenaline ebbed from veins, followed by a seeping numbness. "Koloso?" he whispered. "Koloso."

Tristan rose to his feet and walked to where Kale knelt. "You had no choice." He placed his hand on his friend's shoulder. "He left you no choice."

"Koloso?" Kale said again. The heaviness spread, the night's events a horrific blur. "Brother. Please, Koloso."

"He's gone," Tristan said.

"Please," Kale pleaded as he collapsed, his head falling on his brother's blood-covered chest. "Koloso, please." He spoke the question that could never be answered, "Why?"

Tears spilled and his words fell to silence as he cried over his brother's body. Time stood still.

The two men who had been escorting Koloso approached. "My lord," one of them said, "he was the king. We had no choice."

Tristan turned back and looked at them. "There is always a choice." He grabbed his blade from where it had fallen.

"Please, my lord, he was—"

"I know who he was," Tristan said flatly, before thrusting his blade into the chest of the speaker.

The second jerked back, scrambling across the field as Tristan stalked him. "My lord, please, no!" Tristan ignored his pleas, driving a sword through his chest as well. He turned back to where Kale crouched, inconsolable over his dead brother's body.

Tristan attempted to pull Kale back, but Kale fought off his hands. "Kale," Tristan spoke softly. "My friend."

"No."

"Please, Kale, there is nothing else you can do for him. He's gone." He placed a hand on Kale's shoulder and his friend's body shuddered under the touch.

"He's my brother."

Tristan replied in a voice thick with sorrow, "He was." He again attempted to maneuver Kale away. This time, Kale relented, turning enough to allow Tristan to slide his arms around the distraught man. "I'm sorry, my prince."

Kale shook for a long time, then pulled back to meet Tristan's green eyes. "We can't tell them what he did."

"Kale, I don't think..."

"We do not tell *anyone* what he did," Kale reiterated. "My brother died a hero, killing the men we sought. Men who were traitors to the realm. The entire kingdom will mourn his death. A hero, Tristan. Koloso died a hero."

Tristan thought about arguing, but looking into the pleading eyes of his best friend, found he could not. "Okay, Kale. Your brother died a hero."

Kale's eyes closed. He fought to force air into his lungs, gagging on the saturation of blood surrounding them. "Thank you."

"My prince," Tristan acknowledged. "My king."

CHAPTER XXXII

WE WORKED IN SILENCE TO secure Koloso's body to one of the golden horses before riding back to the temple. What happened next was a blur. We told a story of the bandits being knights of the realm. A plot to overthrow the royal family, by killing both Kale and Koloso, naming Jerald as the leader and scapegoat. That Koloso had died valiantly killing five of the attacking men, saving both Tristan and Kale's lives. A true king. A hero. A knight worthy of the halls of the temple gods.

When we arrived back at the palace, a massive gathering of mourners greeted us, Lady Rachel at the front, her face shrouded in a black veil. "I was not married to him," Rachel had said, "but I feel a widow, just the same."

Her glassy gaze is one I recall to this day. The profound sadness of a kind woman who had loved our king, in spite of his cruelty. I wanted to tell her the truth. To tell her he was a villain unworthy of such devotion.

My promise to Kale staid my tongue. It would continue to do so, until this very moment, when I've poured our deepest secrets into paper, which will be tucked away, possibly to never be seen by another soul.

Kale, whom the populous believed avenged his brother, was never the same. A streak of cruelty haunted him on the throne, which had never been there before, as his dreams of leading a temple vanished. His first act was to disband the Temple of Aurum. It had created too many of the traitor knights, he said. Far too many. The students were scattered to other temples. Once abandoned, Kale secretly had a fire lit, burning half the building to ruins before it could be extinguished. Kale was only sorry he could not wipe the hated land from the face of the kingdom.

His second cruelty was to Lady Rachel, the woman who had loved his brother and would, true to her prediction, love Koloso until the end of her days. Speaking with Rachel's father, the High Lord of Serenitas, Kale declared he would honor his brother's alliance and take Lady Rachel as his queen.

I was present when he told her, in a cold, flat voice I had never heard from him before.

"No," she had said. "Forgive me, Your Majesty, I have been invited to be trained as a temple master. I intend to take my vows and live my life according to the ancient traditions, and in honor of the gods."

"You will do no such thing, my lady. You will be my wife and queen to this kingdom, performing all duties required of one in such an esteemed position." A cruel edge to his voice matched the expression on his face.

Surprise crossed Rachel's features, brunette hair framing her green eyes. "Please, my lord, I do not wish to be queen."

"You were perfectly willing to be so when my brother was alive."

"I..." She drew a slow breath. In a voice that spoke volumes of misery, she tried to explain, "I loved him. Please...I—"

"Loved him? Since when did one's heart ever dictate the marriage of a high lord's daughter?"

"My lord—"

"Silence! This is not a discussion. You will marry me, if you have to be dragged screaming down the aisle."

Panic filled her eyes as I stepped between them, taking Lady Rachel's arm. "This way." I pulled gently, leading her from the room. "I will speak to him," I assured her. "I'm confident Kale will relent."

He did not.

A month later, they were wed, her begging until the final moment for him to choose another bride. I stood beside him, knowing his anger was a mask for the pain deep within, but the wound was not one I, nor anyone else, could seem to touch nor soothe.

What was I to say? That it was okay he was forced to kill his brother? That his brother had tried to kill him? That it was... A suitable phrase of comfort does not exist.

Kale went on to lead great battles. He had more victories than any could recall a king ever achieving before. By the time his two sons were grown, the kingdom was a secure, safe land of prosperity and peace. Yet to his closest confidants, Kale was never the way he had been before. Every year, on the anniversary of his brother's death, he raged against the gods. He existed as a man with only half a soul. Born a twin of a shared destiny, which only one could live to fulfill.

When my friend, Kale, died two years ago, he charged his sons with the protection of the kingdom. I was asked to preside over the selection of a new team of knights, who would be drawn from the temples, sworn to defend the kingdom from all harm. And I, a twenty-year Temple Master of Demetrion, became the first member of this defendant team.

After the king's death, several temples were renamed. The one I served as master would henceforth be called the Temple of Desoto. The Temple of Kale and the Temple of Koloso were also newly named. A man of whose treachery the world will never know, Koloso will be remembered a hero, celebrated by all those to come. Such is the will of my friend and lord, King Kale Dektra.

Should you find this letter, you whom I shall never meet, know you have been conveyed a sacred trust. Treat it delicately. The world needs heroes. Shining examples of all they should strive for. To take away that aspiration, as illusionary as it may be, is to destroy everything this hero once stood for.

Learn from this story, and know that twins of the ancient bloodline come in both darkness and light, from which only one can emerge.

Fear to the fearless. Hope to the hopeless. Mercy to those who hate you. Death to those who love you. Heir to Kale. Heir to Koloso. Heir to both. Two heroic figures with only one destiny.

I was with my friend when he died. The last word Kale ever spoke was his brother's name.

With broken faith,

Lord Tristan Desoto
First Golden Defendant

CHAPTER XXXIII

PRINCESS MARIANA WALKED IN THE *grassy field, toward the statues of the gods. Previously a place of disrepair, Mariana's first act as queen was to have the statues and tall pillars restored to their former glory. She walked alone up the marble steps until she reached a stone basin, which rested on a short pedestal. Kneeling down, she withdrew a thin knife made of metal from the river mines outside the Temple of Ziazan. Taking the slight blade into her hand, Mariana sliced down the center of her palm, from the heel of her hand to the pad at the base of her middle finger, allowing her blood to splash into the basin. She lowered herself into a traditional Kalian bow, shifting to one knee. Head down, neck bared, she moved her arms straight to her side, allowing only her fingertips to touch the marble floor. She held this supplicant position, offering prayers to the gods.*

"Please," Mariana prayed, "*grant me the strength to rule this kingdom. Guide my hand. I...*" She could not keep the pain from her voice. "*I am surrounded by advisors, yet, I am alone. I don't know who to trust. I don't know what is right. I beg your guidance.*"

Tears gathered in her eyes. "Please forgive my offenses."

"Fear to the fearless," *a voice whispered, sending a cold chill down her spine.* "Hope to the hopeless. Mercy to those who hate you. Death—"

She jerked her head, tears staining her cheeks, and screamed, "What does that mean? What, by the gods, does it mean! Haven't you taken enough?" *A sob escaped her lips, a single, solitary sound, which echoed the anguish in her heart.* "I sent him away. I sent him...Please. Please."

"Princess of Kale. Princess of Koloso."

Mary stood and raced down the marble steps, searching for the creature. "Where are you?" *she demanded.* "Show yourself."

Rain splashed from the gray sky.

"Why are you doing this? What does that mean?"

The rain went from cold to warm. She raised her hand and realized the droplets collecting on her golden robes were not clear, but red. Her breath caught as she gazed up and saw—it rained blood.

Mary woke with a scream, golden sheets twisted around her. Heart racing, she struggled in their grip to fall to the side of the bed, and scrambled across the floor. Her entire body shook, and her breath came in broken gasps and pathetic sobs. She grabbed her sword in a panic, placing her back against the wall. Propping her blade beside her, she pressed the back of her left hand against her lips.

Another nightmare, each more real than the one before. Each with the wraith's prophecy ringing in her ears, laced with the deaths of friends she had lost. Those she had been unable to save—had been responsible for.

"Dammit!" she cursed between short, constricted gasps, fighting through fear. A soft knock rapped against her door. She tried to answer, to stop her tears, but found she could do neither.

The door opened. Master Jiro entered the room in robes of silver, and found her where she sat, her back pressed against the wall. "My queen?"

"I'm..."

"It's all right, my lady."

"Please, don't..."

Jiro moved closer and knelt a few paces in front of her. "My lady—"

"Don't," she pleaded.

"Okay, Mary."

"I'm sorry."

Jiro shook his head. "There is no need to apologize, my lady. You are far too young to have been through so much death."

"I'm supposed to be queen." Her terror receded, replaced by an anger born of self-loathing. "I don't want to do this anymore. I can't do it! I need my father. I need Leo."

Jiro answered, his voice thick with sorrow, "I know that I am but a poor substitute. We all are."

"Leo knew what to do. He always knew."

"Yes," Jiro spoke of his old rival and friend. "He did."

"Marcus. Jace. My father. Leo. I killed them all."

"No, Mary." He shook his head. "They were defendants and princes. Honored to serve the realm. They knew the risks."

"But I killed them. They told me I killed them." Her voice fell to a hushed whisper, so low he had to lean closer to hear her next words. "All my fault."

"Mary, what are you talking about?"

She stared into his green eyes, so like her own. How much did she trust him? This master of a temple she had been raised to scorn. This man, so unlike the one who had trained her. A more patient man. Perhaps even a kinder one.

"Please, Mary, I cannot help you if you won't confide in me. I am not Leo, and I wish to the gods he were here now for you—I would give my life to make it so. But, my lady, he is not here. I am. I swear, upon the temple gods, I will help you the best I am able, and would never betray your confidence, for any reason."

"You swear to keep this secret from every living soul?"

He held her gaze. "To the gods of Kale and Koloso."

"I called upon the gods, the night Kyle lay dying by our twin blades." Her voice was a mere breath. "They answered."

He showed no hint of surprise at this confession.

"They told me to save him, a price must be paid. That someone would die in his place. Someone I loved."

Comprehension filled the temple master's gaze. "They took Marcus' life."

She nodded. "I forfeited my partner's life for the life of my sister's."

"You didn't know it would be Marcus."

"Does it matter?" Her voice sounded bitter. "It could have been anyone I had ever cared for. Anyone I had ever loved. And I chose Kyle."

"Mary—"

"They said people would die. They said *death* to those who love me. That is my destiny. Repeatedly. Night after night. Dream after dream; sometimes even when I'm awake."

"Who?" Jiro asked.

"The gods. The wraith."

"The...wraith?"

Tremors resumed their path along her spine. "I want Kyle," she confessed as another tear ran down her cheek. "I want him here, but I swore an oath. And the wraith..."

"Demands you fulfill it."

"I..." Her voice trembled. "I am forbidden to love. I vowed before the gods never to do so, but I..."

"Mary," he spoke softly, "if anyone deserves to love, it is you. Yearnings of the heart cannot be controlled, my lady. And I would have to be blind not to recognize he loves you too."

She shook her head. "I wish he did not. Or, that I loved him...more than..."

"Than the crown," Jiro finished for her.

"No, I do love him more than the crown. I would gladly trade the title for him, if only..."

Then, Jiro understood. "If only your sister were Kalian."

Mary bit her bottom lip, her teeth sinking through the tender skin until she tasted blood.

"I wish I could tell you, my lady, if it were your sister sitting here, that I'd tell her to follow her heart, instead of ensuring a member of the Koloso Temple sat on the throne. That I would counsel Ameria, the student I trained, to give up everything for love. But..."

He considered the question, not wanting to lie to this young, vulnerable woman before him. Would he encourage Ameria to follow her heart, instead of her temple? Would he advise her, had the situation been reversed, to put a Kalian, and not a Kolosian, upon the throne?

"I can tell you, with no hint of doubt, Master Leo would never have allowed you to surrender the throne to a Kolosian. The same, I believe, can be said of your late father. They were good men—the best—but temple loyalty came above all else. They would direct you to do your duty. As for me, I think this rivalry has never been what is best for the kingdom, yet it is the very foundation on which the temples are based."

Jiro shook his head and continued, attempting to answer honestly. "Were it your sister asking me if she should give up the throne, I don't know if I could tell her to do so. Temple loyalty is so fiercely ingrained, in me, as it is in both you and your sister. If I could go back, knowing all I now do, perhaps it was unwise to separate the two of you. To train you as rivals. Had you been on the same team, one of you would have been silver, it is true, but..." He searched for the words to complete his thoughts. "But this would be an easier choice. Passing the crown to the sister you trained with, had loved, and fought beside instead of against."

"Why?" she asked. "Was my parents' hatred of each other's temples so great they did not care their choice would transform sisters into adversaries? We could have been friends, partners."

"No, Mary, that wasn't the reason."

Mary looked surprised. "What do you mean?"

Jiro stilled.

"What do you mean?" Mary asked again, more emphatic.

"My lady, tell me, do you remember anything about your visit to the Province of Serenitas? Of visiting your grandfather, Lord Riccard, there?"

Mary stared at him blankly. "No. I don't recall ever being with my grandfather, outside of tournaments."

"I figured as much. You were very young and the events were—"

"What are you talking about?"

Jiro sighed. "A group of temple masters and defendants had gathered to determine which temple you and your sister should be sent to. Most argued for Kale. A few, for Koloso. Some thought you should go to the same temple, for the reasons you are speaking of now. Others, to separate ones. The high priest arrived and it was decided that you both would, to your mother's dismay, attend the Temple of Kale."

"Why didn't we?"

"Because that night there was a disturbance. A scuffling sound, followed by screams coming from both your and Ameria's room. The guardsmen attempted to knock down the door, but...it would not fall. The screams continued before abruptly stopping. The doors flew open, everyone fearing the worst." He drew a deep breath. "There were bodies strewn around the room, in pieces."

Mary's heart skipped. "Torn apart?"

"Some of the men swore they saw something. A creature."

"A wolf," Mariana guessed. "They saw a wolf."

Jiro nodded. "I did not see the apparition with my own eyes. Your grandfather, and others, thought it was as you say, a wraith. Others, a trick of the imagination in response to their horror at the bloodbath."

After considering the implications, Mary found her voice. "The wraith saved us."

"The next morning, the high priest decided, given the assassination attempt, it would be too dangerous to house the two of you in the same temple. For your protection, you should be separated. That way, if another attempt were made—"

"Only one of us would die," Mary finished for him.

"Yes," Jiro confirmed. "You and your sister would have been sent to the same temple, had it not been for that scare. If you had, this would be easier. To hand over the throne. To follow your heart. But, alas, it is not."

"I want to love Kyle more than tradition. More than the temples. But another part of me wants to hate him. For standing beside me when he should not have done so. I—"

"Mary, believe me, as someone who has watched Kyle become the man he is today, he could have done no less. To not have helped you would have crushed his soul, no matter what it may cost his heart."

She stared at him, struggling to place a particular tone in his words. "You speak as though..."

"We all have secrets of the heart, my lady. Even a man who vowed to devote his life to the temples before all else."

"Was she pretty?"

He stared at Mary, her face framed by the same black hair that cascaded over her mother's shoulders. "She was meant for another path, one differing from mine. She would go forth to perform her destiny and I, a chivalrous knight, would love her from afar."

"How did you bear it?"

"It was our choice. A difficult one, yet a choice just the same."

"How did you choose?"

He looked at her before answering. "You choose the path you can live with. It's as simple, and as agonizing, as that."

CHAPTER XXXIV

KYLE LEANED BACK IN HIS chair, his mind whirling from what he had learned. Kale had killed Koloso. Had forced his brother's intended wife into an unwanted marriage. Had led multiple battles in an attempt to rid himself of the guilt and, he guessed, ordered the creation of the defendant team to permanently keep the crown's power in check.

"*Yes.*"

Kyle jumped. He turned to find himself facing the reflective eyes of the wraith.

"*To ensure no king would ever hold unlimited power.*"

Kyle nodded, unsure of what to say in the presence of, what he now knew to be, the messenger of the gods.

"*Come, doubtless you have learned more than why the defendant team was formed, Lord of Koloso.*"

"The story," Kyle answered.

The wraith nodded, encouraging him to continue.

"They..." He sorted through the words. "You keep saying..." He tried to recall the exact words. "'Heir to Kale. Heir to Koloso. Heir to—'"

"*Both.*"

"That means..." His struggle for understanding transformed to a sense of horror.

"*Say it, Lord of Koloso. Speak what you know to be true.*"

"There can only be one." He hesitated. "Only one."

"*Yes.*"

"One destiny. Two heirs. Only one...will live."

The wraith remained silent, allowing the truth to seep through Kyle's desperate desire not to believe. The dreams came in a flurry of flashes. Two men. One in gold. One in silver. Fighting at the edge of a burning forest. Inside the rooms of a stone castle. On the un-scorched surface of the Temple of Ziazan. The fight always resulting in the death of one.

"Twins," Kyle said. "They were all twins."

The wraith lowered his head in confirmation.

"No. It can't be. They would never..."

"*Never what, Lord of Koloso? Attempt to kill each other?*" The light in the wraith's eyes bled from jewels to a silver sheen. Kyle saw his reflection, including the scar that ran above and below his eye. Put there by Mary's sword, when he had stepped between the twin blades. A strike which had been meant for Ameria.

His eye a reminder of the sister's wrath, the truth became more difficult to deny. "No."

"*This is their destiny. Their legacy. Required by the gods since the dawn of time.*"

"Why?" he asked, fear leading to desperate anger. "Why are you doing this to them?"

"*I do nothing. The choice, always, lies with them.*"

"Do you mean it can be stopped?"

The wraith laughed. "*How many times have I heard that question over the centuries? Millennia? Many have tried. Many have struggled, begged—raged.*"

Kyle stared at the wraith, afraid to utter the question burning in his mind. He forced himself to muster enough courage. "How many succeeded?"

The wraith's laughter died as he leaned closer to the silver lord and said, "*None.*"

Kyle attempted to deny the truth. "They wouldn't do it."

"*Heir to Kale. Heir to Koloso. Heir to both. One and the same. One heir. Never two. Twins are born. The prophecy begins anew.*"

"I don't believe you."

Something close to pity crossed those soulless eyes. "*I have heard these words before—right before Kale drove his blade through his brother's heart.*"

CHAPTER XXXV

LORD ANDREW SLOWED HIS HORSE as they neared the end of the dirt path that opened to a grassy field. He wondered how it had come to this. His father had disowned him. Fully aware he'd never been, and would never be, the son his father desired, being disinherited still came as a shock for which he was ill-prepared. "He took everything!" Andrew grumbled angrily as he rode across the blue grass.

When he reached the hidden village, he rode straight through, grateful the late hour shrouded his approach from the majority of those who would have been present in the open-air market had it been mid-afternoon. Against the setting suns, he made his way down the quiet path through the closed booths, before reaching his destination.

Many centuries ago, the Temple of Aurum had been the grandest of all the Kalian Temples. Now, it stood a sickly shadow. Abandoned since the time of Kale, the temple was a mess of broken statues and tattered colors, its very existence stricken from the scrolls of history and known to only a select few. Towering doors stood atop a series of marble steps, the gold once plating them only visible in patches, pieces having been removed by those brave enough to enter doors declared cursed by the sons of Kale.

He was not surprised to find three men, dressed in drab, gray clothes standing watch. As Andrew pulled his horse to a stop before the temple steps, one of the men with sandy brown hair stepped forward. "Who goes there?"

"I am looking for Lady Angelia," Andrew answered.

The man walked down the steps to gain a closer look at the new arrival. "Who are you?" he asked. "I don't recognize you."

"I assumed things might be a bit tense. Her son, after all, killed the crown prince."

Alarmed by the bold assertion, the man drew the sword at his side. "I ask again, who are you?"

"I am Lord Andrew, future High Lord of Serenitas." *Or at least I was.*

Not understanding the connection, the guard's eyes narrowed. "What is your business here?"

"That is none of your concern. Please, inform Angelia of my arrival."

The man turned back to where the others stood, one of whom vanished inside the mutilated doors. A few minutes later he reemerged, a woman in an ankle-length blue velvet gown beside him.

Andrew finally dismounted as she approached.

Surprise showed plainly as she took in the sight of a man she had not laid eyes on in over twenty years. "Andrew?"

"Hello, Sister. It has been a long time."

She continued to descend the marble steps. "Yes, it has. It's all right, Warren," she added to the guardsman standing between them, sword still drawn. "He's family."

Warren sheathed his blade and stepped aside.

"It's really you," she spoke softly.

They stared, then Angelia took another step and slid herself into his embrace. He hugged her fiercely, gripped by an unexpected sense of guilt.

"Andrew," she whispered.

"Sister. My little sister."

When they pulled back, a warm smile lit her face, lost in the joy of their ended separation. "What are you doing here? Did father send you? Did he…"

"No, I'm sorry. He did not send me."

Her smile vanished. "Then why are you here? What are you—"

"He disinherited me, Angie."

She stared at him blankly, as though he had answered in a foreign language. "What do you mean?"

"We have much to discuss, Sister."

"Of course," she answered, motioning up the steps. "Please, come this way."

Together they ascended the stairs and entered the temple. The walls had been gold, but the paint had faded and chipped. Angelia led him down a series of hallways until they reached a square room with a mahogany table standing in its center. She motioned for her brother to take a seat when another man walked into the room.

Younger, the man was undeniably related, sporting the same impressive height, sharp cheekbones, and emerald eyes so common in the Kalian line. "Peter," Angie greeted him.

"Mother," the young man replied before shifting his gaze to Andrew. "Who is this?"

"Peter, allow me to introduce you to Lord Andrew, your uncle."

"My what?"

"Nice to finally meet you." Andrew offered his hand, which after a moment's pause, Peter grasped. "You resemble your father."

"By uncle you mean..."

"My brother," Angie clarified. "Heir to the High Lordship of Serenitas."

"Former heir," Andrew corrected. "Recently disinherited."

Angie took a seat before asking, "What happened?"

"A terror of a princess, that's what."

"Why would Mariana be declared the heir of a province when she is heir to the entire kingdom?"

"Not the future queen, though that may be debatable. The other one—Ameria."

"The blonde-haired one?" Perter inquired.

"Yes," Andrew answered bitterly. "Annabelle's blonde-haired brat. She arrived at the castle, demanding to see Father. They spent a few hours conversing. Next thing I know, she is *declared his heir* and I'm ordered to go settle some petty village squabble on the far edge of the province. I, his own son, tossed aside like..."

Across the table, Angelia absorbed this information. Even as a young girl, she'd realized Andrew was a disappointment to their father. No matter how hard Andrew tried, nothing he did pleased the most influential of the kingdom's high lords. She and her sister were the apples of Lord Riccard's eye. At least, until she had betrayed him by running away with Nathan into exile.

At one point, her father had been willing to forgive her transgression. When Nathan died, her sister had come, offering her children places in the Kalian temples. "Your children can train beside my own," her royal sister had said, "and you can go home to Serenitas. Father offers you back your rightful place in the province."

"Father?" She'd been shocked by this offer from the man seen by so many to be stern of heart. "He wants me to come back?"

"Yes," Annabelle had answered. "And if you can regain his trust, you will perhaps be named his heir."

The discussion had been followed by more visits, but in the end, Angelia had spurned her sister's offers of forgiveness, clinging to a deep-seated anger that her husband had been wronged by those they should have been able to trust most. An anger she'd been unaware had taken such a deep hold in her children's hearts, until it was too late.

"Did you hear me?" Andrew asked, drawing her mind back to the present.

"What? Oh, sorry. I was lost in thought."

"I said, Father knows, or at least I think he knows, your children are the ones who killed the crown prince."

Angelia shivered, a chill at the confirmation of what she had suspected to be true. "I figured someone would piece it together."

"I believe our father intends to come after you."

"Father?"

Andrew nodded.

"He wouldn't."

"You—or rather, your sons—killed the man who made his daughter royal, and his granddaughter queen. Also, if what I hear is true, they killed a Golden Defendant, a couple of well-respected knights, a silver student of Kale—"

"We never killed a silver student," Peter interjected. "I had heard he died, but we had nothing to do with that particular death."

Andrew turned to eye the younger man. "Does it really matter, given the list of those you did kill? A prince, a Golden Defendant, and the Temple Master of Kale? Even one of those deaths would be enough to send every high lord and defendant in the land after you."

Angelia interrupted, "What, exactly, brought you here after twenty years of silence? Did you come to lecture me on what I already know?"

"No, Sister. I came to learn your plan, and stand by your side, should the need arise."

"Why? Why now, after all this time? I mean, there are better places you could've gone, dishonored or not."

"I came to warn you the blonde princess is coming, and she will soon have the power of Father's knights at her side." He drew a deep breath. "As to why I am here now, I guess..." He shifted. "I guess I wanted to talk to the only other person who's experienced what it's like to lose Father's love. To say I didn't..." He shook his head. "I didn't understand why, Angie. Why you would leave. I was angry with you for breaking our family. But now, seeing how easily Father chose to toss me aside..." He exhaled before raising his eyes to meet his sister's more directly. "I came to say I am sorry, Angelia. I'm sorry."

His eyes shone with pain, prompting his sister to stand and walk to his chair. "Andrew, I understood your anger. I abandoned everyone, including you. But I..." She searched for the words. "I loved him, Andrew. I can't justify or explain it, but I loved him. And that love meant I could not allow Nathan to go into an unjust exile alone. For what it is worth, I am sorry for hurting you, Brother. I never wanted to." Her voice cracked.

Andrew looked at her and held out his arms. "May I?"

She went to her knees and allowed him to wrap his arms around her, reunited at last.

Outside the decaying temple, Lord Yarin rode cautiously through the forest. When he was certain he'd moved well outside the temple grounds, he dug his heels into his horse and rode with great haste to report what he had witnessed to Princess Ameria.

CHAPTER XXXVI

❖

KYLE DREAMED, NOT OF DEATH or bloodshed, but of Mary. With her in the sanctity of his mind, they walked under a clear, violet sky. She wore a gold dress with thin straps baring her shoulders, and their hands intertwined in the mist of the Rainbow Mountains. At ease, he inhaled the soft scent of lavender carried on a breeze that cooled his skin from the heat of the Kalian suns. Neither spoke, safe in each other's comfort. When they reached the mountain top, Mary walked toward the edge and gazed over the horizon at the shadowed valley below.

He stepped behind her and pulled her against his chest. She twisted her neck, flashing him a heart-soothing smile before turning back to the view. "I don't ever want to leave," she spoke softly. "Do we have to?"

Kyle cast his eyes past her, taking in the brilliant, endless sky, the scent of lavender becoming stronger as he leaned down and placed his cheek on her bare shoulder. "My lady." The words a bare whisper on his warm breath.

"Mary," she corrected, in a voice that was a caress. "Only Mary."

His resolve waning, Kyle turned Mary in his arms to stare into her emerald eyes. "My lady, I..."

Her body trembled at the use of the title. Tears gathered. It was too much.

He pulled her forward until his lips met hers. She returned the kiss, her tears banished by his touch. Desire coursed through him as the kiss deepened, prompting Kyle to pull her more tightly into the embrace. "Please," she pleaded. "Please...Kyle."

Giving way to both their hungers, he pulled her fully against him, her arms sliding around his neck. She clung to him. He fought his desire, desperately wanting to grant her request. To love her. To crush her in his arms and forever cast out the sorrow that clouded her emerald eyes.

"My lady," he tried to reason, but the words came breathy, unsteady. "Mary, I can't. We can't." Drowning, he lowered his head, squeezing his eyes tightly as he hid his face in the soft locks of her ebony hair.

"So sweet," the wraith's deep voice echoed around him.

Kyle opened his eyes, and there, in the shadowed valley below, was the wraith. He moved Mary behind him, shielding her with his body. "Leave her alone," he demanded, attempting to be brave as fear creeped along his skin.

The wraith gave a deep laugh. "Do you think your love will be enough to save her?"

"It was you, wasn't it?" Kyle challenged. "The night she asked me to take her away, you forbade it."

The wraith laughed again. "To think I hold the power to make such a choice. No, Lord of Koloso, I merely reminded her that with every choice, comes a price. A choice, which always remains with her."

Mary stepped around him and moved closer to the cliff's edge.

"No," Kyle demanded, grabbing her wrist. "Mary, please, stay behind me."

She moved her free hand to caress his left cheek, then leaned forward and kissed him. A soft touch which nearly overwhelmed Kyle's better judgment. Mary removed her other hand from his grasp and pulled back, smiling sadly. "It's all right, my love. Everything will be fine."

With that promise, she turned and stepped off the cliff.

"No!" Kyle woke, his heart racing. "Mary!"

A knock at the door made him jump. Without waiting for an answer, dressed in pink robes with the silver mark of Koloso on his breast, Brandan entered the room.

"Forgive me," he said. "I heard you scream and wanted to make sure—"

"A dream," Kyle answered.

"Another nightmare?"

Kyle nodded.

"Do you want to talk about it?"

"No, I—"

"Something is wrong. You don't have to tell me what it is, Captain, but I must ask, is there anything—absolutely anything—I can do to help?"

Kyle parted his lips to say no, but ended up closing them without speaking the assurance.

Brandan walked around the room, the light of the first rising sun filtering through a series of windows. He took the chair from the desk and put it beside the bed. After taking a seat, he tried again, "Please, Kyle, talk to me."

Kyle considered aloud, "If I asked you to do something for me, knowing the request went against the crown princess' wishes, would you consider it? Without need for a detailed explanation?"

Brandan paused briefly then said, "Yes, I would."

148

"The princess asked for you to come with me, but...I'm afraid for her."

"For her life?"

Kyle nodded.

Brandan bowed his head. "What would you have me do, my lord?"

"Return to the palace. Stand guard over the princess in my stead. Be her captain until I return. I am aware that Mary...the princess...said she would feel safer if you were traveling with me. But I would rest more easily if you were with her."

"I'm honored by your trust," Brandan answered. "I will return immediately, if it is your wish. I'm sure the princess will understand."

"I will relax knowing there is someone she trusts guarding her. She trusts you, Brandan. Queen Mariana never would have sent you with me if she didn't."

"Then I am further honored. As you've requested, I will return to the palace and explain." Brandan smiled. "Though I would ask, my friend, for you to take extra precautions on this journey. I do not know what plagues you, but tread carefully, and trust few."

"I promise. You should follow your advice as well."

Brandan stood from the chair. "Is there anything else you would like for me to convey to the princess?"

Kyle considered the question, a million choices flitting through his thoughts. "Tell her..." *I love her with all my heart,* he wanted to say, a truth so desperate he had to draw a deep breath to suppress it.

Brandan did not speak, but allowed him time to gather his words.

"Tell her," Kyle tried again, "I will keep my promise, to serve her in whatever capacity is within my power to give."

Brandan stared, as though waiting for him to add the words he fought to prevent himself from speaking, and then gave a low bow. "As you wish, Captain."

He left before the majority of the men had risen for the ride to Sanguis Castle, where the High Lord of Serenitas had long-ruled the largest of the Kalian provinces.

Resuming his quest, Kyle rode with great haste, attempting to outrun the nightmares based on chilling truths. One of the sisters would die and he had to warn them. To stop them before they did something from which there could be no forgiveness. Before they committed a sin which would rip the very fabric of their souls. He rode through the Rainbow Mountains, surrounded by the twirling mist. The peculiar fog seemed thicker than usual as he urged his silver mount forward.

He heard the gruff voice on the wind. *"Be warned, Lord of Koloso."*

Kyle looked to the men riding on his left. Their steady gaze told Kyle he alone could hear the wraith's words.

"*Try to save them, if you wish. But know this and remember, for I shall only say this once. Should you attempt to reveal the truth behind the prophecy to anyone, be it the sisters or those who stand by their side, you shall be dead before the words pass from your lips.*"

Kyle leaned forward, burying his face into his mount's mane as he urged the horse into a run. But even the silver stallion was not fast enough to escape the echoing laughter.

CHAPTER XXXVII

MARY SAT AT A TABLE, listening to the monthly reports sent in from the high lords. Flos had recently dedicated a new structure for distributing food to villages suffering from the spring drought. Mary signed an order for neighboring provinces to also provide assistance.

"Last," Chiro said, "we have a report from Serenitas."

"Lord Riccard's kingdom?" Mary straightened against the uncomfortable chair.

"Correct. There had been a series of raids along the Rainbow Mountains. A few weeks ago, a warning was issued to the temples, and towns, in the affected areas. Now Lord Riccard reports the threat has been contained." His eyes scanned the parchment lying on the table in front of him. "It would appear, Your Highness, Princess Ameria handled the situation herself."

"My sister?"

Chiro nodded. "She led a group to find the bandits and oversaw their punishment with the help of Serenitas knights."

This was news to Mary. She knew her sister was with her grandfather. That's why she'd sent Kyle there. However, to learn Ameria was out protecting local villages was surprising. *What is she doing?* Mariana wondered. Aloud, she said, "Well, let us be grateful the threat is no more."

"Yes," Lord Chiro agreed. "That, at least, is a blessing."

Mary nodded. "Is there anything else?"

"Nothing that cannot wait for another day."

"Good." She moved her hand in a dismissive wave. "I am going to my chambers."

"Yes, Princess." Chiro stood and they left the room, separating near Mary's private chambers. A guardsman opened the door at her approach and she smiled gratefully. But as she entered the room, a familiar voice caused her to pause.

"Princess!"

Mary turned, her heart quickening at the sight of the man walking toward her. "Brandan," she greeted. "You have returned."

"Yes, Your Highness," he answered, lowering himself to one knee.

"Please, Brandan, rise. There is no need for that."

He did as she bade, rising to his feet, noticing her eyes were glued to the hallway from which he had appeared. "He's not here, my lady."

Her eyes flicked back. "What?"

"Kyle is—"

"What do you mean 'he's not here'? Has something happened?" Fear gripped her.

"No, please, it's nothing like that. I did not mean to frighten you."

"Oh," escaped her lips. The fear ebbed. "Where is he?"

"May I speak with you privately?"

Mary nodded and proceeded to enter her room, Brandan following. The guard closed the door behind them, granting the two privacy. She motioned, indicating sofas covered with golden cushions. "Would you like to have a seat, Brandan?"

He moved toward the seating arrangement, but waited for Mary to take the couch across from him before lowering himself into the upholstery. She parted her lips to speak, when Brandan interrupted, "Kyle is fine, my lady."

"Why is he not here? Where's my sister?"

"I left him at the Temple of Desoto. He planned to ride to Lord Riccard's keep the following day."

"I don't understand."

"Kyle, he..." Brandan straightened on the lush pillows. "He's been having dreams. Only dreams, but still, they disturb him greatly. He asked me to return, to protect you in his place."

"No." Mary shook her head. "I sent you with him for fear of *his* safety. I wanted you with *him*."

"Yes, my lady, but whatever is going on in his head is distracting him. And I think—I know—the best way to allow him to focus, is to put someone he trusts near you."

"I have the entire defendant team. Temple masters, high lords, golden students...all at my call."

"Yes, and some of those temple masters and defendants tried to kill you, in this very palace, which should be the safest place in the entire kingdom for our queen." Brandan shook his head. "If you order me to return, I will ride back to join Kyle's party. However, my lady, I would ask you not to. I am but a shadow of the masters actually protecting you, but I think it's worth the peace of mind allowing Kyle to ease his fears for your safety. However..." He paused briefly. "As you are the crown princess, I shall do as you command."

Mary drew a deep breath. She let it out. "Fine. If this is what Kyle wants, then this is how it shall be." Her words softened. "I don't want to upset him, not when he's out there."

"He did not want to distress you, either."

"Did he have a message for me?"

"Yes, my lady. He said he would serve you with anything in his power to give."

A flash of pain flickered across her face, slipping past her mask. "Yes, he would say that."

Brandan stood only to kneel on one knee. "I have upset you, my lady. It was not my intention to do so."

"My disappointment has nothing to do with you, my lord. In fact, I am glad to see you."

"Kyle will be fine, my lady. He will fetch your sister and return to you shortly."

Mary nodded. "I'm sure you're right." A half-smile formed on her lips, but not enough to make the lie convincing. "You may join the men outside my door, if you wish. I assume Kyle intended for you to stay close."

"Thank you, my lady."

Standing, with a final bow, Brandan left the room, the door closing with a soft *thunk* behind him, leaving Mary seated alone on the golden sofa.

Chapter XXXVIII

Princess Ameria stood across from Lord Stephen, upon the gold and silver mats, her blade clutched tight in her palm, when their sparring was interrupted by one of the guardsmen.

"Forgive me, Princess," the man said, bowing at the waist. "Lord Stephen."

Ameria turned, lowering her silver blade. "What is it?"

"A riding party has arrived. They report they have been sent from the palace to speak with you. Their leader is Lord Kyle, the son of—"

"Kyle's here?" Ameria asked, surprised.

"Yes, Your Highness."

"Bring him in." Ameria reached down and grabbed her sword's sheath from where it had been discarded beside the mats. *What is Kyle doing here?* After securing the belt against her left hip, she straightened her robes in preparation for Kyle's appearance.

As he walked toward her, Ameria could not help but stare. He looked as though he had been riding hard. His hair, usually neatly pulled back from his face, was wind-blown, stray strands having slipped from the silver band. His robes were wrinkled. Yet her eyes eagerly trailed across his broad chest, the defined lines of his face, and finally, his emerald eyes.

"Kyle." Her voice was soft. It had been so long since she'd last seen him. Far longer than ever before.

Kyle moved forward until he was only a few paces from her. "Princess Ameria." He moved to kneel.

"Don't you dare," she instructed.

He hesitated, then straightened.

"Kyle, what are you doing here?"

"I came to find you."

Ameria's heart skipped. He had come for her. But his next words crushed that assumption.

"Your sister needs you to come to the palace."

"My...sister?"

"Yes."

Ameria shook herself, the momentary spell broken. "I see," her voice grew colder with each word, "and instead of sending a message, Mary decided to send you."

"Ameria, I have much to tell you."

"Because, of course, I would listen to you, right? The partner who left me."

"I..." He looked like she had struck him; in a way, she had. "Ameria, please."

"No." She saw his pain, but was too angry for it to affect her. "How nice of the *queen* to send her *personal captain* to fetch me home. How...sweet. She must be awfully concerned for my safety to send *her* personal bodyguard. Tell me, Kyle, what is it like to stand by her side day in and day out, knowing she can never be yours?"

"Ameria," he pleaded.

"Tell the queen I am grateful for her concern, but not inclined to heed her summons."

"Ameria."

"No." Her words seeped with anger. "Tell my sister, if she wants to see me, she had best come to the tournament. And I expect her to bring the crown, which I intend to rip from her perfect hands."

Kyle reached toward her, but she jerked away.

"Don't touch me!" she said, before rushing past him out of the room.

CHAPTER XXXIX

◄─►◦❉◦◄─►

AN HOUR LATER, AMERIA STILL seethed, hiding in the confines of her mother's old room, one she had come to see as her own. She was not normally quick to anger; even less so to fantasy. Yet when Kyle had arrived, she allowed herself to hope he had returned to her of his own accord. Had finally recognized it was she, and not her bleeding-heart sister, in whose hands his future should be intertwined.

"She really does get to have everything," Ameria spoke aloud to no one. She finally lay across the bed and closed her eyes. While sleep remained elusive, her fury slowly ebbed.

A knock at the door interrupted her attempt to rest. She ignored it. A second, louder knock echoed in the stone chamber.

"Come in," she finally yelled.

Kyle walked into the room. Everything in his expression radiated with pain and regret. He stopped in the doorway, wondering if she would send him away. Curse him for coming against her will.

Instead, Ameria motioned him into the room with a wave of her hand. He stepped forward and knelt down.

"Princess," he began, "Ameria, I..." His words were laced with the same pain she had seen in his expression. "Ameria."

"I apologize, Kyle." Her tone held a cold formality. "I should not have become angry with you, and am sorry if my words hurt. I did not mean them."

He looked up at her from his kneeling position. "Yes, you did."

She drew a sharp breath, the bold assertion enough to break through her attempt at indifference. "Fine, I meant them. But I am sorry for the way in which they were delivered. Kyle, I—"

"It's okay. I deserved them."

"No. Maybe." She shook her head. "Regardless of the merit, that's not how a princess should conduct herself. Especially not to someone who has meant as much to me as you have."

Kyle shook his head. "Harming you was not my intent. I only did what I thought was right."

"Of course," Ameria answered, her words now laced in a mix of bitterness and regret. A pang which worsened as she reached down and brushed a strand of black hair from the side of his face, bringing the scar running both above and below his eye into full view. With her own scarred hands, she ran her fingers down his disfigurement. Kyle closed his eyes at her touch so she could trace the entire length.

The scar should have been a complete line. His enchanting green eye should have been a ruined mess. His vision had been saved by the wraith. She slid her fingertips down his face until she reached his neck and found the second scar, this one running over the artery of his neck, and disappearing into his silver shirt, where Ameria knew it continued down his upper chest. A mark left by the stroke of her own silver blade. One which should have claimed his life when he stepped between sisters who intended to claim the other's life.

"Kyle." Her voice came softer this time. The regret something she was unable to hide.

He reached up and grabbed her hands, his fingers touching the ridges that covered them. They were similar in that way. Two people who should not have survived their injuries. Both saved by the same creature. Both eternally bearing a visible reminder of their pain.

"What is it you came here to tell me, Kyle?"

The truth lay on his tongue. The truth he knew, yet he could not utter. Neither could he bring himself to speak a lie to this woman, to whom he had confided secrets his entire life. Instead, he settled for part of the truth. "Your sister requests you come home. She wants to go after your father's killer, but needs you to do that."

Ameria paused, reading him far too well. "There's more?"

Kyle shifted uncomfortably.

"What is it?"

"Ameria," he began, then shook his head. "This is all wrong. Asking you like this. It's...too fast. Too..."

She looked at him and saw what she had missed at first, distracted by the scars. Circles loomed under his eyes, as though he had not slept in weeks. His expression was raw, absent the normally perfect mask. "Kyle, what's wrong?"

"I..." He shook his head again, not knowing what to say. "I'm so tired."

Concerned, Ameria nodded. "Get some sleep," she urged. "We can speak when you wake up."

Kyle wanted to argue, but he was exhausted. Physically, emotionally, spiritually exhausted. The wraith's revelation, combined with the lack of sleep, had claimed his last ounce of strength, and so instead of arguing, he nodded.

"I'll put you in the chamber next to mine, if you'd like. Lord Stephen has been sleeping there, but he's on guard duty tonight, so he won't mind."

Drained, Kyle followed her into the next room. Ameria watched him crawl on top of the covers and, before his head fully settled on the pillow, sleep claimed him.

Ameria turned and left the room, apprising Lord Stephen of Kyle's whereabouts before returning to her own chambers and again lying down. She was unsure how long she had slept when a muffled sound drew her from her dreams. Still black night, the only light in her room came from the fire's glowing embers. She listened, and when she heard nothing further, put her head back on the pillow.

Again the unusual sound came, only this time louder. A muffled cry. She jumped from the bed and went toward the door, grabbing her blade as she moved. Her threshold opened a second before she reached it and Stephen burst in, his own sword drawn.

"Are you all right?" His eyes searched the room.

"It wasn't me."

Stephen turned back toward the door.

"Kyle," Ameria said, prompting both of them to rush into the hallway and throw open the door to Kyle's borrowed room. He sat on the bed, knees drawn up to his chest, head cradled in his hand. "Kyle?"

He jumped at the sound of her voice. "Sorry," he apologized unsteadily. "I had a dream. I'm sorry I alarmed you."

Stephen scanned the room anyway before turning to Ameria. "I'll be right outside."

"Thank you," she answered.

Once they were alone, Ameria moved to the fire against the far wall and added several pieces of wood, coaxing the embers back to full, blue flames.

"I can do that," Kyle said from behind her, rising from the bed.

"I've got it." She stirred the flames so they brightened. "There, that's better."

Kyle stepped to the fire and held out his hands before the flames, then rubbed his arms.

"Kyle?" Her concern grew. "What is going on?"

He drew a shaky breath and turned toward her, his eyes hauntingly sad in the firelight. "I must ask you something, Ameria, and I don't know how."

"What is it?" She took a step closer to him. "You've always been able to ask me anything."

"Yes, but...this. To ask you this is, something else."

Her body stiffened at his lost tone, earlier anger completely forgotten. He sounded confused, desperate even. This was not like him. Not even close. Something must be terribly wrong. "Kyle, please, just say it."

At her words, Kyle fell to his knees before her. "Drop your challenge for the throne." The words tumbled beyond his control. "No good can come of it. Please, Ameria, I am asking...begging you, don't do this, my lady."

Ameria stared down at the kneeling man, for once unsure how to respond. "How can you ask this of me, Kyle? To drop the challenge now, with the tournament so close. Why? Is the thought of my sister spilling blood so unappealing you would sacrifice our honor in order to see it prevented? My *sister*," she made the word sound foul, "for whom you betrayed me so easily?"

"I never betrayed you, Ameria."

"Like hell you didn't!" Anger flared through her voice. "Leaving me would have been one thing, Kyle. But for my sister? My *twin* sister? The same sister who was given true golden status whereas mine is silver? Who was given the crown, despite never having taken an interest in politics once in her entire life? The title, status, our birthright, the crown, Father's love— it all belongs to her. Why should you be any different?"

"Ameria," Kyle replied, "I didn't become her captain to hurt you. I would never have purposefully hurt you. I'm sorry I did." He paused, searching desperately for the right words. "You are my partner, my best friend, and I never meant to cause you pain."

"But that didn't stop you, did it?" she said bitterly.

"Ameria..."

"Admit it, you love her." He kept his head down, knowing he would not be able to hide the truth from his eyes. "You love my sister, and you are here to beg me to..." She shook her head in disgust. "Give me a reason, Kyle. One good reason as to why I should not fight in that tournament. Why I should not take the crown, and all that goes with it."

Because one of you will die, the silent words unutterable. In their place, he said, "Because no good can come of it. A fight between the two princesses of the realm? You saw what it did to your father and Leo. They were haunted by that match until the day they drew their last breaths. Do you really want that destiny with your twin sister?

"And how about for the kingdom? The people are recovering from the death of their king and prince. Are we to add a bitter feud? Please, Ameria."

The princess stared at him with cold eyes. "While eloquent, those are not the real reasons you're asking, are they, Kyle?"

"I..."

"The truth."

Silence followed before Kyle finally raised his gaze to meet Ameria's enraged blue eyes. A thousand reasons raced through his mind, but what finally escaped his lips was, "Because I am asking you not to."

"For Mary?"

"No. For me."

Ameria turned from Kyle to face the far wall. Time clicked by, seconds transforming to minutes as the room filled with a painful silence. Ameria closed her eyes, breathing deeply as she attempted to come to terms with what he'd asked of her. Decided, after inhaling deeply, she turned to face him. "Okay, Kyle. I will withdraw my challenge for the throne. I will give up the crown, my birthright, and a piece of my honor as a Princess of Kale. I will let my sister be queen, and defend her right to the throne against all challengers. I will do as you ask."

"Ameria," Kyle began, relief filtering through his voice, "I can't—"

"On one condition," her voice disrupted his words. "I will withdraw from the most revered and sacred of all temple traditions. I will allow my sister to be queen. However, I have one, single condition."

Kyle stared at the princess and gave the only possible answer, "Name it."

No smile crossed her lips as she gazed down at him and said, "You. Consent and I shall do as you ask. Refuse, and I will have my sister's throne."

"Ameria, you cannot mean..." Staring into her eyes, Kyle knew without a shadow of a doubt, she did.

CHAPTER XL

◆◄◊►❋◄◊►◆

"I WANT YOU, KYLE. I have always wanted you. This is my price. You, for my sister's throne."

Kyle stared up at her in raw disbelief. "My lady, I—"

"The choice is yours," Ameria interrupted. "My sister can have your love, but she'll have to fight for both her throne and your hand in the thirteenth tournament. Or she can have her claim to the throne unchallenged, but you will belong to me."

A thousand answers came to his mind, all silenced by the deadly demeanor of the princess' cold eyes. No rage to be cooled, nor flames to be extinguished. Instead a powerful determination, one which Kyle knew all too well.

"Ameria."

"Me or her, Kyle. Your decision is quite simple."

"Ameria," he again spoke her name. "I hurt you deeply." He paused, searching for the words. "That was never my intent."

"I do not care what you intended, only for the choice you must now make. Tell me, Kyle, are you captain to the Queen's Royal Guard? Or my sister's would-be-lover? I know you too well to presume you are her actual lover. Even you, my cold, practical partner, have too much integrity to take my sister's virtue, and she reveres the gods too much to tarnish yours."

Minutes ticked by. Ameria stood as calm as he had ever seen her, waiting.

"Why are you doing this, Ameria?"

"Because you are mine," she replied, but this time her voice betrayed her pain. "At least, you were. You loved me, or as close as people such as you and I are capable of. A Kolosian version of love. One based on reason instead of passion, practicality instead of romance. And yet, it was love nonetheless. Did you banish me from your heart so quickly?"

"You know I have not," he answered. "I could never banish you. I could never..."

Ameria knelt to one knee beside him. "Tell me, Kyle, do you really think you could make my sister, my soft-hearted, teary-eyed, oh so gentle Kalian sister, happy? Come now. We are not like her, you and I. We are not soft, nor warm, nor gentle. We are the heirs to Kolsoso—cold, emotionless. We do not wear our hearts on our sleeves.

"How will my sister react when she realizes you can never be the emotional support she needs? When she opens those pretty green eyes and comes to understand all you have to offer is brutal strength and unwanted honesty. How will my beautiful, child-like sister react the day she sees behind the carefully placed mask you wear? When she realizes you...are just like me."

Kyle's heart beat harder as her words washed over him.

"Come," she spoke honeyed tones, which did not match her cold eyes, "you must see this is what's best for the kingdom, the temples, and our future queen."

"Ameria, I..." He searched her eyes for answers that would not come. "I love her." The words slipped out against his will. "I wish to the gods I didn't, but...I love her."

"Then protect her, Kyle. Let Mary have the throne and we will defend her from all who would challenge, as silver to my gold. From where you belong; where you have always belonged. We will unite the provinces, my grandfather's lands with your father's. We will support her, Kyle, as long as you remain by my side."

"I..."

"I won't require that you love me to do your duty to this kingdom, but you must stay by my side." She reached out her hand and caressed his cheek, sliding her fingers down the side of his face with a cruel, deliberate touch. "Love her from afar if you must, but make me your bride." Her fingers pressed up on his chin, raising his face to more fully meet her own. "Your choice, Kyle."

It was my choice. Mary's words plagued his mind. *My choice.*

"Your heart for her throne. Choose carefully, because I will not make this offer again."

Kyle closed his eyes and could see the depths of Mary's emerald gaze. The streaks of exhaustion and fear, a reflection of her haunted dreams. He attempted to draw a deep breath, but it rose harsh and unsteady.

I chose you, Mary's words haunted him. *It could have been anyone I had ever known; anyone I had ever loved, and still, I chose you.*

I'm sorry, Mary, he spoke the silent words to the vision standing before him. *I'm so sorry.*

Kyle opened his eyes. Mary's emerald scrutiny transformed to Ameria's sapphire blue. He reached forward and placed his hand gently on the side of her right cheek. When she didn't pull away, he slid his hand lightly down her pale skin, the tips of his fingers brushing against the strands of her blonde hair. Wrapping his hand partially around her neck, Kyle guided her forward, until all he could see were her green—no blue—eyes. Slowly, Kyle closed the last breath between them and kissed the golden-haired princess for the very first time.

CHAPTER XLI

WORRY FILLED MARY'S THOUGHTS. SHE had assumed Kyle would return a few days after Brandan. A full week had passed, and he had not yet come home. Receiving only a brief message that Kyle's party had arrived safely, Mariana waited their return on bated breath. Every day she would jump at the announcement of new arrivals to the palace grounds. And each time was stung by disappointment.

She spent her days attending as few meetings as she possibly could, and training for the upcoming tournament. During the long nights, she attempted to avoid her dreams, which only seemed to grow worse with each night of Kyle's absence. She dreamed of Master Leo, dying in her arms, his final words an echoing curse. *"What a Golden Defendant you would make."*

What did he mean? She wondered for the umpteenth time if Leo had changed his mind on his insistence she become queen. Was it even possible for him to do so? How long had he planned her ascension to the throne? From the moment she had been dropped at his temple? Since the day of her birth? Or, a more chilling thought, before even that? When he'd arranged the marriage of her parents, against her father's will.

Late on the twelfth night since Brandan's return, the dream Mary feared most came again.

She rode through the forest, the horse's hooves dipping into the wet ground beneath her. She knew this path, one she had taken to avoid the rising river that led into the forest of Periculum. Under a gray sky, the trees cast ominous shadows over the pebbled trail. They rode, their speed restricted by fallen branches from the storm that had raged the prior night.

With a terrible screech, the horse beneath her collapsed, landing on her leg. Mary cried out, from pain and fear, as she struggled to pull herself from under the horse's now lifeless body. She turned her head, knowing to her right would be a White Defendant facing off with one of the men attempting to end her life. Only, when she turned, instead of a defendant, she saw Kyle.

"No!" Mary exclaimed, struggling to free herself. But no matter how she twisted, she could not seem to pull her leg from beneath the dead weight.

A loud hiss turned her attention from her efforts back to where Kyle now crossed blades with the hooded man.

"No, please. Kyle!" She pulled harder, desperate to escape. Then, before her helpless eyes, she watched as the faceless man plunged the tip of his silver blade through the center of Kyle's chest.

"Kyle!" Mary screamed, writhing, twisting, turning, doing anything and everything to come to his aid. Kyle managed two steps in her direction before falling to the ground with an audible crash. "Please," the word a sob, wrenched from her heart. "Kyle, please."

He looked at her. "Mary," he spoke her name, but the word was low and faint. "Mary."

"Mary, wake up!" Brandan's voice called her from the dream.

She jerked to a seated position, clawing the sheets as she did so, disoriented. She drew a trembling breath as she looked at Brandan, recognition dawning.

"Forgive me. You were calling out in your sleep."

"I'm sorry."

"It's fine, my lady." His voice was soothing.

Mary pressed both hands against her face before sliding them down in an attempt to help steady her rapid breathing. "Forgive me."

"No need, my lady." He hesitated before adding, "I'm sure Kyle is fine."

"What?"

"I mean...sorry, never mind."

"Tell me."

He looked down, avoiding her gaze. "You were screaming Kyle's name."

Mary's voice was less steady than she would have preferred. "I'm sorry,"

"There is no need to apologize. I only wish there were some way I could be of better service."

"You do a great job, Brandan, and I appreciate everything. Please know that."

He nodded at the compliment. "I wanted to offer, well..." He drew a breath. "If you want to talk about it—the dream—I'm here to listen."

Mary squeezed her eyes shut at his words. A mistake. Again the blade plunged through Kyle's chest. A memory of the hero who had died protecting her, replaced with her deepest fear. "Just a dream." Her breath came faster. "A dream, I...Kyle, they killed him."

"My lady—"

"Mary," she corrected. "Please, I can't take being your princess right now."

"Okay, Mary."

"I dreamed he died," she forced the words out. "Kyle was as close to me as you are now. I wanted to help him, but I was trapped. I couldn't get to him."

"Only a dream. Kyle is safe."

Mary shook her head, her trembling grew worse. "No, it wasn't. You don't understand. The scene happened, in the woods when they tried to kill me. I wanted to help the White Defendant. I wanted to so badly, but I couldn't get to him in time. He died protecting me and I..."

Brandan fell to his knees beside the bed and placed his hand on top of Mary's. "I am sorry, my lady. Sorry it happened, and even more so that those who helped to plan such an attack have yet to pay the price. I promise you, Mary, they will in time. Every single one."

Mary slid her hand more firmly into his.

"It wasn't him," Brandan assured. "Kyle didn't die."

"I know," she answered. "But, for a terrifying heartbeat, it was. He died and—" Fresh tremors disrupted her words. "Where, by the gods, is he? Why hasn't he come back? I thought sending him away would protect him. Would keep him safe. But now, all this time has passed, and no news as to why he has not returned. What if I was wrong? What if by sending him away, I sent him to his death?"

"Don't think like that, my lady. Kyle is fine. I don't know what is keeping him, but he will return soon. If you'd like, I will dispatch a messenger."

"Yes, please."

Brandan nodded. "It will be done. In fact, give me just a moment." He stood and walked across the room. Opening the door, Brandan spoke to someone on the other side. Turning back to Mary, he explained, "A rider is being dispatched now. By this time tomorrow, someone from the Temple of Dektra will be on their way. They will ensure nothing is amiss."

"Thank you."

"Think nothing of it. I, too, would like to know what is taking so long. Though as I said, I'm sure nothing is wrong."

Mary nodded.

"I'll be right outside if you need me," he said, before closing the door.

Mary sat on the golden sheets and struggled against overwhelming fear. "*Sutis*," she cursed. "Kyle where are you? Please," she spoke to the gods she could not see. "Please, don't harm him." She lost her battle with tears, drawing her knees up to her chest and pressing her face against them. "Kyle, I'm sorry. I'm sorry. Please come back."

With his death flashing through her mind, she realized she didn't just love Kyle, she loved him more than the throne. More than her life. More, even, than her temple.

Kale must be reunited with the crown, Leo's words echoed through her mind. *No Kolosian can ever be seated upon the Kalian throne.* The lifelong lectures a direct contradiction to the last words the temple master would ever utter.

"I'm sorry, Leo," she whispered to the ghost who haunted her. "I can't be your queen."

No sooner did she draw this startling realization than she fell into a deep slumber, which was blissfully free of dreams for the rest of the night. She spent the next two days anxious, nervous, waiting for the return of the man for whom she was now ready to surrender her crown. She would tell him when he arrived, and they could be done with it. Surely the gods had no need for either of them once the crown was surrendered. They could compete in the tournament, take their rightful place on the defendant team, and eventually join the temples to teach the next generation of defendants.

With the decision came a newfound hope, mixed with an overwhelming sense of relief. She had never been fit to be queen anyway. She saw that clearly now. Her sister would fill the role with a grace and poise that Mary herself had never possessed. Ameria would be thrilled at the endless round of court politics. Playing peacemaker at the meetings Mary abhorred attending.

She would be allowed to follow her heart, a luxury not normally afforded to a queen of the Kalian bloodline. Remarkably content in her choice, she celebrated when the messenger arrived back at the palace, stating all was well with Kyle's riding party. Apparently Ameria had a few outstanding issues to resolve before she would be able to journey back with him. The relief of this report added to her contentment and the nightmares faded entirely.

Two days after the messenger had arrived, Mary worked through a particularly brutal sparring session with Master Jiro. Exhausted, she stepped into a hot bath, allowing the water to soothe her aching muscles. After the soak, she wrapped herself in a thick, golden robe and called for a maid to help brush the tangles from her hair.

Julia entered the room and picked up a brush from the dressing room table, nimbly running it through Mary's hair, which smelled of lavender from her soap.

A typical chatterbox, as girls of her young age were prone to be, she babbled on about various palace happenings. After a particularly long pause, she commented, "I'm surprised to see you here, Your Highness."

"What do you mean?"

"Well, I just...forgive me, Princess. I spoke out of turn."

"It's fine. Why would I not be here?"

"Well..." The young woman appeared uncomfortable, her eyes avoiding Mary's reflection in the golden mirror.

Mary turned and took the brush from Julia. "What is it?"

"I thought you would be at the wedding."

"Wedding?" Mary shifted in her seat to better view Julia's expression. "What wedding? What are you talking about?"

"Forgive me, my lady." Julia's posture shrank with every word that passed her lips.

"What wedding?"

"I must be mistaken. I heard from my cousin, but she likely misunderstood."

"Julia, what are you talking about? Who did your cousin say was getting married?"

The maid trembled as she stared into Mary's emerald eyes.

"Julia, what's wrong?"

"I'm sorry." The words tumbled from her lips. "It made no sense. I questioned the news because it didn't sound true. And if you don't know, then it must not be. I mean, I've seen the way he looks at you, Your Highness. It couldn't be true."

"'The way he looks at me'?" Mary questioned with an increasing sense of foreboding. "Julia, tell me what, in the name of all the temples, you are talking about."

When the girl remained silent, Mary added, "Answer me, Julia. It's not a request."

The girl's explanation came in scattered pieces. "Forgive me, Princess. I was told your sister was—this week—getting married."

"My sister?" Mary asked in confusion. "To whom?"

Julia again grew silent.

"To whom is my sister said to be betrothed?"

"My princess." Julia drew a short breath, then raised her gaze to meet her future queen's. The look in her eyes revealed the answer long before she spoke.

Mary's heart stopped beating.

CHAPTER XLII

"JIRO," MARY'S VOICE RANG DOWN the hall. "Jiro!"

"Princess," Jiro answered, walking toward her from a side corridor. He had been in a conversation with the Golden Defendant when he heard her call. Both turned in her direction.

"Is it true?" she demanded. Her voice was wild; out of control.

"I'm sorry, my lady, I don't—"

"Kyle and Ameria?" she interjected. "Look me in the eye and tell me you did not know. You, Master of Temple of Koloso."

"Princess," Jiro spoke slowly, "please tell me, what has upset you? I have not heard from Kyle since he left the palace."

Mary cast her enraged eyes upon the pair in front of her. "Is my sister marrying without royal permission?"

"Marrying?" Jiro asked in confusion. "What are you—"

"Do you expect me to believe you don't know?"

"My princess," Lady Rebecca's voice joined the conversation, "I have no idea of what you are speaking."

"Oh, don't you?" She turned rage-filled eyes on the Golden Defendant.

"I swear," Rebecca answered, "to the gods of Kale."

Mary restrained her next words, digging her teeth into her bottom lip.

"My princess, I will have Kyle brought to the palace immediately. If that is your wish," Rebecca added.

"You do that," Mary replied coldly, before turning back toward her chambers, using all of her will to keep from breaking into a run to escape the eyes behind her.

The two masters watched in silence until the door to her chambers slammed shut. "Do you think Master Leo was wrong?" Rebecca asked the man standing beside her. "She is so young."

"So were we," Jiro reminded her.

"No, we were never that young. She wears her heart in the open. Leo might have raised her, but she's her father's daughter."

"Eadmund was a good prince." Jiro paused in thought. "He would have been an even better king."

"Eadmund paid a high price for his position, perhaps too high. I am uncertain if it's a price Mary is willing, or able, to pay. And to be honest, do we truly want her to?" Rebecca shook her head and voiced the forbidden question, "Would Ameria make the better queen?"

Silence fell between them.

Minutes passed before Rebecca called for the guards and ordered the Red Defendant to her presence. Shortly after, a young woman appeared, garbed in the robes of the defendant team's third-highest rank.

"Sasha," Jiro greeted the red-haired woman with the same emerald eyes that occurred frequently in the Kalian bloodline.

"Master Jiro," Sasha addressed him, bowing before her former teacher.

Rebecca motioned for her to rise. "Crown Princess Mariana has ordered Lord Kyle back to the palace. My understanding is he's with Princess Ameria at Lord Riccard's castle."

Sasha glanced at her. "You require a defendant to fetch—"

"Bring Kyle to the palace immediately," Rebecca stated. "In chains if necessary."

If Sasha was shocked by this, she covered the emotion well. "As you command," she said. "Should Kyle be made aware of the reason for this summons?"

"If rumors are true, no explanation should be needed. He will know why you are there. Also, issue orders for Coco to come to the palace as well. The puppy has a way of calming Mary when she needs it most."

"I shall do so at once." Sasha offered another bow before turning to carry out her orders.

As she disappeared down the corridor, Jiro turned to the Golden Defendant. "Sasha?" he asked in surprise. "Last time I saw her, she wore pink, not red. When did she advance?"

"A few days after the king's death."

Jiro drew a deep breath. "From seventh to...?"

"Third," Rebecca answered. "She beat them all."

"But not Stephen?"

"She has not challenged for silver."

As a former golden student of Koloso, Sasha had been offered a place on the defendant team during a non-Championship Tournament year. Because of this, Sasha had to start in the lower ranks, despite having won ten of her twelve Temple Tournament rounds. It surprised no one when she did not stay in the bottom ranks for long, winning all fifty of the fights required to reach the top ten ranks. From there, she advanced, reaching the seventh-highest-ranking defendant position.

To the best of Jiro's recollection, Sasha had taken the pink rank almost a year ago, advancing to sixth after the death of the Golden Defendant. To achieve third so swiftly was impressive. Now he found himself wondering... "Why did she not challenge for silver? It makes no sense."

"Actually, it makes perfect sense."

"How so?"

"She is in this for the duration. Tell me, Jiro, what happens after the thirteenth tournament, now that Leo is dead?"

"You will step down to become Master of Kale?"

Rebecca nodded. "One sister becomes queen; the other challenges for gold. I step down, Sethrick loses. One of the princesses becomes the new Golden Defendant. Then Sasha challenges and, should she win, moves into the silver—"

"Without having to fight either princess," Jiro finished for her. "And in a perfect position to take over the golden role when the princess steps down to assume other royal duties."

"Correct."

"What about Kyle?"

"If Mariana and Ameria win the tournament, Kyle will come in third, at best. As such, he will be required to enter the defendant team in the lower ranks, as Sasha once had to do. It will be years before he has the right to challenge for leadership. Sasha, as silver, will outrank him, and should she reach the golden rank, it will be forbidden to challenge her."

"If Sasha becomes the Golden Defendant... Do you think she wants to be her father's heir? It would be difficult to refuse if she were the Golden Defendant. Combine this with Kyle angering the crown princess..."

Rebecca considered his words. "It would be difficult for Lord Chiro to declare Kyle his heir, if his daughter is the one graced with golden robes."

"Do you think she would prefer my position?"

Rebecca shook her head. "Sasha has been seeking a way to become her father's heir since the day Kyle drew his first breath."

CHAPTER XLIII

LIFELESS. KYLE STARED INTO THE golden-rimmed mirror. His green eyes were flat, expressionless. The past few days were a jumbled blur of secret preparations and whispering voices. He stood in a silver robe overlaid with a green, representing his additional status as the heir to the High Lord of Turbamentum.

He fought the urge to walk to the wooden desk in the corner of the room, but eventually found himself drawn to it. The letter, written in Brandan's unmistakable handwriting, lay on the otherwise clean surface.

Kyle,

I write this letter in secret and pray it arrives to your eyes alone. I am uncertain what keeps you, my friend, yet have no doubt whatever your reason, it must be one of utmost importance. However, I must implore you to return home at once. These dreams which plague you—forgive me, my lord, but they do—also curse the princess. I cannot help but think more is going on here than meets the eye.

As for Mary, you were right. She's not okay. Not even close. I think she's worse, my lord. I try to help her, we all do. But I now recognize the only ones who can truly do so are yourself, and the ghosts of those who are no longer here. I am asking, my friend, please return soon. I fear how you will find her if you do not.

Forever faithful,
Brandan

The letter had arrived two days ago. Every line had ripped into him like a fresh wound. All he wanted to do was rush to her side. Yet, to do so would destroy all he had done in an effort to save her. To secure her crown and protect her life. All would be for nothing if he surrendered now. He glanced again at the mirror, his reflection showing none of the ache in his chest.

Am I doing the right thing?

It mattered little now. He had agreed to Ameria's heart-breaking demand, her reasoning undeniable. Join the two powerful provinces, which had worked to destroy each other for centuries. Put an end to the feud at last. Pledge the armies of both to fully support and protect the newly crowned queen. The more he attempted to argue, the more logical Ameria sounded. Best for the kingdom. The sacred duty and honor of the high lords and royals who had come before. The continuation of ancient traditions, established to ensure the safety of the people was always first, the duty of both lord and defendant alike.

Everything made sense, except for the harrowing knowledge that Mary would never understand. He had sworn to serve her. To love her. To never leave her. Now he wondered if those promises had been hollow, even as they were uttered? She was bound to marry another, in all likelihood. The chances of him winning, against the thirteen years of temple champions, were slim even under the best of circumstances.

"*Never forget what she is*," his father had said. "*She's the queen. It is your job to protect her and her crown, even from herself.*"

He had hated his father for saying those words, because deep down, he knew they were true. His love for Mary was forbidden. Something that should never have been and could never be. Yet...

"She won't understand." He spoke the words and their utterance pulled at something deep inside. The thought of the pain shining through her emerald eyes, of knowingly adding to her suffering, was too much to bear.

The way they were doing this was all wrong. He should go to the palace. Tell her why. Try to explain this was best for the kingdom. For her crown. For—

A knock interrupted Kyle's thoughts. "Come in."

Lord Riccard entered the room, garbed in gold, his right as the former Golden Defendant. "Lord Kyle."

"My lord?"

Riccard studied the younger man, trailing his eyes up and down as though in consideration. His eyes went to where the piece of parchment lay open on the desk. "Would that be from the crown princess?"

Kyle turned his head, his eyes following the high lord's gaze. "No, my lord."

Riccard turned back to Kyle, motioning to the opposite side of the room where a pair of chairs sat in front of the fireplace. "Come," he said as he moved toward them, his cane striking the stone floor with every step.

Surprised, but not about to argue, Kyle followed, taking a seat upon a golden cushion across from the high lord.

"You have impressed me, Lord Kyle, with your willingness to see the advantages of this match. Though I regret it must take place in such secrecy. My granddaughter has explained to me, should her sister learn of this intended union between our provinces, steps might be taken to prevent it." Riccard cleared his throat. "Tell me, my lord, is she correct?"

"Correct?"

"Will the crown princess be upset by this union?"

"My lord, I..."

"I know my title," Riccard reprimanded. "What I do not know is the answer to my question."

"Ameria is correct."

"Tell me about her."

"About...Princess Mariana?"

"Yes. I have only met her once, as a child, despite also being her grandfather."

"I'm not certain what you would like to know."

"I want to know if she is soft, like her father? If Ameria is afraid of her objecting to a marriage as sound as this one, she must be."

Kyle shifted in his seat. "I do not think 'soft' is the right term, my lord."

"No?"

Kyle shook his head. "She's just..." His thoughts trailed again to his green-eyed princess. "She's seventeen and running the kingdom. That's not soft, nor is it easy. Leo died in her arms. That's not easy either."

"I'd agree, it is not. Yet this was the destiny for which she was born. As being a high lord is yours. If your father were here, he would tell you the same, but since he is not, I shall do so in his stead."

Kyle turned in his chair to stare more directly at the gray-haired lord.

"What I tell you now is something I expect you to keep between us."

"Yes, my lord."

"I had two daughters. One married according to her duty. One married for love." The trace of a bitter smile crawled on his lips. "The one who married for love ended up banished, exiled, and disowned. The one who married for honor, became mother to a queen."

Kyle digested this information. "The daughter who was banished?" he began the question, uncertain how to finish.

"She had three sons, and a husband who died before the youngest was old enough to remember him. Three sons, who grew up to kill a prince, a temple master, and a Golden Defendant."

"Wait. That means Ryan..." Kyle shook his head. "Ryan is their cousin? Your grandson?"

"Yes. My traitorous grandsons who could not let their father's sins be enough. They blamed those in power for the loss of their birthright, when they should have blamed their mother, who refused to send them to the temples even when promised her children would not be held accountable for the sins of their parents."

"Forgive me, my lord, but why are you telling me this?"

"Because I want to know what kind of woman my other granddaughter is. Is she like her mother? Or her aunt?"

Kyle considered the question. "I think, my lord, there is a strength and beauty in following the heart, though it may appear quite different from the kind that comes from making a more rational choice."

Riccard moved his cane from his left to his right hand. "Wise words," Riccard answered. "Evasive as well."

"I do not mean to evade, my lord."

"Then answer this in plain terms. Which are *you*, Lord Kyle? You have agreed to marry the younger twin, yet you look broken." He paused. "Will you be able to endure the pain of the heart you must break for the good of the kingdom?"

Kyle drew a slow breath before answering. "Did your daughter?"

A single chuckle emanated. "Annabelle never had a heart to break. I made sure of that. She was watched closely, even in the temples, and reminded of her duty at every turn. She never knew the meaning of true love, or following one's heart. I kept her too tightly controlled. Something I should have done with my younger daughter, but with already having two heirs before her birth, thought unnecessary. Which, of course, was a terrible and ultimately tragic mistake."

Kyle shook his head. "Forgive me, but I still don't understand what it is you are trying to ask."

"Determine is more like it. You are the future high lord of a very powerful province. You have consented to marry Princess Ameria, strengthening the ties between our two lands. Yet your heart bleeds from the corner of your eyes. In order to go through with what you have promised, your pain is something you must be able to hide, if not altogether banish. Otherwise, it will rip apart both you, and the kingdom you are breaking your heart to protect."

"Are you saying I should not wed Ameria?"

"I am saying that if you do, you must do so completely. You cannot spend your life pining for the woman you could not have." Riccard shook his head. "This does not mean you must love Ameria. But you cannot allow your heart to scream for another woman every time you look at the one you are about to marry."

He stood then, supporting his weight on the golden cane. "Tell me, my young lord, can you bury your heart enough to fulfill your duty to both our provinces? To rule them, as the heir to both myself and your father, Lord Chiro?"

Kyle closed his eyes, having to fight down the image of the woman he loved. He opened them again to stare at the high lord. "I will find a way."

Riccard attempted to read the look in his eyes. "Very well, Lord of Koloso. Tomorrow at high noon, we shall join our lands, affirming our loyalty to Mariana's crown, and crown you a prince of this kingdom."

"We shall," Kyle answered, his voice hollow.

"You are aware, without the presence of the high priest and queen, this marriage must be consummated with more than words."

"I will perform my duties, in all ways."

Riccard stepped toward the door. "Good night, Lord Kyle."

He departed, leaving Kyle alone in the room, his gaze on the dancing blue flames before him.

"I'm sorry, Mary. I can't let you die." Tears gathered, stinging his eyes. He refused to allow them to fall.

The next morning, he rose early and bathed before donning the ceremonial robes. It had taken a team of tailors working around the clock to complete them on such short notice. The green and silver blended together, a mixture symbolic of both the temple he rose from and the province for whose care he would one day be entrusted. He wondered briefly if this marriage would please or anger his father. On one hand, he was becoming a prince, which was an advancement for his family. On the other, he did so in secret, without the permission of the queen or Lord Chiro. The status of the marriage itself would protect him from public repercussions, but in private...

Kyle pushed the thoughts from his mind. Too late now. In a few hours, the marriage would be complete, as would his betrayal of both the woman he loved and his own heart. "I'm sorry," he whispered again, reaching for his blade and securing it around his waist. He sat silently, attempting to rid himself of conflicting thoughts when the door opened. He turned to find the Silver Defendant standing in the doorway.

"Lord Kyle," Stephen said, "they await your presence."

He looked down, struggling to calm himself, and nodded. "Let's get this over with."

Stephen stepped back, holding the door open for the future prince, and then walked beside him down the hallway. When they neared the castle's outer doors, they found Ameria waiting. He briefly considered asking her to name another prize. Anything other than this. Yet, he knew there was nothing he could offer that would satisfy her. She had been planning this since they were children. Assuming as paired partners of the same temple, she had always been his destined bride.

He could not deny she was lovely, standing in a full-length gown of deep Serenitas blue. The ribbons, which tied the front and back, were of thick, gold fabric that also outlined the edge of the gown, accenting her long locks of blonde hair. Her face was shrouded in a golden veil, edged in rose-patterned matching lace. Underneath, he could detect the outline of a slender silver crown; a matching one would soon be placed upon his own brow.

Ameria turned at their footsteps, her blue eyes distorted by the veil, and watched them approach. She laughed, but Kyle did not see the humor. "Oh, Kyle," her voice was honeyed, "you look like you are walking toward a funeral, not your wedding." Her eyes cast down. "Am I such a horrific sight?"

"You are a vision, Ameria." He meant it. She was stunning in the blue and gold. "A lovely vision."

She looked up and reached for his arm. "Come, Kyle, let us unite the kingdom. The rest will happen, in time."

Banishing all thoughts except those of the woman who stood before him, Kyle took Ameria's arm, leading her out the doors, and down the stairs along a stone path. When the trio reached the castle prayer grounds, a distinguished group awaited them, including Lord Riccard, and the Temple Master of Dektra, who had agreed to serve as a temple witness at Lord Riccard's request.

They ascended the weathered marbled steps. Like the Temple of Ziazan, this ancient structure was composed of high, round pillars, which held up a vaulted roof. Kyle felt a chill when he reached the top of the steps and realized that, where traditionally a statue of two horses pawing the air stood, there was instead a pair of wolves guarding the sacred grounds of Sanguis Castle. The same grounds where Kale himself had once married his unwilling bride.

The sight of the wraiths, even in stone replicas, sent a cold tingle along Kyle's spine. So real, they looked. A silent reminder of the words he was not permitted to utter, and the dire consequences should he falter in his purpose to thwart their dreadful prophecy.

The pair walked between the statues to where the highest-ranked of those gathered stood on either side of a marble basin. Knowing what was expected, Kyle turned to Ameria, taking her hand in his own.

177

The Temple Master of Dektra addressed them, "Before we begin, I must ask both of you to confirm you are here of your own free will, and you consent to this union?"

"I am," Ameria answered.

Kyle was slower to respond. "I am, and do."

"Face each other."

Kyle turned toward the princess.

"Do you, Lord Kyle of Turbamentum, heir to the high lordship, and silver trained of Koloso, accept Princess Ameria to be your bride and lady?"

"I do." Kyle gave the confirmation, far more calm than he'd imagined.

"And do you, Princess Ameria, heir to Serenitas, golden trained of Koloso, accept Lord Kyle to be your husband, lord, and prince?"

"I do."

"Please turn to seal the ceremony, which is not complete until you have both made your offering to the gods of Kale and Koloso."

As one, the two Kolosians knelt before the stone basin. On either side waited thin, silver knives. Bowing his head, Kyle reached forward and picked up the knife, moving it to the center of his palm. But, as he was about to press its sharp edge into his hand, a voice drew his attention back to the marble steps.

"What is this?" High-pitched, and feminine. A voice he knew well. "My brother to wed and I, his only sister, receive no invitation?" She *tsk*ed her tongue.

The knife clattered to the marble floor, leaving his hand untouched. "Sasha." Kyle stood as his sister walked to the top of the steps. She was not alone. Behind her followed a sea of defendants, covered in their brilliant robes of status. "What are you do—"

"Shouldn't I be the one asking that particular question, Kyle?" She glided over the marble floor. "Marrying a princess without consent of Father, the high priest, or your queen?" She shook her head, keeping her words soft, though they carried in the still air. "I didn't believe it, not for a single moment. Yet, here you are. Kyle, what are you thinking?"

"Lady Sasha," Riccard addressed her. "It has been a long time."

"Yes." She nodded in acknowledgment. "With all due respect, my lord, are you aware all royal marriages must be approved by Queen Mariana and High Priest Louis?"

"Traditionally, yes," Riccard replied. "Unless those who oversee the union are of sufficient rank to qualify as substitutes."

"Hmm," Sasha considered. "Yes, I see how you could mistakenly believe this group would be sufficient. A temple master, a Silver

Defendant, and of course, yourself. Their esteemed presence does not change the fact, my lord, that you are attempting to marry a Princess of Kale without royal permission, nor consent from the High Lord of Turbamentum, to whom the groom is heir."

"Sasha, please," Kyle interjected, "if I could explain."

"I was not sent here to entertain excuses."

"Sasha, I—"

"No," she cut him off angrily. "I came to defend you from rumors, and instead find myself forced to escort my brother to the palace in chains."

"What?"

"Your actions have caused a great deal of distress to our fair queen." She gave him a cold stare. "What I fail to understand, Kyle, is why. This behavior speaks of irrationality and foolishness. Neither of which are words fit to describe you." She again shook her head and leaned closer, pressing her lips to his cheek so not to be overheard. "What *were* you thinking? Anyone can see the queen loves you above all others. And, if rumors were to be believed, you love her as well. A folly to be sure, but this? To marry her sister in secret? I don't understand."

"Sasha, please."

"Save your explanation for the queen, if she will consent to see you, after learning of this betrayal." She motioned to the two defendants behind her, garbed in bright red robes identical to her own. "Bind his wrists. We will be returning to the palace immediately."

The men moved to carry out Sasha's command as she spoke the formal words required, "Lord Kyle, in the name of Queen Mariana of Kale, you are to surrender yourself to temple authority."

"Please, Sasha," Kyle said, eyeing the thick length of rope in the hands of one of the men approaching him. "Restraints are not necessary. I will come with you of my own accord."

"These are my orders, and how it will be done, nevertheless."

She turned toward Ameria and offered a bow. "Forgive me, Your Royal Highness, I am afraid your sister has a dire need to speak with you."

Ameria did not answer, but instead simply smiled. This was not the reaction Sasha expected and she wondered if the princess had anticipated this union would be stopped all along.

Not having time to dwell, Sasha turned to Lord Stephen. "The Golden Defendant, Master Rebecca, charges you, Lord Stephen, to escort both High Lord Riccard and Princess Ameria to the palace."

In response, Lord Stephen nodded.

"Sasha, please," Kyle tried again as he found himself sandwiched between two Red Defendants.

She stepped forward and her face softened. "I'm sorry, Brother. Please save your explanation for the queen."

Without another look back, she walked down the steps as Kyle's arms were drawn behind him with a thick, coarse rope. They escorted him to the waiting horses and began the long ride back to the palace.

CHAPTER XLIV

◆ ►☰◆✳◆☰◄ ◆

MARY SAT ON THE SILVER throne while another lord offered a list of petty grievances. "Enough," she snapped. "You are lords of this kingdom, for god's sake! Figure it out peacefully, or I'll have both your statuses stripped and put someone in your place who can, in fact, work together!"

"My lady," the lord whose name Mary could not recall exclaimed, "I—"

"The princess has heard enough for today." Brandan, who stood a few paces behind her guarding the throne, stepped forward.

Master Jiro agreed, "Forgive me, my lords. The queen is tired."

Neither lord argued with the Kolosian master. Mary stood and moved down the steps, Brandan and Coco, who had arrived the day before, following after her as they traversed the hallways, eventually reaching her private chambers. Coco trailed Mary inside, whereas Brandan hesitated at the door. When she did not command him to stay outside, he followed the pair into her room.

When the door was closed, Mary whirled to face him. "Go ahead and say it," she spat.

"My lady, I—" Brandan looked to Coco for assistance, but the puppy jumped onto Mary's bed, turning three times before flopping with a dramatic sigh.

"That is not how a princess should behave. Not how a queen should rule. Patience is a virtue. I must treat the lords with respect. Go ahead, Brandan, lecture me on court etiquette."

"With all due respect, Your Highness, you seem to require no help from me."

Mary glared then drew a raspy breath. "I know better, gods I do!"

She walked over to the table between two golden sofas. Grabbing a glass from the wooden surface, she threw it against the wall. After it shattered to a thousand pieces, she sank down in the cushions, burying her face in her hands.

Feeling helpless, Brandan approached her cautiously. "Princess."

Mary pressed the back of her hand against her lips. "I'm sorry."

"No, Mariana. No."

Brandan eased onto the sofa beside her and, much to his surprise, she lowered her hand and pressed her cheek against his shoulder. Likewise, with Mary's transition from anger to pain, Coco roused himself from the bed, approached her other side, and curled up behind her, his warm weight offering silent comfort because no words would have been sufficient. Brandan lifted his arm and turned toward her, moving Mary's cheek to his chest.

"I'm so tired," she admitted, sandwiched between her two confidants.

"I know, Mary. I can't believe what you heard is real. Kyle...he wouldn't do that to you."

Leaning against him, her words came in a hushed whisper, "I was going to surrender the throne."

"What?"

Coco raised his head curiously.

"When he came back," she confessed. "I was going to..."

"Shh," Brandan coaxed. There was no romance, only comfort. He held her as one might hold a child frightened by the dark. Only this was the queen, and the monsters were real.

With another deep huff, Coco settled in more securely against Mary, his head angled to take advantage of a convenient pillow.

"Mary," Brandan whispered, but her eyes were closed, having fallen asleep in the momentary comfort of his arms. He lifted her gently and laid her on the couch, her legs now angled around Coco, before covering her body with a thin blanket that had been draped over the back.

Abandoning the pillow, Coco rested his head on Mary's thigh.

Brandan wondered how many nights she had spent sitting here, fearful of dreams. If they were as Kyle's, he guessed far too many. Yet, she was the queen, and by that fact alone, there was little he could do other than watch over her when she asked.

Knowing her distaste for being alone, and despite Coco's presence, Brandan moved to the opposite sofa and took a seat, allowing himself to become lost in thought until a soft knock interrupted the silence. Lord Jiro entered, noted the puppy's presence with a brief nod, and motioned for Brandan to come with him. Brandan rose quietly, so not to wake the sleeping princess, and managed to leave the room without disturbing her; only Coco's somber eyes followed his departure.

"Sorry," Brandan explained to the temple master, "she really doesn't like—"

"To be in there alone," Jiro finished for him. "It's fine, as long as she doesn't mind."

"She was...upset."

Jiro nodded in understanding. "The defendants Lady Rebecca dispatched to Serenitas have returned with Kyle."

Intense relief washed over Brandan. "Thank the gods. He can clear this up. Mary will be so relieved, she needs to—"

The look on Jiro's face pushed back his exhilaration.

"No."

Jiro lowered his head, and cast down his eyes.

"He wouldn't. Without even telling her?"

Jiro's continued silence confirmed the unbelievable truth.

"I..." He hesitated. "Let me speak with him, before we wake her."

"She would want to know, Brandan."

"Please, she just fell asleep. What would an hour hurt?"

The temple master stared, then nodded. "He was taken to his chambers, guards stationed outside his door. I shall walk with you and ensure they allow you inside."

Both men turned and walked down the marble hallway, through a series of turns, before approaching the men guarding Kyle's doorway. Both were garbed in Red Defendant robes, and Brandan gave a brief bow of his head in acknowledgment of their higher rank. Across from him, the two men did the same in regards to Master Jiro.

"Open the door," Jiro instructed. "Brandan would like to speak with Lord Kyle."

The men stepped aside at the temple master's instruction. Brandan moved between them before entering the room to find Kyle seated on a silver sofa. He looked tired, his elbow on the end of the couch with the palm of his hand cradling his forehead. Kyle did not look up at Brandan's entrance, but remained still, eyes shut. Brandan moved to the desk and grabbed a chair, moving in front of where his friend sat.

"Kyle."

At the sound of his voice, Kyle's eyes opened and he lowered his hand from his face. "Brandan."

"Is it true?" He searched his friend's eyes and saw a sadness he did not understand.

"Yes."

"Why, Kyle? By the gods, why? Is this the reason you sent me away?"

"I did what I thought was right—"

"You've never loved Ameria. In all the years I have known you, I have never, not once, seen you look at her the way you do Mary."

"It doesn't matter if I love her. She's the future queen. I'm not allowed to love her, even if I wanted to, nor is she allowed to love me." Kyle spoke in a way that made Brandan wonder which of them he was attempting to convince.

"So what, you just...flipped a switch? From being so concerned for Mary's safety you forced me to return to the palace—to marrying her sister?" Brandan shook his head. "I don't believe that for a second."

"Brandan, please, you have to understand what I do is for the kingdom. Ameria has been named Lady of Serenitas. With her, we can unite two provinces that have been stabbing each other behind closed doors for centuries. We can support Mary. We can—"

"I don't care about the provinces, Kyle."

"You were not born the son of a high lord. You never had to worry about the kingdom as a whole. How one wrong action could send thousands into war. What I have done is for the best of the—"

"Lord Kyle," a third voice entered the room. Both men turned to find themselves facing one of the Red Defendants who had been standing guard. "The queen has asked for you."

The two men rose at the guard's words.

"Kyle, please," Brandan said, "don't hurt her."

Kyle did not reply, but headed to the door with a heavy heart.

Brandan added, "She needs you, Kyle," as his friend left the room.

CHAPTER XLV

MARY HAD BEEN CALLED TO the throne room by Lady Rebecca, who was speaking with Lady Sasha. At her entrance, both defendants bowed.

"What is it?" Mary asked.

"Lady Sasha, my third-in-command, retrieved Kyle from Sanguis Castle."

A flicker of hope and relief washed over her. "Where is he?"

"I have sent the guards to fetch him, my lady. It is your choice though, if you wish to see him."

She stared at Rebecca's solemn face. "Oh, I see."

"I am afraid so, Your Highness."

"It's true?"

"Yes."

She forced herself to ask the unwanted question. "Are they?"

"No, my lady. Sasha's arrival interrupted the ceremony."

"Ceremony? You mean?"

Lady Sasha took a step forward. "The ceremony had begun, but was not finished, nor sealed."

"Okay." The word came unsteadily, more of a long exhale. "I..."

"You do not have to see him now, Princess, if you would rather not."

"I want to."

"I am not so sure—"

"Now. I wish to see him now."

The two defendants exchanged a glance. The one in gold nodded. "As you wish."

Mary walked across the marble floor and stared along the glass wall, which framed the background of the silver throne atop a series of steps.

Why would he do this? she wondered, her mind racing through a thousand explanations, none of which were acceptable. Kyle loved her. She knew he loved her, there was no doubt of this. Yet he had agreed to wed Ameria?

What happened? Did he see her and instantly forget everything he felt for me? Everything he had promised? I could say I was willing to give up the throne, but then...No. Mary shook her head in angered confusion. No, she would wait to see what Kyle had to say for himself.

Footsteps interrupted her thoughts as Kyle entered the room.

"Leave us," she issued the single command.

Those in attendance filed out.

Before the door closed, she heard Brandan say, "I'll be right outside if you need me." A pause, then he added, "Either of you."

She did not respond, but waited until she heard the soft thud of the closing door, before turning to face the silver lord.

CHAPTER XLVI

❖ ►⊙◄✳►⊙◄ ❖ ─────

HE FORCED HIMSELF TO MEET her piercing eyes. As expected, they were filled with anger, perhaps even rage. But beneath lay something worse—an agonizing pain.

"Kyle."

The sound of his name passing through her lips pierced the emotional shield he had worked so valiantly to put in place. "My lady," he answered, his voice unsteady. He prayed for the strength to do what he must.

"I don't understand." Her words were soft, which only served to unnerve him further. "What's happening, Kyle?" She drew a breath, her eyes staring at the silver floor.

Kyle fought to control his voice. "My lady, this will be difficult to hear, but I beg you to try and understand."

"I'm listening."

"My lady, your sister is my partner. She has always been my partner. We are a match, her and I. Kolosian. Silver to her gold." He forced more air into his lungs. "I belong by her side."

"What?" Her eyes snapped from the floor. She searched his features uncomprehendingly. "Her side?" A tremor slid down her spine. "Why are you saying this?"

"My lady," Kyle tried again, "it's better this way. You should be with a Kalian king, and I a Kolosian bride."

"I don't believe you." Her voice trailed to a defiant whisper.

Unshed tears shone in her eyes, causing Kyle's next words to die upon his lips. He had been prepared for anger, but this—her soft words, broken pleas, her soul's pain radiating through those emerald eyes—he couldn't breathe.

"I must be with your sister," he tried again, desperation seeping over him. "You must..." His words trailed as Mary stepped closer.

He stood mute as she moved across the room, shattering the silence with each step of her heels against the marble floor. When she reached him, she paused, searching for the answers he would not speak as though she could see through his thin flesh to the tortured soul within.

She reached out a trembling hand.

"Don't," he whispered, but stopped as her fingers touched his skin, pressing her palm against his left cheek. He shuddered, closing his eyes as his only defense against the tenderness of her caress. "Mary." Her name fell from his unwilling lips, the single word betraying him.

"Why are you doing this?" she pleaded, as her fingers slid down, tracing the lines of the scars she knew so well. "Please, Kyle, tell me why."

I can't watch you die, his soul screamed the words he was forbidden to speak.

He opened his eyes, but his words were broken by uneven breaths. "My lady. My prin—"

"Please, Kyle."

"I have to be with Ameria," he tried desperately to place conviction in his words.

"Why?"

"Because it's where I belong."

"You're lying." She pulled her hand away. The first touch of anger entered her voice. "Why are you lying?"

"My princess—"

"Stop it!" Her words increased in volume. "Just tell me the truth."

"I am," Kyle replied, but even to him, his words sounded false. "What was between us cannot be, my lady. You are the Kalian Queen. This cannot—"

"Why?" she demanded, digging her teeth into her bottom lip in an attempt to control her emotions from becoming words. She lowered her head, squeezing her eyes shut as the first tear fell from her stinging eyes. "Why are you doing this?"

He could not seem to draw the breath required for speech.

A whimper emanated from Mary's lips and his entire body jerked at the sound.

"Mary," he said without thought, reaching out in a hopeless attempt to comfort her. She twisted out of his reach.

Desperate for her to understand what he could not say, he grabbed her arm, this time forcing her to him. She fought half-heartedly, but was inexorably drawn forward. Only with his arms fully around her did she lose her battle with grief, her entire frame shaking as Kyle held her, helpless.

"Please, Kyle," she sobbed, "please don't do this."

"Mary, this is for the best. I know it doesn't seem like it right now, but...it will be."

Her trembling grew worse.

"My princess, please. I'm trying to protect you. You must understand." His eyes squeezed shut, not knowing how to continue.

Kyle held her until her sobs lessened, and she removed herself from the circle of his arms.

"I'm sorry, Mary. This is how it must be."

With those words, Mary again leaned closer. So close, her hot breath fanned his skin. "Why, Kyle?" she demanded. "You at least owe me the truth."

"My lady."

"You promised me your heart, your soul, your very honor!"

"My lady."

"You love me," she accused.

At these words, the last of Kyle's strength vanished. He collapsed, placing his hands on the cold, marble floor and lowered his head, closing his eyes tightly as his shoulders shook.

"Kyle." Mary slid to her knees beside him. He kept his eyes on the floor until her hand touched his chin, raising his gaze.

"Yes," he spoke the unwanted words. "I love you, Mary. Gods I do. I love you." He forced a deep gasp of air into his burning lungs. "But...I will not be your king." The words were brutal, broken, and undeniably true.

At their utterance, Mary's sobs ceased. Her tears slowed and her body stilled. The air grew thick with silence. She pulled away, still kneeling on the floor. Her fingers clutched the edge of her golden robes. Her eyes squeezed shut. Her lips moved, but made no sound. Her anguish transformed, before his eyes, to a numbness far more terrifying than any anger could ever hope to be.

"I'm sorry," his words tumbled forth uncontrollably. He reached his hand forward, but she pushed it away. "Mary, please."

"Get out."

"I need to tell you—"

"Get out."

"Mary." He again reached for her, no longer caring about the gods, the wraiths, or even his own life. None of it mattered. He would do anything, risk everything, to take back the words that had finally broken her.

It was too late.

No sooner did he touch her, she again yelled, "Get out!"

"Mary."

"I am your queen!" she screamed, rising to her feet to escape his touch. "The Queen of Kale. And I am ordering you to get out!"

Frozen, he stared at her.

"Guards!" she shouted. "Guards!"

Seconds later, Brandan and another man dressed in the crimson robes of the Royal Guard raced through the tall doors on the left side of the room. Mary kept her back to the newcomers, refusing to face them as she said, "Remove the Kolosian from my chambers."

"Mary," Kyle tried again, but the woman he loved was no longer there. "Now!"

Kyle stared, realizing no word or plea would penetrate the shield protecting Mary from the heart-wrenching pain. He stood and walked toward the two men with a heavy heart.

Several steps from the door, he turned briefly back to the princess. "I'm sorry," his voice exposed his soul, "but it was my choice, Mary. My choice."

With those words, Kyle continued toward the silver doors. The Red Defendant had moved back out of the threshold, when Brandan stepped past Kyle and pushed the door closed before he could walk through.

With only the three of them in the room, Brandan leaned toward his friend. "Kyle, what are you doing? This isn't you."

Kyle pushed him aside, grabbing the door handle without answering.

Brandan touched his arm. "Kyle, please." He sounded as confused as Mary had moments before.

"I'm sorry," Kyle replied, jerking the door open and stepping outside the chamber.

Brandan leaned forward, lowering his words so not to be overheard. "Kyle, she was going to give up the throne—for you."

The color drained from his face, but before he could articulate an answer, someone from the other side grabbed Kyle's arm and pulled him from the room.

The door closed.

Alone with the princess, Brandan approached her, resisting the urge to offer the comfort of touch. "Mary," he spoke gently.

She did not respond, merely staring across the silver room to the glass walls. "I traded his life for Marcus'," she whispered the confession on a broken breath. "I loved him so much I traded the life of my friend, my partner, my...I—"

"Mary." Brandan's heart crumbled at her shattered voice. "Please."

"I killed Marcus. Traded his life away as though it meant nothing. Thinking of nothing except for...for—"

"Mary, you didn't kill Marcus. That wasn't your—"

"*Your choice, Princess.*"

Brandan's words died as he heard the deep, gruff voice. He turned to where Mary's gaze was fixated. There, the wolf-like creature stood before the glass window. Instinctively, Brandan drew his sword, placing himself between his queen and the wolf.

"*Brave*," the wraith growled. "*So brave.*"

Mary touched his shoulder and he looked at her. "It's all right," she mouthed, then pushed gently on his arm, lowering the sword.

She turned to the wraith. "My choice?" she asked. "What kind of a choice is that? To kill the man I love, or the one who had stood by my side." Her voice rose in volume. "What kind of a choice is that? There is no choice! There is only death!" Her breaths were unregulated. "My father. My partner. My master. My protectors. My friend."

"*I did not kill your father. Nor your master. You know who did*," the wraith corrected. "*He lives still. A choice, Princess. A choice that lay with you.*"

Mary screamed, her arms crossing over her chest as she bent down.

Brandan grabbed Mary, pulling her against him as he faced the wraith, the blade once again held between his god and chosen queen. "Enough!" he said. "She's had enough."

The wraith narrowed its strange, cat-like eyes to thin slits, which reflected all light, but held none. "*Not yet*," the wraith growled. "*But soon, Knight of Koloso. Soon.*"

With those words, the wraith vanished, leaving Mary crying against his chest. Her body shook with fierce sobs.

"Mary."

He searched for the words to comfort her but knew—there were none.

CHAPTER XLVII

KYLE REACHED THE DOOR TO his chambers with no recollection of how he'd gotten there. The crimson room had been masked in silver, from the curtains covering the tall windows to the blankets lying over the bed near the center of the room. He stepped toward the bed, but instead of sitting on the soft comfort it offered, he sank to his knees, reaching forward to bury his fists into the cloth.

"What have I done?" He slid to the floor, fully collapsing. He raised his right knee and wrapped his arms around his leg, a struggle to simply draw breath. More sobbing than speaking, Kyle spoke to the silent room surrounding him. "What have I done? I'm sorry, Mary. I'm so sorry. Oh gods! What have I done?"

The look in her eyes as he left her—the broken spirit they reflected—would haunt him every night for the rest of his life. His fierce, brave love broken by the same man who had sworn his life to keep her from harm. To love her, no matter the cost.

You were saving her life, a voice reminded him from somewhere deep inside.

"But is it truly a life she will deem worth living?"

The passionate, romantic princess forced to marry a nameless tournament champion. Compelled by duty to enter the bed of a man she did not love. The very thought made his stomach churn.

She was going to give up the throne—for you.

What have I done? His mind attempted hopelessly to grapple with the revelation. She had been willing to sacrifice everything. To give up the throne, her birthright. She loved him more than the crown, more than her temple—and he had betrayed her.

The thought made him physically ill. His head pounded painfully. He could have taken her away, as she had begged. Could have swept her into his arms. Could have changed everything, if he had simply trusted his own heart. If he had returned sooner. If...If...

His grip tightened on his leg as he drew a deeper breath. His heart ached as he cursed the gods above. "Why are you doing this? Hasn't she suffered enough?" He gazed into the room, night having shrouded the light of Kalian suns. "I know you can hear me. Why?"

"Please" he prayed. "Don't make me do this."

"*Make you?*" a sinister voice entered the room. "*We do not make decisions, Heir to Turbamentum. The choice,*" he drew out the word, "*was yours alone.*"

"Not to save her? To let her die?"

"*A terrible choice, but a choice just the same.*"

"How can you do this?"

Shadows gathered in the corner of the darkening chamber. They danced and shimmered across the air before twisting to take form before him. They weaved together, transforming from shadow to the black, mangled fur of the gods' chosen messenger.

Kyle's heart beat faster as the creature fully materialized, its slanted eyes glowering with reflective light. "*He does not see,*" the wraith spoke in a low growl.

"*No,*" a second voice answered. Kyle's muscles tightened, realizing another had appeared on the opposite side of the room.

"*Shall we tell him, Satius?*" the second wraith asked with a chilling tilt of his head, further exposing his fanged teeth to Kyle's vision.

"*As always, Brother Proteus, the choice lies with you.*"

Proteus took a step closer to where Kyle knelt.

"Why are you doing this to her?"

The wraith shook his mangy head. "*I did nothing to the princess.*" He turned his inhuman eyes to stare into Kyle's. "*You, on the other hand, have done everything required to ensure their fight will come to pass.*"

"No. I made sure it would *not* happen." He drew an unsteady breath. "I don't understand. Why are you doing this to her?"

"*Don't you see, Lord of Koloso? Everything comes back...to you.*" He paused. "*Two undefeated champions. The crown on the line. Yet never had one sister raised so much as a hand against the other, until you took the boy's life.*"

"*The boy she loved,*" Satius interjected.

"*Yes,*" Proteus affirmed. "*A result that caused them to enter the woods unguarded, exposed to the eyes of their enemies. Enemies who had never thought to fear them, until the day Jace died. Exposing others to the realization that the royal twins hold a power not seen since the day Kale drew his last breath.*"

"What are you talking about? I don't—"

"*Oh, but you do,*" Proteus countered. "*You were the reason the sisters fought that day. The reason they were in the woods when they were attacked. The reason your father was placed upon the council instead of their grandfather, a man far more dangerous*" *than the High Lord of Turbamentum. One who even now plans to place his younger granddaughter upon the throne. And ultimately..."* Here the wraith paused, allowing his words to fade completely before he said, *"The reason she was forced to choose between her destined partner and the man she had come to love."*

Kyle wanted to tell them they were wrong. He had been trying to help them; to save them. Would give his life for theirs.

But the wraith's words rang with a horrifying truth.

He had accidentally killed Jace, and in doing so, exposed both sisters to a rivalry that could not be undone. Had forced Mary to stand helplessly as her partner died. He had made her love him, and sworn upon his honor that his love was true...

It could have been anyone, Mary's words echoed through his mind. *Anyone I had ever known; anyone I had ever loved. And still, I chose you.*

Proteus continued as though he too could hear Mary's words. *"I may have threatened her life, but you, Lord of Koloso, you skewered the very heart that beats in her chest. Something I never could have achieved on my own."*

Silence filled the room for a long time as Kyle sat defeated on the floor, the scope of his actions falling fully upon him. The pounding in his head grew worse. He was forced to shut his eyes, struggling to breathe through the pain.

Proteus broke the silence. *"Long live the Queen of Kale."*

With this sinister revelation, Proteus vanished as he had appeared, his physical form blurring to shadows before completely fading in the darkness.

Satius remained, observing Kyle on the floor with his knees drawn up and his arms wrapped around them. He studied Kyle's hopeless expression, and the anguish which wracked his body and mind.

"The outcome was destined," Satius spoke quietly. *"The prophecy is a never-ending cycle. Take comfort in that, if you can."*

"I want to save them."

"There is a choice, Heir to Turbamentum. Which part do you seek to save?"

Kyle raised his eyes to meet those of the wraith. "I don't understand."

"Her heart, her life, or her soul. You must choose."

"What?"

"Wed the golden-haired princess, and you sacrifice the heart of the Kalian heir." He paused. *"Beg the forgiveness of the raven-haired sister and you will save her heart, but risk her life in death, or the soul she will lose as she claims her sister's life."*

"I want to save them both. They are my life."

The wraith looked upon him with something akin to sympathy. *"So young."*

"Why are the gods doing this?"

"Punishment."

"For what? What did we do to warrant such torment?"

"Not you, and not her. Society, the world, the oath that was broken."

"The king who broke that oath is dead. Mary is the new queen. She will make things right. She will return the gods to their rightful place. You do not have to do this."

"She will, because the gods have decreed it."

"Then what is this prophecy? Is it hopeless, unchangeable?" A harsh breath escaped Kyle's throat. "How do I save them?"

The wraith shook his shaggy head. *"Heart, soul, or life, Heir to Turbamentum."*

"Don't do this," Kyle pleaded. "Let me fight, if someone must. But please, she's been through enough."

"It is her role to play. As this choice is yours."

Kyle lowered his gaze, unable to continue staring into the wraith's emotionless eyes. "She can't take any more. Don't you understand? Tell me what to do. I'll do anything."

"I cannot," Satius answered. *"The choice must always lie with you."*

Kyle's heart fell further.

"I will say only this: To whichever princess you choose, you must surrender yourself fearlessly, completely. And should you choose your raven-haired love, you will forsake every oath, every vow, and every semblance of honor. Both yours, and hers."

"How can I do that? How can I destroy what I have sworn my life to protect?"

The wraith did not answer immediately, but simply stared at the young Kolosian, before finally repeating Mary's echoed words, *"Your choice,"* he whispered. *"The choice always lies with you."*

CHAPTER XLVIII

PRINCESS AMERIA CHANGED INTO HER golden clothes. She had always known of her sister's susceptibility to emotional outbursts. However, she found it jarring to see those moments of irrationality enforced by the power of the temples and crown alike. "Queen" they had called her, not princess. Despite her objective knowledge of Mary's status, she was shocked to have heard her sister referred to as such, and to watch her orders be carried out by the highest-ranking of the defendants.

"Queen Mariana Dektra." Ameria weighed the title on her lips. "Queen Mariana, first of her name of the Kalian bloodline."

Would her sister punish her for this attempted act of defiance? It had never occurred to her Mary was in a position to do so. Now, she was not so sure.

She sighed. It didn't matter. Ameria would travel to the palace and maintain her usual air of neutrality. She would explain her logic for such actions. Mary, in all likelihood, would refuse in her oh-so-Kalian way to accept this was best for the kingdom. However, her advisors, Ameria knew, were of a far more logical persuasion than her overly-emotional sibling. They would explain the logic of her choice. Mary would rage, and then...

A smile curved Ameria's lips. Mary would be forced to make her choice. Either relent and surrender Kyle to her, or refuse, allowing Ameria to challenge for the throne after all. Either way, Ameria intended to have her prize. Whether it be Kyle or the crown, the choice rested with Mary.

"My lady." Stephen entered the room with a bow, interrupting Ameria's thoughts.

"I am almost ready," she told the Silver Defendant.

"Thank you, my lady," Stephen answered. "Only, it is not that."

"Then why are you here?"

"Lord Yarin has returned, my lady. He has asked to see you."

"Lord Yarin?" In the commotion, Ameria had forgotten about the lord she had sent to follow her uncle. "Bring him to me."

"Yes, Your Highness." He left, but returned shortly, her grandfather's captain in tow.

"Princess Ameria," Yarin said with a bow.

"My lord," she answered. "Do you have news of my uncle?"

Yarin gave a curt nod. "I do."

"Did Uncle Andrew go to the villages, as ordered?"

"No." He exhaled sharply. "He did not."

"Ah," Ameria said. "I see."

"He..."

Ameria's voice grew icy at Yarin's obvious discomfort. "And where, pray tell, did my dear uncle venture instead?"

In a flat tone, Yarin resigned himself to answering. "You were correct, Princess."

Ameria leaned forward, slipping closer to the tall lord who stood in deep blue robes, the color of Serenitas. "He went to the Periculum Mountains?"

"Yes."

"And where, exactly, did he stop his travels?"

"At the Temple of Aurum."

"Aurum?" Ameria pulled back in confusion. "What do you mean? There is no such temple."

"Not one you would know of, my lady. It is a temple forsaken long ago. Condemned and cursed by Lord Kale himself after his brother was slain before it."

"A forsaken temple?"

"Yes, my lady. The structure has not seen a battle since Kale. A fire destroyed the majority of it, or so the story goes. Only a single building remains. Kale ordered all students who trained there to be disbursed among different temples, and Aurum became a thing of forgotten ruin."

"And you were led to this forsaken temple by Lord Andrew?"

Yarin nodded.

Putting aside numerous questions, which materialized at mention of this "forsaken" temple, Ameria forced herself to focus on the only question that mattered. "Tell me, Lord Yarin, can you take me to this lost temple where my father's killer lives in careful refuge?"

"Yes, Princess, I can."

Ameria's smile tightened, her expression turning cruel. Hard. Her gaze slid past Yarin to where Lord Stephen stood a few paces to his left.

"Change of plans," she informed him. "It seems we will not be returning to the palace after all."

"My lady," Stephen stepped closer, "with deepest respect, Princess Ameria, I do not believe the acting queen made her directive optional."

"The man killed my father, Stephen. I am going to avenge him, my sister be damned."

"My lady, I'm aware there has been an agreement for the two of you to fight for the throne," he spoke carefully. "But until that fight has been won, she is the queen."

"No," Ameria corrected. "She is place-holding, warming the seat that belongs to me, along with everything else she holds dear."

"My lady, I still must insist we heed—"

"No!" Ameria straightened, tall enough in her heels to meet Stephen's gaze. "I asked you once, if you would be willing to follow me, silver to my gold. I did not insist upon an answer that day. But now, it is time to make your choice, my lord. Follow me, and become the trusted advisor and hero who lurks deep within you. Or return to the palace, empty-handed, and face my sister's wrath. Mariana or me, Stephen. Choose your queen. Choose now, Lord Stephen, knowing whichever path you choose, your destiny shall be forever intertwined."

The room fell to absolute silence as the Silver Defendant gazed into the sapphire eyes of the Kolosian Princess. Ruthless in politics. Dangerous in battle, and with a blade, absolutely lethal. A woman whose rule would know little forgiveness, and never mercy. Not a girl, or even a lower member of royalty, but a powerful queen poised to rule, over the defendants or the kingdom, only the gods knew for certain. He drew a deep breath and knelt to one knee, lowering both arms to his side so only the tips of his fingers touched the ground. "My Princess of Koloso," he stated, "I offer you my service and swear to you, heir to the Kolosian title and Kalian bloodline, my service unto death."

Ameria stared down at the kneeling Silver Defendant. "And I," she answered his vow, "Princess of the Kalian bloodline, Heir to Koloso, and Lady of Serenitas, so swear to you, Lord Stephen, to live worthy of honoring this sacred trust you have seen fit to bestow upon me." She held out her hand, which he clasped in his own before pressing it to his lips.

"Arise, Lord Stephen. We ride out with the morning light. My father's killers will face *justice*." She emphasized the word by placing her hand on the hilt of her silver blade. "At last."

The Story Continues In...

RISE OF THE TEMPLE GODS:
HEIR TO THE PROPHECY

Expected: Fall 2017

Read on for a preview...

HEIR TO THE PROPHECY

KYLE HAD SAT IN MISERY, under guard, for two nights with no distraction from his anguish. His sister was his first true visitor. Though her flaming red hair had been inherited from a maternal grandmother, her piercing green eyes were as Kalian as his own. She stepped forward, her Red Defendant robes wrapped around her, silver blade eclipsed in the black leather scabbard on her left hip.

"Have you come to gloat?" Kyle asked, casting his eyes in her direction.

"No," she answered, in a cordial professionalism.

"What *are* you doing here?" he asked miserably.

"I came to check on you." She moved to the sofa across from him. "I am, after all, your sister."

"Oh come on," he baited, his tone disgusted. "You must be pleased."

"Actually," Sasha answered, "I'm not. Far from it."

"Why not? Surely Father is already planning to name you his heir, as you have always wanted."

"I have always coveted the title. As the eldest, it should have been mine to begin with."

Kyle sighed. "Just say what you came to."

"You're being unfair, Brother. I wanted the title, yes. I wanted to show our father that I, and not you, was worthy of being his heir. But..." Her voice held sadness. "I did not wish to gain the honor like this. I didn't beat you, Kyle. If we had fought for the title, to face you in this upcoming tournament, and to win. That is what I wanted. But this..." Sasha shook her head. "Not the way I wanted it."

Kyle stared at his sister and, to his surprise, found himself believing her. "I made a mistake, Sasha. A huge mistake, with horrifying repercussions. But I swear I did so with the best of intentions." His breath escaped with a harsh sound. "I messed up," he confessed, to one of the last people in the kingdom he had ever considered confessing to before.

With five years between them, Kyle had not yet been born when his sister had begun her temple training. They'd only met on one occasion, before he himself was sent to train in the younger class, where she was already in the upper. The year he turned twelve, his seventeen-year-old sister had competed in the tournaments, and been named to the defendant team. After that, her appearances in his life had been sparse at best, with brief visits perhaps thrice a year, though some years fewer, or not at all.

"Please believe me, Kyle, I never wanted you to fall from favor. I merely sought an opportunity to prove I was the more worthy. This business hurts not only you, but also our family's status and reputation." She shook her head. "Marrying a princess of the realm in secret. Gods, Kyle, what were you thinking?"

"I...I don't know. I wasn't thinking. I was only..." He drew a harsh breath. "I was trying to do what was best for the kingdom. What was best for Mary."

Sasha stared at him, her eyes studying his face. "So, it *is* true? You have fallen for our dark-haired princess?"

"I..."

"Don't bother to deny it, little brother. A lie would be beneath you."

"I wasn't going to."

"Good."

"I have to make this right. I have to tell her I was wrong. That I..."

"Oh," she answered, drawing out the word. "I take it you don't know."

He leaned forward. "Know what?"

"The princess has gone to find her father's killer."

"What?"

Sasha nodded. "She left with the morning sun."

The wraith's words whispered through Kyle's mind. *Beware the twins of Kale.*

"No." He stood from the sofa. "We must stop her."

"It's too late," Sasha answered. "She's gone."

Though the words were faint, he heard the unmistakable voice of the wraith. *Hope to the hopeless. Fear to the fearless. Mercy to those who hate you. Death to those who love you. Heir to Kale. Heir to Koloso. Heir—to both.*

ACKNOWLEDGEMENTS & THANKS

I WOULD LIKE TO OFFER a special thanks to a few people who both assisted and supported me throughout the creation of this novel.

I would like to thank Scott of the Vancouver Taekwondo Academy for his assistance in my research, both through an extensive interview and allowing me to observe his classes. Second, to the instructors and students at East West Martial Arts of West Vancouver for also allowing me to observe their courses and for making themselves available to answer questions.

To my family for their never-ending love and support. This never would have been completed without them.

I would also like to thank my longtime writing mentors, Kate, Pam, and Mike for instilling within me a passion for writing and reminding me of that passion when it was needed most.

To the friends and fellow artists who have listened patiently while I ranted, raved and driven them crazy as I went through the writing process, and who understand, because they have had the same frustrations writing their own characters—Becket, Greg, Sarah, Raven, Shane, Christine, and Stina. Also to the non-writers who listened anyway—Robert and Steven.

To Carol of Star Angels Promotional Services, for putting together the wonderful review and blog tours for these books.

I want to thank my brilliant illustrator, Raven. Thank you for helping to bring my mythical worlds to life in such vivid detail and being a true inspiration in all that you do.

To my fabulous content editor, Melissa, who worked above and beyond, tirelessly reading through draft after draft, assisting me in making this story the best it could be. You've kept me straight through this entire process and gave me the courage to stay true to the story. I love working with you!

Also to my second editor, Tara, your willingness to work with me, challenge me, and passionately debate the various aspects of this story has helped me to become a better writer. I appreciate all that you do!

Finally, to my cover designer, copyeditor, and formatter, Skyla, who takes the jumbled pictures in my head and consistently turns them into beautiful covers. Your work is nothing short of marvelous! Thank you for being my friend and mentor on this journey.

ABOUT THE AUTHOR

K.L. BONE IS THE AUTHOR of the Black Rose Guard dark fantasy series, the Rise of the Temple Gods fantasy series, and a stand-alone science fiction novel, *The Indoctrination*. Bone has a Master's degree in modern literary cultures and is working toward her PhD. She wrote her first short story at the age of fifteen and grew up with an equally great love of both classical literature and speculative fiction. Bone has spent the last few years as a bit of a world traveler, living in California, London, and most recently, Dublin. When not immersed in words, of her own creation or studies, you'll find her traveling to mythical sites and Game of Thrones filming locations.

Follow her at: www.klbone.com
On Twitter: @kl_bone
Or on Facebook: https://www.facebook.com/klboneauthor

GROWING UP DEAD

Mortimer Drake discovers that he is the product of a supernatural mixed-marriage. His mother is human and his father is a 925 year old vampire. His life is completely turned upside down as he struggles with this knowledge and his emerging vampiric nature. The truth behind the myths and legends of the vampire are revealed as Mortimer enters into a centuries old war of the Undead.

Read on for a preview...

PROLOGUE

THE CLOAKED FEMALE DESCENDED THE spiral staircase. Her movements were graceful and fluid as she floated across each step. She moved quickly, a sense of urgency guiding her feet. She tread on the landing and made her way down the long corridor that ended outside two arched wooden doors. She hesitated for a brief moment before pushing them open.

The large room was crowded. Shrouded figures stood in clusters along the drab grey walls lined only with bright torches, while others sat at an ornate table centered in the room. Every chair was filled except for one.

She slid behind those seated to the right side of the table and took her seat. The room was thick with silence and she felt the weight of many eyes pressing down on her. "Well," the male seated at the head of the table spoke from under his white hood, his voice deep and smooth.

"It has started," she said. "And it is worse than I feared. We must go to him immediately if we hope to survive."

The hooded man raised his head and looked at the woman before he asked, "Are you certain that he's changing?"

"Yes, Minister. I'm positive it's happening," she answered as she slid the hood from her head. Thick curls of black hair framed her olive-skinned face. Her large crimson eyes reflected the flickering torchlight. She opened her mouth to speak with her fangs extended. "Narkissos, you must put your anger aside. After all, he is our grandson and this crisis is bigger than our family. If you won't go to him, then I beg you to let me."

"Aldora, you're sure that it has come to this?"

"I'm sure, but there's more that concerns me," she added cautiously. "There's someone else who wants him and we may already be too late."

CHAPTER 1

A FIGURE SOARED HIGH ABOVE the forest that stretched out for miles in all directions under him. Mist spread beneath the tree trunks covering the ground in white clouds. His eyes searched madly for his prey until his gaze locked on the quick movement in the thickness of the damp woods beneath him. He smiled, revealing sharp fangs that sparkled in the brilliant moonlight. The hunger and thirst that had forced him out into the night was no longer simply pangs in his stomach or a scratching in the back of his throat. This hunger had grown to such a frenzied crest that it sent painful waves of heat through his veins. His primal instincts told him only one thing would quench this thirst and satisfy this unbearable hunger. He needed living blood.

Landing in the long branches of a moss covered oak tree, he leaned forward and perched precariously, being careful not to create any noise. His ears filtered out the sounds in the air around him. His eyelids flittered as they lowered to cover his deep ruby eyes. The scent of the lone human that hiked unwittingly below him filled his nostrils. The hunger pounded through every inch of his body. The black hairs that covered his pale skin tingled in response to the breeze that moved across his arms. The sound of breaking twigs snapped him out of his deep, seductive lull. The hiker had sensed something and darted off into the thickness of the trees.

Pushing up from the branch, he was airborne again, but not for long. Hungry eyes quickly found the human as it fled through the forest. He did not take any more time to enjoy the chase. The hunger was now beyond his control. He dove through branches, tearing past limbs and leaves, making his way towards his frantic prey. With arms outstretched, he tackled the terrified hiker and they tumbled to the ground. His victim screamed out in fear. His legs kicked madly in a futile attempt to break free from this unseen attacker. Using his hands, the hunter grabbed the hiker's head and twisted. In one powerful jerk, the neck was broken and the body went limp. He lifted his prey's head and opened his mouth. His red lips spread wide as his fangs grew to a fine point before he sank his teeth into the sweat covered flesh.

He took in the blood. The burning desire and hunger that had propelled him to hunt and attack was subsiding with each swallow taken. His heartbeat was slowing and his mind was now focused only on the joy of the moment. He relished in his kill and he took pleasure in the feeling that now engulfed his entire body. The warmth of the hiker's blood filled every inch of his body. His veins carried new life to his undead body. He was, at last, satisfied.

He opened his eyes slowly in response to a familiar, unwelcomed sound. Raising his head, he looked from side to side in search of the source of this noise. The high-pitched screaming was rhythmic. It irritated the predator and it hurt his ears. He released the dead hiker and stood, wiping the warm blood from his lips with his triangular tongue. The noise became more intense, more deafening. He raised his hands to the sides of his head and knelt down on one knee in an attempt to shield his ears. The sound continued to attack him. It was steady and purposeful. Finally in desperation, the hunter raised his head and howled in protest into the night air.

Mortimer Drake jumped in his sleep, torn from the nightmare by the sound of the alarm clock that beeped furiously from his bedside table. He sat still in his bed and breathed heavily. He was drenched in sweat. This was not the first time he'd had this dream. He jumped again when he heard his mother knock on his bedroom door. "Morty," she said in her soft, morning voice. "Are you alright?" He reached over and switched off his alarm. His hands were still shaking.

"Yes, Mom, I'm fine. I just had a bad dream that's all."

"Well, don't stay in bed too long or you'll be late for school," he heard his mother say. "I'll see you downstairs."

Mortimer tossed the covers from his legs and swung his feet off the side of his twin-sized bed. He rested his hands on his knees trying to calm himself. Sweat rolled down his forehead and down the small of his back. He felt sick to his stomach. This dream always made him feel sick. He stood and walked over to the mirror that hung over his dresser. The window shade was cracked just enough to allow a sliver of morning light to invade his room.

He turned on the small lamp next to his dresser. His eyes blinked in response to the harsh first light of morning. He rubbed his face and looked at himself in the mirror. His thick black hair was matted and oily. He tried to smooth it out with his hand, but it was obvious that he would need a shower this morning. He slid his hands down his long, pale face. His brown eyes were blood shot from another night of restless sleep. Mortimer leaned closer to the mirror and opened his mouth. He inspected his teeth and stuck out his tongue. He didn't look good.

He turned and saw the red numbers on the black radio next to his bed. It was already seven o'clock. He wondered how many times he'd hit the snooze button. Mortimer usually woke up at six so that he could finish his homework before getting ready for school. He walked to his bedroom door and pulled it open. He peered out in to the hall, looking first to his left to see if his parents' bedroom door was opened. It was closed. That meant his dad was home from his third shift job and already in bed. Rarely did Mortimer get to see his dad before he left for school. That was another reason he got up at six. He could sometimes catch his dad coming in from work.

Mortimer walked down the hall to his right and flipped on the light switch just inside the bathroom door. He crossed the threshold and closed the door behind him. He pulled back the shower curtain. The metal hooks shrieked across the metal rod. He turned on the hot water. It took a minute or two for the water to heat up. That was one of the drawbacks of living in an older house. Mortimer turned and grabbed his toothbrush from the pedestal sink, then squeezed the last remaining dollop of toothpaste out of the rolled up tube onto the bristles. By the time he had finished brushing his teeth, he had to wipe the mirror with his hand. The entire room was filled with steam. *This is going to feel good* he thought as he stepped out of his boxer shorts and into the tub.

Mortimer entered the kitchen and saw his mother reading the morning paper and drinking her morning cup of coffee. The *River Turn Times* headlines told about another killing in the downtown area. She shook her head in disapproval. Mortimer was dressed for school in his khaki pants and blue polo style shirt. "Good morning, Morty dear," his mother greeted him warmly from behind her newspaper. "Want some breakfast?"

"No. I'm not hungry this morning." Mortimer was never hungry for breakfast. He opened the refrigerator and pulled out a two-liter of soda. His mother stared at him. He knew that she would prefer that he have milk or juice. "I don't feel very well this morning. My stomach is a little upset. I was hoping that some Sprite would help." He removed the plastic lid and began to drink straight from the bottle.

"Mortimer Drake!" his mother shouted. "Use a glass for heaven's sake. We all drink that Sprite you know." His mother stood and walked over to the wall of cabinets next to the fridge. She handed Mortimer a small blue glass for his Sprite, then she poured herself another cup of coffee.

"I don't see how you drink that stuff," Mortimer said to his mother. She took a sip of the hot, black liquid from her white cup.

"It's an acquired taste," she responded and smiled at her son. She leaned in to give him a peck on the cheek but he resisted and turned away from her. "Don't be so dramatic. Can't a mother give her son a kiss before he heads off to school?"

"You're so weird, Mom," Mortimer said. "Can't you just wave or something?"

"I think you're safe," his mom responded. "I don't believe anyone saw. You're still the cool eighth grader who doesn't want his mother to love him and besides—" A series of car horn honks interrupted her. "Oh well, there's your ride to school." She walked over to the window above the sink and looked out. She waved to the driver of the car. "Are you sure that William's sister is a safe driver?"

Mortimer rolled his eyes. "Don't start that again, Mom. Jennifer has been driving for over a year now. William's parents can't take us to school today so they asked his sister to drive us. We'll be fine," he said then he grabbed his book bag from the chair where he had dropped it. "I'll be home late today. I have a newspaper staff meeting today after school. I'll get a ride from someone." Mortimer darted out the door, down the steps of his house and bounced into the back seat of Jennifer's car.

"Had any more bad dreams, Mort?" William asked. He chuckled as he turned to look at Mortimer from the front seat.

"Shut up, man," Mortimer said. "Those dreams are not funny, and as a matter of fact, I did have one last night. It was pretty sick, too." Jennifer was talking on her cell phone while she drove so she only heard bits and pieces of the conversation. She rolled her eyes in the review mirror. Mortimer described his dream to William who, of course, ate up every gory detail. By the time they arrived at school, Mortimer had finished his story.

Mortimer and William walked through the two large glass doors that led to the main lobby of their school. Allen Academy's halls were packed and loud, the

212

usual welcome of a middle school. Teachers corralled the students as best they could towards open classroom doors. Laughter, shouts, and slamming locker doors filled the air. Mortimer stopped briefly to speak to his other best friend and final piece of his best friend trio, Christopher Roberts, known to most of his friends as Tofer. The shrill ringing of the first morning bell sent students running in every direction, scattering like frightened birds. "I'll see you later at lunch," Mortimer shouted to Tofer before he dashed up the stairs to his first block class.

Mortimer walked into Spanish class and grabbed his folder from the shelf. Dr. Jones' reputation as a strict teacher was known throughout Allen Academy. Students either loved him or hated him. Mortimer loved him, and Spanish was one of his favorite classes. He had always had a talent for languages.

Even as a young child, Mortimer loved to read and tell stories. He excelled at spelling and grammar. He never seemed to mind doing work for teachers of these subjects.

"Buenos días, Señor Drake," Dr. Jones said as Mortimer passed. "I am so glad that you were able to make it on time."

"Hola, Señor Jones," Mortimer answered in Spanish then he plopped down at his assigned seat. "What are you looking at?" Mortimer snapped at the two girls that sat opposite him. "I was on time today." Mortimer's classmates ignored him and began to copy the morning's assignments from the board as Dr. Jones checked the class attendance. Another day at Allen Academy was off and running.

The day crept at a snail's pace. When Mortimer glanced down at his watch it read eleven-thirty. He looked up at the clock on the wall above Mrs. Woodruff's head hoping to see a different time. She was going over the results of yesterday's test. Mortimer hated math, any math, but his parents had made him take algebra. His father had preached all last summer about the importance of taking algebra.

All Mortimer could think about now was lunch. He looked down again at his watch just as the bell sounded. He slammed his book shut and grabbed his notebook from under his seat. He nearly knocked three students down as he hurried out the door and darted down the stairs towards the school cafeteria.

William and Tofer were already in line. The cafeteria was an open and unstructured area but it operated under strict unwritten protocols. On the far side of the room, all the athletes and cheerleaders gathered. Anyone knew that unless you were a jock or very popular, you had to be invited to join that section of the cafeteria. It was definitely the cool place to sit.

Just inside the main doors was a series of round tables. This is where the teachers normally sat when they ate in the cafeteria. On most days, these tables were empty as almost all teachers ate in their rooms or left campus to run through a drive through, relishing those precious minutes of liberation away from school and the noisy hoards of teenagers.

Mortimer spotted William as he entered the cafeteria. He pointed to the table against the wall of windows. Mortimer nodded and made his way over to their usual place. He dropped his books and went to join his friends in line. "I'm starving," Mortimer exclaimed. "What's for lunch?"

"Who knows?" Tofer smirked. "Looks like burgers and sandwiches again."

The boys grabbed Styrofoam trays, cartons of milk, and made their way through the line. Once they were back at their table by the window, Mortimer started in again about his dream.

"It was totally gross," he said. "When I woke up, I felt so sick to my stomach. My legs were shaking and I was covered in sweat. I could barely move. I felt like every muscle in my body was locked." Mortimer took another bite of his sandwich and washed it down with chocolate milk. "Every time I have the dream, it seems more and more real."

Tofer looked up from his empty tray. "Yeah, what was that first dream you had? Didn't you say some sort of vampire was floating outside your bedroom window, calling your name?"

"I forgot all about that dream," Mortimer said. "That one gave me the creeps for a long time."

"You need to write this stuff down and make a book," William added to the conversation. "You're always going on and on about how you want to write a book about vampires. Why don't you try it and see what happens?"

"Well, maybe. I don't know." Mortimer shrugged. His eyes watered slightly as he wiped his left hand across his face.

"What's up with you?" Tofer asked. "Your eyes are all red and bloodshot. Don't cry if no one wants to read your writing."

William laughed then added, "Seriously. You should just let Mr. McDaniel read some of your scary stuff. I bet he'd go for it."

"I'm just a kid. Who'd read anything I'd write?" Mortimer said as he stood to throw his tray in the garbage. "Maybe I will write it down and show it to Mr. McDaniel. He's always pushing me to write a short story for the school paper— Jeez!" Mortimer shouted and he raised his left hand to shield his eyes. "That sun is really bright." He squeezed his eyes closed. "My eyes feel like they are on fire!" This wasn't the first time Mortimer had had this reaction to the sun, but this was by far the most painful that he could remember.

William and Tofer stood and looked at Mortimer. His eyes were shut, slightly watering. "You alright, man?" Tofer asked as he looked out the window at the hazy blue-grey sky. "The sun's not even out dude, look." Tofer nodded his head to the window.

William looked outside. Tofer was right. The sky was cloudy, only splinters of sunlight managed to make their way through. Mortimer lowered his hand and opened his eyes briefly before he dropped his tray and cupped his hands over his face. "That's not funny!" he shouted. "That sun is too bright." He turned quickly, tripping over his chair and falling to the floor. Laughter erupted instantly. Tofer and William sat back down, embarrassed for Mortimer.

"Dude, get up. You just busted it in front of the whole school," Tofer said, trying not to laugh. "Are you alright?"

Mortimer struggled to stand, his eyes still closed. By this time, Mr. Lee, the assistant principal, had made his way over to the scene. His presence loomed like a shadow. He helped Mortimer to his feet. "What's the problem, son?" Mr. Lee asked Mortimer. He panned his glare around the cafeteria, giving the students

214

that look that meant get it together or call your parents to come and pick you up. Mr. Lee was tough as nails. Nobody dared to make him angry. He demanded total respect and compliance to school rules. "What happened here?" he asked, this time looking at Tofer and William.

Tofer was still holding back his laughter, so he nodded for William to answer. "He was just standing up to throw away his tray." William pointed out the window. "He said that that sun was too bright and that it hurt his eyes. He turned to leave and that's when he fell." William's answer was followed by Tofer's full blown laughter. He had lost all control of himself. He leaned back and grabbed his stomach.

"Get it together, Mr. Roberts, or we'll have a conversation after lunch," Mr. Lee said sternly. He turned to Mortimer. "Are you okay? What's wrong with your eyes? Why can't you open them?"

"The sun's too bright. I can't see a thing," Mortimer answered pleadingly. "Can I please go to the restroom and put some water on them?"

Mr. Lee looked outside. He, too, only saw a dull sky covered in clouds. He turned his head back so that he could see Mortimer.

"Come with me. Let's get you down to the nurse. You don't look so good." Mr. Lee helped Mortimer steady himself. "Can you try to open your eyes?"

Mortimer lowered his head and slowly opened his eyes. The glare from the window was now behind him. His face, stained with the water from his burning eyes, was splotchy.

He wiped his face with his hands and raised his head. Blurred visions of bodies gathered around, some watching with concern while others pointed and snickered. Mr. Lee continued to help Mortimer out of the cafeteria.

"I am feeling a little better now," Mortimer said quietly. "I think I can make it to the nurse by myself."

"Okay, people! Show's over. Get back to your tables and finish your lunches. The bell will be ringing in about ten minutes and I won't be giving any late passes to any classes," Mr. Lee announced as he watched Mortimer exit the cafeteria. "You boys clean up this mess and take Mortimer's books to the nurse's station." Mr. Lee pointed to the spilled tray on the floor next to William and Tofer.

"Yes, sir," William responded and then he picked up the tray, quickly dumping it into a large black garbage can in the center of the room. He returned to the table and grabbed his books and followed Tofer out the door. The other students settled back into their lunchroom conversations. It was as if nothing had happened.

Made in the USA
San Bernardino, CA
30 November 2016